Shadow

New Species - Book Nine

By Laurann Dohner

Shadow

by Laurann Dohner

Beauty resents being labeled Gift Species. Everyone is way too overprotective, males aren't even allowed to speak to her and so far true freedom eludes her. Then a big, sexy Species officer mistakes her for the enemy and takes her to the ground.

Shadow is dumbfounded. He has a Gift pinned under him—a big no-no. But Beauty is fascinated and wants to know Shadow a lot better. She is full of newly discovered, unrequited passion and he's just what she needs to satisfy her curiosity.

For Shadow, sex means pain and revulsion. For Beauty, it was enslavement and ridicule. Two lonely souls who have never known a lover's touch, together in a cabin in the woods. Each touch, every discovery brings them closer to a life they never thought possible…beyond even their dreams.

Dedication

As always, a special thanks to Mr. Laurann. He's an endless source of help in so many ways—wrangling kids to give me time to write, understanding the many hours I put into each book. And he's the man who always has my back. He's...*MINE!* LOL.

I want to thank everyone who reads this series. I began it a long time ago when I just had a dream of becoming published and an imagination when my spare time allowed. Thank you for seeing why I love New Species and how they could become an obsession for me. I hope to bring you many, many more stories about the males and females of the NSO.

Kele Moon is the BEST critique partner ever. She's always there to bounce ideas off and she's become my best friend.

New Species Series

Fury

Slade

Valiant

Justice

Brawn

Wrath

Tiger

Obsidian

Shadow

Moon

True

Darkness

Smiley

Numbers

Shadow

Prologue

Freedom

She wouldn't be called Mud any longer. *Beauty.* She silently repeated the new name the woman had given her, determined to remember to answer to Beauty instead of Mud. That distraction helped her battle the confusion and deep shock she had suffered after being led out of her cage by the woman named Jessie. The chains were gone and she'd overheard her rescuers say her guards had been killed during the fight to free her.

Beauty would have stumbled but a firm arm around her waist helped steady her as they walked through the well-lit house. Jessie swore she was taking her somewhere safe, to others like her who had been locked away. The concept of such a thing seemed completely unreal. It had to be a lie, some kind of mean game of cruelty. Beauty glanced around and spotted the blood on the floor, which she could smell. Evidence that her guards were really dead.

A sense of hope filled her that the redheaded woman might be telling the truth. She would be free from Master. The promise of being able to see sunlight again seemed impossible. She only had dim memories of the rare times she'd been allowed outside.

Stars dotted the sky and a partial moon hung to her right. Fresh, wonderful air filled her lungs, and joy struck. *I'm outside!* She nearly tripped on her own feet, her body weak from lack of food, but the woman hugged her tighter to her side. A big man called Trey kept silently at their side, but she refused to look at his face. She could feel his glances but she tried to hide her fear. He hadn't tried to touch her.

A large black thing with wheels waited close to the door. She balked a little but Jessie kept urging her forward. "That's what will take us from here and then we're going to do something really exciting. We're going to fly in the sky to get you some medical help and you're going to meet your family. They are going to be so happy to see you."

"You won't leave me?" Beauty was terrified the woman would abandon her to the group of men.

"No, honey. I'm going to hold your hand the entire time." Jessie smiled. "I'm not going to let anything happen to you."

The seat was soft and comfortable in the big box. Beauty wasn't sure about the belt that Jessie tightened around her body but she didn't fight. It was supposed to be for her safety and she was just happy not to be shoved into the back, inside the hole with no light. That's how they'd moved her to the house.

"I'll sit right next to you and Trey here is going to drive us. He's a very nice person." Jessie checked the belt, leaned over to push Beauty's hair behind her ear and smiled again. "He's a good friend of mine and you can trust him too."

She met Jessie's gaze and her really bright, red hair shone in the lights from the big house. Her features were nice, pleasant. A sense of peace filled Beauty. She trusted this woman. She wasn't sure why but she did.

"Everything is going to be fine, Beauty. I—" Jessie jerked once violently where she stood and her mouth opened. The sheer pain reflecting on her face sent terror through Beauty. She screamed, not sure what else to do. Jessie's blue eyes widened before she suddenly threw her body into the vehicle. The impact knocked Beauty over on the seat.

"Sniper!" Trey shouted the warning.

"I've got you," Jessie promised, her arms hugging Beauty tightly until she jerked again, her tense body becoming limp.

Beauty shrieked, too gripped with fright to do anything else. Jessie wasn't moving. The smell of blood pierced her panic but she knew it wasn't her own.

The box they were in shook, swayed, and the door closed. Another one opened above her head and hands dug between her body and Jessie's. The weight gently eased and she halted her screams. She opened her eyes and watched as another man dragged Jessie off her body. They disappeared to the ground but another big man suddenly launched through the opening. He slammed the door and climbed over the seat in front, hunching down.

"The glass will protect us," he panted, out of breath. "It's going to be okay, Beauty." He withdrew a weapon. "I'm Shane. Nothing is going to hurt you. Just stay down."

The door in the front opened suddenly and another man leaned in. "The sniper is from the east. He can't nail this side. Hand her over." The one who spoke was older than the rest but not as wrinkled as Master. He was the one who'd dragged Jessie off her body.

"She's safer here," Shane argued. "I've got her, Tim. Take care of Jessie. How bad is she?"

9

"Bad. Trey is assessing her." The door closed as the older man disappeared.

That left Beauty alone with Shane. Her terrified gaze met his where he crouched in the front seat.

"Stay down," he ordered again softly.

Soft dings sounded and he cursed, suddenly climbing over the seat into the back with her. She shrieked when he grabbed the other side of the seat behind her, hanging his upper body over the top of hers. Only inches separated them and she felt trapped. He reached between them and the belt holding her middle let go. She gasped in air to scream again but he released the seat to clamp a big hand over her mouth. It silenced her and her heart felt as if it would explode as his face drew closer.

"Damn it," he rasped. "Don't look at me that way." He threw a leg over the seat to climb closer. "I'm not attacking. I'm trying to protect you. I want my body between you and a bullet. You need to stop screaming, okay? I'm afraid the sniper can hear it and he's not going to stop firing until you're dead. Can you be quiet?"

She fought the panic and nodded. His hand eased away from her mouth. She stared at him with fear as his big body crowded her. He got on the seat with her and a heavy thigh wedged between her leg and the seat. He wiggled an arm under her too and braced his body to hold his weight to avoid crushing her down.

"I'm just using my body to cover yours," he assured her. "That's all. I'm not sure what kind of rounds the sniper has but it's better to be safe than sorry. All he's managed to do so far is blow out the side mirrors and the tires. By now he has to realize he's not breaching the SUV and could be reloading with armor-piercing ones. I'd rather a bullet strike me than you."

Surprise made her study his eyes. She didn't see cruelty inside them — they were really kind. Her fear eased somewhat, allowing her to breathe normally, and his scent filled her nose with each breath. He smelled clean and nice, even pleasant. The warmth of his big body seeped through his clothing and some of the coldness that gripped her faded.

"They'll find the sniper and take him out. It's going to be fine." He looked away from her to peer over her head through the glass. "Tim? Is Jessie breathing? Is she alive?"

She realized he spoke to someone else and had to have one of those ear listening devices that Jessie had shown her. He closed his eyes and hung his head, until his lips almost brushed hers. It made Beauty tense. He softly cursed.

"Understood. Thank God she's breathing but that's bad. Fuck. How did this happen? The victim is secure. Traumatized as hell though. I'm on top of her to keep her down but she's not hit."

His eyes opened and he stared intently into hers. He adjusted his upper weight to rest on his elbows and his big hand touched the side of her face. She allowed him to turn it a little as his thumb brushed her cheek gently.

"It's okay, honey. Easy. You look so terrified but you're safe with me. Does your face hurt? You've got a little cut. I think Jessie nailed you with her fingernail when she landed on top of you."

She wasn't aware of the injury but it didn't surprise her. Everything had happened so fast and she knew she was too stunned to register it all. His thumb paused and she turned her head enough to meet his gaze again. He looked at her with an expression she'd never seen before and it was kind of nice.

"I'd never hurt you. I'm nothing like the assholes who kept you in captivity. Do you know what my job is? I find ones like you and take them home. You are going to be happy from now on. No more chains, cages or pain." His voice deepened. "I would die for you."

Warmth spread further than just her skin. It seemed to radiate inside her chest at his words. He meant them and for some incredible reason she believed him. All her fear faded and she curled her hands to grip his strange-textured shirt.

"Easy, Beauty," he rasped. "Don't scratch me up. I'm your friend."

"I—" She closed her mouth, worried he'd get angry if she spoke without permission.

"You what? Talk to me."

No rage darkened his features or flashed in his compelling stare. It encouraged her to speak again. "You want me to be nice to you?"

"Yes." He smiled. "We're friends." He grew serious. "I'll kill anyone who comes after you. I'm here and you're totally safe with me. The team has secured the immediate area. They will find that sniper and take him out. No one is going to get close to us."

He wants to protect me. He'll kill others if they try to hurt me. The astonishment that flooded her made thinking difficult. His clean, wonderful

12

scent was really nice, his body scary big and bulky, but she didn't fear him. He was careful not to crush her under him, had touched her with gentle brushes of his skin against hers. He'd be a kind master.

He lifted his head, peered around again and shifted some of his weight before he glanced down. "I'm going to take off my vest and put it between your head and the door. The sniper could change locations to avoid detection longer."

She said nothing as he tore at the covering on his chest. It made loud noises as one of his hands ripped at the thing and he shrugged out of it. He placed it against the door above her head. Her gaze fixed on his shirt and she saw buttons running down the front of it. His chest was wide and his arms looked really thick. She'd thought they might only appear so because of the thing he'd just removed.

He touched his ear. "How is Jessie doing?" He paused. "Good. How far out is the other team?" He paused again. "We're fine in here. Just find that son of a bitch." He tapped his ear again and his arm dropped along the edge of the seat to brace his upper body on both forearms. He met her gaze.

"They haven't found the sniper yet but teams are moving in and a helicopter is nearby for air support. It shouldn't be too much longer. How are you doing, Beauty? We're friends, right? You know I'm not going to hurt you, don't you? Just stay calm for me."

She swallowed her fear and asked again, "You want me to be nice to you?"

"That would be great." He smiled at her.

He had an attractive face and no "mean" lines marred his tan skin. She never wanted to go back to Master. He was coldhearted and punished her for any offense. Shane promised not to hurt her and she believed him. She took a deep breath, knowing anything had to be better than going back to her old life. At least Shane gave her hope of a future without misery. He didn't even mind when she spoke without permission. He didn't slap her and that was enough to convince her he was a much better man.

"I'll be nice to you."

"Good. We're friends, Beauty. Just relax, okay? You're totally safe with me."

Her hands shook as she touched his chest. This material was softer and she could feel the warmth of his body. Beneath the thin shirt, firm muscle met her fingertips. She wanted to stay with him. It couldn't be worse than what she'd survived in the past. Nothing ever could be.

She waited to see how he'd react but he didn't do anything. It confused her. She said she'd be nice to him but he only watched her silently with his mesmerizing eyes. They really were pretty and she liked the way he stared at her. It was almost as if he were waiting for her to do something.

I can do this. He must want me to start. She swallowed, wished she were clean, and hoped she didn't look as bad as she feared. She slid her hands on his shirt and gripped the thick curve of his shoulder, while her other one ran down his stomach. He gasped in air and jerked his upper body away from hers enough to give her room. She used the space to rub the front of his pants.

"Fuck!" His eyes widened as he gaped at her. "What are you doing?"

She froze.

"You've got my dick." His voice shook. "I thought we were playing nice. That's going to hurt but I'm not going to fight you, damn it. You're a woman. Please don't do what I think you are. I'm your friend."

Confusion gripped her until she realized he thought she was going to attack him. He thought her touching him was a threat to cause him pain. She gently massaged her hand over him to show him she was being nice. She'd said she would be.

He stared at her, his gaze still wide, and he gasped again. She knew she did it right when his man-part grew hard against her hand.

"Stop," he rasped.

She froze. "Do you want my mouth there instead? I said I'd be nice to you."

He twisted his hips away from her palm. "No! Shit! I didn't mean 'nice' that way. Oh hell." He shifted his hips lower down her body until the front of his pants were out of her reach. "I...son of a bitch. I didn't mean I wanted sex from you. I just meant...shit!"

She'd displeased him, made him not want her, and had done something wrong. Terror filled her that he wouldn't protect her from Master anymore. She fisted his shirt with both hands.

"Please give me another chance. I can do better. I'll do anything you want. Just tell me what to do. I'll do it."

He stared at her with something akin to horror and tears filled her eyes. She'd failed by making him angry. She turned her head away and jerked her hands off his body, curled them against her chest, hoping he

15

wouldn't hit her. He was much stronger than Master and he probably could inflict more pain.

"I'm sorry," she whispered. "I'll do anything. You seem kind and I'll look better when I'm clean." She dared to glance at him, only to see him still staring at her with that same horrified look. "Please decide to take me. I want to be nice to you. Don't leave me here."

"Oh hell, baby. I can see you're beautiful, despite the dirt, but that's not it." His voice softened and so did his expression. "You don't have to offer sex for me to protect you. I'll kill anyone who comes after you but I don't want anything in return. I just want you to be happy. I'm your friend."

She sniffed, fighting tears. "You'll be my master now?"

"No." More horror filled his eyes. "You're free. No one owns you."

She closed her eyes and turned her face away. She didn't speak again, guessing she'd done something to upset him. Her silence would hopefully calm him and maybe give her another chance to prove that she was worth keeping. She couldn't stand to be returned to Master.

The more she thought about that concept, the more panicked she became. Her breathing increased—something she couldn't stop. The man on top of her softly cursed and fumbled with something inside one of his pockets.

"Calm down," he ordered, his voice a little harsh. "You're hyperventilating. I'm not going to hurt you."

She wanted to beg him not to return her to Master. She just couldn't get the words out. Her fingers gripped his shirt, ready to beg him to keep her with him, but blind terror gripped her that she'd come so close to

16

freedom only to lose it. A low, keening noise filled the vehicle, it came from her, but she couldn't stop.

He lifted something to his mouth and tore part of it off. It was a syringe. Pain made her scream when he jabbed the needle into her arm. It was over quickly as he yanked it out and tossed it on the floor. His hands gently held her down.

"Easy, Beauty. You're safe." He stared deeply into her eyes. "Damn it, she's freaking out!" he yelled. "I just had to sedate our Gift. Find that fucking sniper!"

A haze clouded her vision as lightheadedness struck. Everything went black.

Chapter One

The Present

Beauty jerked upright in bed, her eyes wide, to discover darkness surrounded her. Believing she was still imprisoned, panic struck. She panted, familiar scents filling her nose, suggesting it had just been a dream.

No, a memory, she corrected. She turned and blindly reached toward the bedside table. Her fingertips brushed along the wood until she found the base of the metal lamp. The bright glow of artificial light that filled the room helped her shake off the dream state.

The small apartment she'd been assigned inside the women's dorm at Homeland was her home now. She'd been freed and wasn't called Mud anymore. She shoved at the covers, stuck her legs out and scrambled away from the bed. Her nightmares were getting worse and all her old fears returned.

She paced the carpeted floor while she battled the strong emotion of shame. She'd never recovered from the humiliation she felt over what she'd done to that stranger who'd used his body to shield hers when that sniper had pinned them down. Shane had really wanted to be her friend but she'd misunderstood his motives. She realized why he'd been horrified when she'd fondled him inappropriately now that she'd had time to adjust to her new life.

It was his job to save New Species. He hadn't been offering to become her new master if she agreed to have sex without fighting him. He just hadn't wanted her to attack and force him to restrain her. She groaned, guessing he must have thought her pathetic or insane. Perhaps a bit of both.

A faint sound reached her ears and she crept closer to the common wall of the apartment next door. Her ear pressed against the cool plaster to listen as Kit and a man shared sex. The sounds of their heavy breathing, growls and slapping bodies always penetrated the walls when one of the women brought someone home on either side of her apartment. It made her long for whatever connection they had.

Kit cried out, the man growled louder, and their breathing slowed.

"That was really good," Kit chuckled. "Thanks, Book."

"My pleasure," he rasped. "Do you want me to go or stay?"

"Leave," Kit answered.

"Are you sure?" He didn't sound happy. "I'd like to hold you."

"No way. You're not a male I want to grow attached to. It's just sex."

"Fine." His tone grew gruffer. "Next time we can use the bed."

"No." Kit had changed locations. "Then I'd smell you longer than it takes to wash away your scent from my body and air out the room. I'd have to do laundry."

"You're cold." Anger changed his voice into a bit of a snarl. "I'm out of here. Good luck with the next male you ask to share sex. Poor bastard." A door opened and slammed closed within a minute.

Beauty cocked her head, listening to the heavy footfalls move past her door in the hallway. The sound of running water came from Kit's

19

apartment. Sadness gripped Beauty. If a man wanted to stay with her she'd allow him to sleep in her bed and would enjoy his scent on her sheets. She wouldn't kick him out as soon as the sex finished. Of course that would mean having a man inside her home but Species men avoided her. They refused to even meet her gaze and kept a wide berth.

Gift Female. Those two words assured her single fate. She sighed and walked into her kitchen, knowing sleep wouldn't return. It was law that all men avoid frightening a Gift Female. It was known they'd been abused, probably feared sex, and they steered clear of her.

She opened the fridge to grab a soda but a deep masculine laugh made her start. Her head turned in that direction and she realized it came from her other neighbor. The wind blew her curtain near the sink where she'd left the window cracked open. She inched closer to it and peered out into the night.

Rusty and a man stood on the balcony next door. They were close enough that she heard their words when they spoke. Beauty quickly backed away, fearful they'd discover her spying. It seemed that almost every woman in the dorm had a man visitor. She was always alone.

She turned away and rushed to the front door, desperate to escape. It wasn't fair and it hurt. The Species women who lived on both sides of her had no idea how lucky they were not to know the deep longing she suffered. Kit had just thrown a man out, done with him. Rusty would probably do the same after she shared sex with the one she laughed with.

Beauty bypassed the elevator to jog down the stairs and used the corridor to exit the side doors of the building to avoid the main living areas.

The last thing she wanted was to run into anyone. She burst outside and paused while the door closed behind her. The sky was filled with clouds, blocking out the stars and moon. She could just feel that a storm brewed.

Part of her knew she needed to return to her apartment. The air felt heavy and the wind a bit chilly on her bare arms and legs. She glanced down to realize she hadn't even dressed. The loose white nightgown fell to just above her knees and her bare feet rested on cool pavement. She spun and tried to open the door but discovered it locked.

"Darn it."

She'd have to go to the front of the dorm to gain entrance. She had fled without her badge and someone else would have to let her inside. That meant she'd have to explain why she was outside late at night wearing so little. It would probably make the women worry about her state of mind. She hesitated.

A fat drop of rain landed on her bare shoulder and she reached up to adjust the thin strap of her nightgown. Another drop wet her nose. Lightning flashed in the sky, highlighting the area with a violent streak of brilliance. She counted to four before the boom of thunder followed.

She'd been promised that life would be better after being freed but things were just different. The chains that had enslaved her were gone but she was still alone. Memories of being locked inside the basement surfaced. She had once dreamed of leaving it to see the world outside but she wasn't living in that world. The facts couldn't be denied as she hugged her chest, pondering her reality. It was almost crueler to see what she could never have. At least in the past she hadn't known what could be possible.

21

Lightning streaked across the sky again and she spun, her hands fisted, and she bolted. Her legs moved fast as she sprinted down the sidewalk toward the park. She needed to feel alive. Rain fell faster, soaked her hair and nightgown, and thunder boomed louder. Her heart raced and she almost laughed. She was running free and no one could take that away from her. Tonight she could go where she wanted, when she wanted, and that had to be enough.

She left the sidewalk and her feet sank into soft, soggy grass. She dodged trees, her vision adjusting to the darkness, which was broken only by the lightning. It was dangerous to be outside in a storm but she welcomed the feel of the rain on her face.

* * * * *

Shadow parked the golf cart and softly growled in frustration as he scooted to the center of the seat to avoid getting wet as the sky opened up. He was off duty and had hoped to make it to the dorm before the storm hit. He hadn't succeeded. He could keep driving and be soaked by the time he got home or he could wait patiently for the downpour to cease.

Movement from the corner of his eye made him turn his head. A flash of lightning blinded him but it illuminated the area. He'd seen something. Thunder boomed. He blinked, his mind trying to make sense of what he'd just witnessed. It couldn't be what it looked like. His eyes had to be playing tricks, otherwise he'd just seen a female in a white dress running off the path toward the pond.

Lightning flashed again and he caught another glimpse of her. The sight of pale legs, long dark hair flying behind her, and that white dress had

22

been real. There was a female intruder at Homeland. He lunged straight out of the cart into the downpour. Heavy rain drenched him immediately.

His boots sank into the wet grass when he left the road and a snarl tore from him, his instincts instantly flaring to life. *Hunt. Find. Capture.* His long stride ate up the ground as he pursued her. He needed to find the human quickly and force her to tell him what she'd done that was bad enough to make her run that fast. Had she set a bomb that would detonate soon? The concept motivated him to increase his speed.

He narrowed his eyes and spotted a streak of white ahead of him. She was definitely fleeing toward the park. There was a place big enough for a helicopter to land if she reached the area near the pond. He glanced up for a second to search the sky but rain blinded him. He wiped his arm across his face as he snarled again. Someone had helped her enter Homeland to do harm but she wouldn't escape. He'd catch her before she made the extraction point and make her tell what she'd done.

He dodged to the left through the thick woods, avoided slamming into any trees and broke through to the open, grassy field where they played sports. Lightning flashed and he saw her exit about twenty feet ahead. Her back was to him and the thunder hid his sounds of outrage as he closed the distance. More details became apparent. She wasn't a big female and she'd ditched most of her clothing, maybe to make it easier for her to flee in the rain.

He dived and tackled her. The feel of her small waist in his hands made him instantly react. He twisted in the air before his back slammed hard into the ground. Her body landed on top of his as momentum made him slide along the slippery grass. The second their skid ended, he rolled, pinning her under his body. He was careful not to crush her. His elbows sank into the sodden earth as he braced his upper chest to make sure she could breathe. He yanked her wrists up and imprisoned her in his hold.

"Who are you? What have you done?" His voice came out more animalistic than he intended but he couldn't help it. His heart pounded from adrenaline pulsing through his veins and the urge to snarl again was strong. "Tell me, female."

He couldn't make out her face. There were no lights in that section of the park. She panted heavily, assuring him she could breathe and speak if she wished.

"Tell me," he demanded again, snarling now. He was enraged. The lives of his people could be at stake.

Lightning sparked above them and lit the ground. Her dark eyes were wide with fear as he stared into them. The light only held for a few rapid heartbeats but he glanced at her face. Astonishment made him curse.

"Shit." Shock paralyzed him for a moment before he hastily eased his grip on her wrists. They were small and frail in his hands. Guilt filled him immediately as he tried to lift his weight off her.

She said nothing and he hoped he hadn't injured her. The rain beat down on his back harder as the storm intensified. He hesitated to roll off her completely. She'd be at the mercy of the storm. Her only shelter at the moment was him.

"Are you hurt?" He forced his tone to lower to a calmer level. "I thought you were human. An intruder."

24

"I'm not hurt," she answered softly.

"I am so sorry." It horrified him to know he'd just attacked a Gift Female. He didn't know her but her features couldn't be denied. He guessed her to be primate from the rounded shape of her eyes and her delicate little nose. It made what he'd done worse. Primate females were even more fragile than the canine or feline ones. "You're safe. I will not hurt you."

He turned his head, frantically searching for help. He needed a Species female officer on scene to handle the Gift but the park was empty. No one would be out in the storm taking a jog. It was just them and he had to fix the mess himself. He wanted to curse again but refrained.

"I'm Shadow." He whispered, hoping it would make her feel less threatened. "I swear you are safe. I'd move but then you'd be in the rain. It's really coming down. Am I crushing you?"

"No."

She didn't move her arms when he released them and adjusted his chest a little higher over her to make certain she was protected from the weather. He just needed to keep her from panicking until the rain slowed enough to move her. His cart and radio weren't too far away. He'd have to call for emergency assistance.

Fury and Justice were going to hand him his ass. Hell, all the males were. He'd hunted a Gift Female. Not only that but he'd taken her down as if she were a deer. He was grateful that he'd recognized she was a small female at least and made certain he'd done his best to take the brunt of the impact with the ground when he'd tackled her.

"I'm Beauty."

The female's whispered words made him stare down at her. He could barely make out the shape of her face in the darkness.

"What were you doing out here, Beauty? Did something frighten you?" He tried to figure out why she'd been running in barely any clothing. A worse thought struck and he darted a searching look around them. "Was someone chasing you?" His voice deepened at just the thought of someone trying to harm her. His protective instincts came fully into play.

"No. I just wanted to feel alive."

Her answer astounded him and drew his full attention to her again. He wished he could see her face. Thunder shook the ground under them. The storm seemed to be drawing closer. He knew then it would be safer to move her despite the downpour. They were in the open. Lightning flashed overhead brightly and his head snapped up to watch the jagged line of it. It was too close. Thunder followed almost immediately.

"I'm moving you. Just remain calm. You have my word as a Species officer that I'd never hurt you, Beauty. I know you must be terrified but there is no reason. I'm not a human."

He hated to expose her to the rain but didn't see any other choice. He rose quickly to his knees, his hands slid in the slick grass under her arms to grip her rib cage and he gently lifted her. She didn't weigh much as he stood with her held tightly against his body. His shoulder hunched and he tucked his head to keep the rain off her as much as possible. He spun and hurried back toward his cart. Her legs rubbed his where she rested lengthwise against him.

"I'm not afraid."

He heard her words and breathed a little easier. "Good. You're very brave." Gift Females were terrified of all males after being abused by humans.

Her arms hugged him around his neck and a second later her legs lifted to wrap around his waist. It made it easier for him to carry her and he appreciated that she trusted him enough to cling to him. He picked up the pace and made it to the thick trees. They'd barely entered them when a loud noise sounded, putting him on full alert. He paused before spinning in a new direction and dashing for safety.

"Hold on. That's hail."

He evaded the tree trunks and lightning flashes showed him the way as he made it to the sports equipment building. He barely paused before lifting his leg and slamming his boot into the door. The lock easily gave under the power of his kick. He stepped inside just as the chunks of ice pelted the roof. He released her waist with one arm to blindly search for the door and slam it closed.

It was loud inside the small building—more of a shed—as the exterior was hammered by the hail. He explored the wall until he found the light switch. The one bulb in the ceiling wasn't overly bright but he was grateful for it as he glanced around the confined space.

"We're safe in here." He leaned back enough to see her face, looking for injuries.

Her big eyes were more curious than afraid as she studied him as intently as he did her. The color of them was a soft brown and she had really

27

long dark eyelashes. All her features were delicate and assured him once again that she was primate Species.

"Are you all right?"

"Yes."

He glanced at the front of her thin nightgown and forgot how to breathe. The material was wet, plastered to her as if it were a second skin and transparent enough for him to see exactly how she'd look naked. The dusky, taut tips of her nipples were clearly visible. They were beautiful temptations he instantly wanted to touch and explore.

Bad. Real bad, he chastised himself, tearing his gaze away to look anywhere but at her. He hated how his body reacted so easily to the sight of her breasts. His dick filled with blood and he had to swallow since he was almost salivating to suck one of them into his mouth to taste.

He'd allowed his instincts to take over while chasing her and they were still too close to the surface for him to easily regain control of his responses. He frantically looked for a safe place to put her down and his attention caught on the large bench-box housing the baseball equipment. He stepped forward and lowered her.

"Sit."

Her arms and legs released him and he let go of her the second he knew she wouldn't fall over. Shadow spun, searching for an emergency radio but didn't find one. He stared at the door. The noise of the storm intensified and wind battered the walls.

"Are you okay?"

Her voice was so soft he barely heard her. *No.* His dick was hard and he couldn't risk her noticing. She'd probably scream, fearing he'd attack. "Everything is fine," he lied, keeping his back to her. "I'm going to go out there and radio for help."

"You can't." Her voice grew louder, less timid. "It sounds dangerous."

He turned his head, tempted to explain why he needed to leave. Innocence stared back at him when he met her gaze. "My cart isn't too far from here. I need to contact Security and let them know what happened. We need a female officer on scene."

"Why?"

He hesitated. "You're Gift."

She blinked and her mouth turned downward as if she didn't understand.

"It's procedure to call in another female to attend you," he explained.

"I'm fine."

She hugged her chest and it hid her nipples but the mounds were still a tempting sight. Her wrists were too small to cover much. Shadow experienced guilt at noting that fact and he jerked his gaze to her face. She was a pretty female with pale features. A few strands of her hair were stuck to her cheek.

"You're wet and not as sturdy as other Species. You need medical care."

"I can't deny the wet part." She grabbed a handful of dripping hair that fell to her waist and glanced at it then looked at him. A small smile appeared. "It's a good thing I'm not part rat."

Shadow stared at her, surprised that she was so calm. She almost seemed amused by the situation.

"You know, 'drowned rat'? It was a joke. I heard monkeys can't swim though. I wonder if that's true. I've never tried it before."

This wasn't going as he'd imagined. He'd thought she would be screaming, perhaps bursting into tears, but she just released her hair to peer around the cramped room.

"What is this place?"

"We store sports equipment here."

"Oh. Are they fun to play? I'm not allowed. I've watched though and it looks enjoyable."

"It depends on the sport." He almost turned around but then remembered why he kept his back to her. His dick refused to comply with his brain, which was ordering it not to be interested in the Gift Female.

A shiver ran down her small frame and Shadow softly growled. Her gaze darted to him and widened. A hint of fear finally showed in her eyes.

"Sorry," he rasped. "I'm not angry or anything. I just hate that you're cold. I need to get you help." He reached for the door.

"Stop!"

His hand hovered over the handle when he glanced back at her. She'd risen to her feet. The white nightgown hugged every curve of her body and made him aware she wasn't similar to the Species females he was accustomed to. Her hips were fuller, her belly softer and she was little. He guessed she couldn't be more than just an inch over five feet tall. One thing was certain. She wasn't wearing underwear. His gaze paused at the thin material plastered to her middle before he stared at the floor.

"Please don't risk your life by walking out into that storm. Just wait for it to pass. This is my fault. I shouldn't have left the dorm but I wasn't thinking rationally at the time. I'd never forgive myself if something happened to you."

"I'll be fine." His chest puffed up a little, his pride injured. "I'm tougher than a little hail."

"I don't doubt that. You look fierce in your uniform and you're very big."

He glanced at her face, worried that she might be afraid if she noticed those things. No fear showed in her gaze though as they examined each other. He wasn't sure what to do.

"Please don't go." She stepped closer. "Would it be so bad to wait out the storm with me?"

He held back a groan. "You're Gift and you need assistance from another female."

Her chin lifted and anger flashed in her eyes. "I know the rules but I'm not afraid of you. It's just stupid to leave here to get help when I don't need it."

"I'm a male."

"I see that."

31

He tried a new line of reasoning. "You shouldn't be alone with one."

She hugged her chest again. "Are you going to hurt me?"

"Never."

"Exactly my point." She glanced around. "We need to get warm first. I read a lot and that's what the books say. We should take off our wet things and find something dry to wear."

His mouth fell open. "What?"

She stared at something above his head to the left and pointed. "What is that up there?"

He followed the direction of her finger. "Those are flags."

Beauty worried that the big man would bolt. He looked ready to as he faced the door once again. Shadow was really tall and his hair was short. It was an oddity to see a Species with it cut so close to his head. His blue eyes were really pretty and she was sure he was canine, the way he growled and snarled.

"Flags?"

He sighed loudly and partially turned in her direction to stare at her calmly. "Flags. We have teams and someone thought it would be nice to put them on the benches when we play."

"Can you hand me one?"

He slowly reached up to the folded material and pulled. She inched closer. He towered over her by almost a foot and a half. Her head didn't even reach his broad shoulders. Shadow was careful not to touch her when he passed it over. The soft, silky material was dry and thicker than she'd hoped. She unfolded it to stare at the white fabric with an orange lion's head printed on the center of it.

"It looks as if it's made out of flames. That's pretty."

"I guess." He shifted his stance. "The other one has a wolf face. Or a dog. I'm not sure which was intended."

"Is there a third one for the primates?"

"No. Just the two. I don't know why but there probably should be one." He appeared uncomfortable.

"These are big. What do you guess? Maybe four feet by two and a half?"

"I am not sure."

"We should wear these."

His mouth pursed into a tight line. "No."

"You could tie it around your waist as though it's a towel and this one will fit me if I wrap it around my body like a dress."

"No." His voice deepened. "I'll go radio your location to Security and they will send out a female officer."

The wind still battered the sides of the small building but the hail had passed. "The rain is still really coming down hard. You shouldn't go out there."

"I must." He grabbed the door handle.

"Don't!" She hated the way she almost pleaded with him but the truth was that she didn't want him to leave. She'd never been alone with a

Species man before but he wasn't frightening to her. Curiosity got the better of her and she just wanted to spend some time with him. "Please?"

He whipped his head around and his eyes narrowed. "You're afraid to be left alone?" His expression softened. "I will radio it in and return immediately."

Guilt ate at Beauty as she flat-out lied. It was wrong to do that but she didn't want him to go just yet. "I'll be terrified. Stay with me."

He released the door. "This building is built well and it's safe."

"Don't leave me."

He relented. "I'll stay."

"Thank you." She realized she'd survive guilty feelings at the deception. "I'll put this on and you can grab that other one. We'll be dry to wait out the storm."

"I'm fine." He looked away. "You change. You're cold."

She backed away from him and dropped the flag on the box where she'd sat. The nightgown stuck to her body as she tugged it over her head. A chill ran down her as the air touched her bare skin. It was cold. She squeezed out her hair as well as she could before touching the flag. It wasn't much protection against the cool temperature but it was dry as she secured it around her body. It covered her from just over her breasts to her knees.

"I'm decent." Her attention focused on him. "I'll close my eyes. You really need to remove those wet clothes. Please? I know you're tough but I'll worry."

34

He turned his head to stare at her. "It isn't a good idea."

"Why not?"

His chest expanded as he took a few deep breaths. "Never mind."

Amusement sparked. She wasn't dense. "Do you think I'll be terrified if you're mostly undressed with me? I won't be. You're Species."

The glint in his eyes turned almost harsh. "I'm male."

He slowly lowered his gaze to sweep down her body. His interest quickened Beauty's heartbeat. He didn't need to say more. She'd heard men were always eager to share sex with a woman. The idea of him touching her didn't send her into a panic. The sounds her next-door neighbors made when they had company pretty much assured her that consensual sex wasn't a bad thing.

"Please take off your wet things and wear the flag?" She purposely turned her back to give him privacy, the way he had her.

A soft growl was his answer but then his clothing rustled. He was doing it. Beauty hugged her waist to keep the silky material in place and smiled at the wall. He wasn't leaving and it would just be the two of them together until the storm passed. She finally would be able to get to know a man.

Chapter Two

"I'm covered."

Beauty resisted laughing at Shadow's gruff tone. She turned to find his back still to her but he'd removed his boots, pants, shirt, and vest. They were neatly arranged in front of the door. The blue flag tied around his waist showed a wolf head covered part of his thigh on the opposite side of where he'd knotted the material at his hipbone to keep it in place.

"I really do like the flame patterns."

"Are you warmer?"

"No." That wasn't a lie. "It's so cold."

"What were you doing out in the storm?" He glanced around the room, seeming to study everything but her. "You could have been hurt."

"I had a nightmare and just wanted some fresh air."

His blue gaze fixed on her immediately. "In the midst of a storm?"

"It seemed the thing to do at the time. It wasn't smart, was it?"

His lips pressed together and he looked away to stare at the long box she'd been sitting on. He took a hesitant step closer but paused. "You're shivering. Do not be alarmed. I will sit down and you could curl into me. I have greater body heat than you probably do."

The idea of getting close to him didn't alarm her but instead it was a bit exciting. "Okay."

He moved slowly, as if he feared she'd bolt, until he inched around her and sat on the center of the box. The flag covered his lap and the top of one thigh, the other side slit up to the knot riding his hip. His gaze held hers.

"There is no reason to fear me."

"You can use my name. It's Beauty."

"I remember." His body looked hard and muscular—unyielding—as his arms parted as if to expose his entire chest to her view. "Allow me to warm you. I won't do more than sit here. You curl into me. I won't touch you."

She wasn't even sure what to do but hesitantly approached. He was so large and his bronzed skin mesmerized her. His legs closed until his thighs were clamped together and he broke eye contact.

"Sit sideways across my lap and lean against me."

I can do this. She sat down on him the way he wanted and peered up at his face. He closed his eyes though and avoided looking at her again. Warmth seeped through the flags in seconds and she dragged her wet hair over her other shoulder to prevent it from brushing the chest she leaned against. He was solid and firm. She opened her hand and pressed it against the tight abs of his lower belly.

He sucked in air but didn't open his eyes as she felt the muscles bunch under her palm. "You're very warm."

"Good." Shadow's voice came out unusually deep. "What was your nightmare about? We should pass the time talking. You are safe at Homeland. There is nothing for you to fear."

Beauty grew braver and adjusted a little on his lap. It was comfortable sitting on him and she rested her cool cheek against his chest more firmly.

37

The smell of him filled her nose as she took a deep breath. It was a nice masculine scent mixed with hints of the storm.

"It was actually a memory of something real that happened. I wish it was just part of my imagination."

She thought he tensed but the motion was so mild that she wasn't sure if he just slightly adjusted or if it was a reaction to her words. He breathed and it rubbed his chest a little against her. She liked the feel of him and relaxed against his frame.

"Do you want to talk about it? We all have things that have happened to us that follow us into our dreams."

"I did something bad when I was rescued."

"You didn't believe they were really there to free you? It's a common mistake a lot of us made. You are not to blame. Who thought we could ever trust humans?"

"It was a man," she admitted. "He asked me to be nice to him. He feared I'd attack him and I…" Her voice trailed off. She was ashamed to admit what she'd done.

His hand tentatively patted her back twice before it stopped. The touch was so soft she barely felt it. "It is understandable if you tried to harm him."

"I did worse."

"Humans harmed us. Nothing is your fault, Beauty."

Her heart did funny things, hearing the raspy way he said her name. She listened to his heartbeat. It was loud in her ear and strong. Steady. It was soothing and nice. "I thought..." She bit her lip. "I don't even want to say it."

"That he would harm you? That's what humans did to us."

She pulled away from him a little to stare up at his face. His chin lowered and he peered back at her. Compassion and acceptance softened them and encouraged her to speak. She wanted to confess to Shadow for some reason.

"I was owned by a man so old his hair was white and his skin was wrinkled. He would yell at me sometimes when I was a child and I didn't know why he seemed so angry. It wasn't until I grew older that things turned worse. He was waiting until I was an adult to get what he wanted from me."

Shadow suddenly growled and his facial expression changed. A flash of fear shot through her and her instincts made her want to bolt. He must have sensed it because his arms loosely wrapped around her.

"Calm," he softly ordered. "I'd never harm you. It's not you I feel the rage toward. I've heard the stories of what was done to Gift Females. There's no need to relive the trauma you suffered."

"I need to talk about it." She wanted to get to know Shadow and hear his story. She hoped sharing hers would make him open up. "He never hurt me physically when I was growing up. I've heard some of the stories too. He didn't molest me as a child."

Some of the anger eased from his features. "I am glad to hear it."

"He waited for me to mature."

His chest under her hand vibrated half a second before a growl was muffled behind his closed lips. She understood it wasn't directed at her. Her gaze left his to focus on his chest. It was easier to talk while not staring into his eyes.

"He wasn't too physically abusive, it was more mental. I didn't enjoy him touching me but I've heard worse stories. It didn't even last long."

"Stop," Shadow whispered. "Please?"

She looked at his face and it surprised her to see unshed tears in his eyes. He hurt for her and it stunned her that a stranger would feel such emotion over something that had happened in her past.

"He got cancer. It's a disease that made him weak and sick."

"I hope he died painfully." Shadow's jaw clenched.

"He survived but he couldn't touch me anymore. It left him in a wheelchair and unable to hurt me."

"Good." He snarled.

She nodded and leaned back against him, closing her eyes. His heartbeat had increased, hammering inside his chest. "The guards never dared touch me. They did say things. I knew what they wanted from me. They'd offer me more food and to treat me nicer if I did things to them and for them."

His arms around her tightened enough that she felt secure in his hold. "We do what we must to survive."

"I never did it." She shivered, remembering how they'd taunt her by eating in front of her and saying crude things. "I was never nice to them.

They scared me but I knew if I told Master that he'd fire them. He made it clear that none of them were allowed to put their hands on me. He would question me a lot about that and made me promise to tell him if anyone tried to come into the basement without him sending them there to fetch me to visit him."

"You remembered this and had a nightmare."

She nodded. "I was scared when I was rescued. I didn't know it at the time but Master had heard his association to Mercile Industries was discovered and he fled the country. He must have feared they'd find out he owned me. He left me with those men. They were always telling me to be nice to them, asking me to do sexual things with them. They had mean eyes and handled me roughly when they took me to a new location to hide. I hated the way they watched me shower." She shivered at the memory, remembering her terror that she'd be attacked. "I often made them angry so they'd punish me by not allowing me to get clean."

Shadow hugged her against his body more firmly. She liked how warm and safe it made her feel. "I think Master hoped no one would find out he had me and he'd threatened the men to keep me alive in case he could get me back. I've thought a lot about it. He must have ordered them not to touch me. It's the only thing that could have kept them from just taking what they wanted."

"Don't call him that. No one owns you."

"It's the only name I have for him. It was a rule."

"There are no more rules."

She nodded. "Not with him."

41

"You're free and never going back. There's no need to have nightmares."

"The man who helped rescue me asked me to be nice to him. I thought he wanted me to do things to him," she admitted softly. "That's what I was dreaming about. He was very kind and I'd been so afraid for so long. They kept me hungry and locked in chains in the dark. They said things about what they'd do to me if Master said to kill me. They were planning on hurting me first." Her voice choked up. "The man who rescued me was so nice. I thought if I was nice to him, he'd keep me safe. I had never given in to someone before but I did with him. I thought if I allowed him to have my body that he'd protect me from my old life."

"What is his name?" Shadow snarled. "A task force member shared sex with you? I'll kill him."

Her head snapped up and rage showed on his face. "No. He stopped me immediately. That's why I feel shame and dream about it. He was horrified. I misunderstood and I touched him wrong. Nothing happened between us."

He leaned in closer, staring deeply into her eyes. "The truth? You can tell me anything. I'll make him pay if he took advantage of you."

"He didn't. It's my shame."

"You were mistaken and scared." He slid one arm from around her waist and his big hand gently cupped her face. "You were trying to survive the best you could. There is no shame in that. Are you sure he didn't take advantage of you? Touch you wrong? Perhaps ask you to touch him?"

42

"He stopped me immediately. I'll never forget the look in his eyes. He was horrified."

"Did you tell the females about this?"

"No."

"Why not?"

She blinked back tears. "He was honestly nice to me. He looked at me in a way that no one ever had. I mattered and was a person to him. I'd have had to admit to the women that I touched the front of his pants. He swore no one would ever hurt me again and I wanted that. He was willing to die to protect me. We were being shot at by a sniper and he used his body to shield me."

Shadow's eyes softened. "Every male at Homeland would give their lives to protect you. That's the truth. You never have to share sex to be safe. You matter and are precious. Do you know this now?"

"I do."

"Good." He glanced away. "It was an honest mistake, Beauty. Don't torment yourself anymore with the nightmares." He lowered his hand from her face to return to the small of her back where he rubbed.

She snuggled against him. He was warm and so strong that she really did feel safe being held by him. His heartbeat slowed. He had large hands but they were amazingly gentle and the soft petting of her lower back was welcome.

"Tell me about you," she encouraged.

His rubbing paused. "I was raised at Mercile. They kept us chained inside rooms and experimented on us."

"How were you freed?"

His body tensed. All his muscles seemed to harden against her before he blew out a breath and relaxed again. "I had been moved to a new place where they did other things to us. I don't want to discuss it. It's not a good story."

"Do any of us have those in our past?"

His chuckle surprised her. "No."

"Please tell me?"

Shadow held the small female secure in his arms. She was dainty and he was afraid he'd scare her by moving too fast. Her skin had been chilled when she'd first rested her cheek against him but she warmed quickly. He was glad for that despite it being torture to hold her so close when he had to trap his hard dick between his thighs to hide it.

"Mercile employees had learned that other facilities had been breached by law enforcement. They were being hunted and they managed to drug and move some of us to a new location. They were desperate for money and we were the only means they had of making enough of it to attempt to flee the country and avoid prosecution." He paused, not wanting to tell her the rest.

"How did they do that? Were they offering to ransom you to the NSO?"

44

"No." He managed to hold back the anger he still felt. "It seems there are a bunch of rich humans who would love to own a Species baby." The idea enraged and sickened him that some infant might be treated as if it were a pet. "It isn't a good story."

She stroked his him gently and he hated the way his dick throbbed. Her palms and fingertips were more human than Species, their texture soft. Beauty had been through a lot and the fact that she trusted him enough to sit on his lap left him in awe of her courage.

"Please tell me? I shared with you."

She had. The thought of what had been done to her seemed to lessen his own trauma. She was so small that she wouldn't have stood a chance at defending herself. At least the bigger females were strong and had lashed out at their captors whenever possible. He was relieved she hadn't been molested as a child but it made him angry that she'd been harmed at all.

"They gave me drugs." He couldn't refuse to tell her his story. "The breeding drugs."

"What are those?"

She hadn't come from Mercile. She'd been spared the testing, had been given away to an investor—a more personal, hellish experience in his mind. Gift Females had been cut off from all others of their kind and most of them had been murdered at the hands of their abusers.

"Mercile invented a drug that increased our sex drives to near insanity." Shame filled him that he'd been used that way. "They did things to us to force out our semen to sell."

"Why would they do that?"

45

"They wanted to freeze it and sell it to other humans who believed they could use female humans to carry our young inside their wombs. They planned to sell the infants."

Beauty snuggled tighter against him. "I'm sorry. Were they able to do it? Do you have young out there?"

"The doctors don't think it worked. I desperately want to believe that is true. I have nightmares about helpless infants in the hands of those monsters. My offspring." His voice deepened but he tried to refrain from snarling. "I would track them down and save them if it was the last thing I did, even knowing I'd die."

She continued to stroke his chest and he appreciated the comfort she tried to give. "The doctors are smart. I'm sure they wouldn't say that unless they believed it. I know Dr. Trisha and Dr. Alli well and they wouldn't lie to us."

"I know. I trust them too. Our sperm dies quickly and they said it wouldn't have survived the freezing process they used to ship it to another country. That's where the buyers were located."

"You should stop worrying about that then."

He hated to do it but he shifted a little. His ass was starting to hurt from sitting too long in one spot on the hard wood under him. Beauty didn't seem to mind or even notice since she didn't protest in any way.

"The storm is passing. I should radio for help."

"It's still raining." She pulled away from him enough to stare into his eyes. He loved hers. They were such a soft brown and so sweet that it

46

amazed him that she could trust anyone after what had been done to her. "Stay with me. Please?"

He didn't want to leave her either. "I'll stay for a little while longer but then I must call in for a female officer. You need to be returned to the women's dorm."

She smiled. "Isn't that funny?"

"What?"

"That we call it that. Do you know what has been difficult for me to learn since I came here?"

"What?" He was curious and liked it when she appeared amused.

"I was raised around all humans and they never used the terms female or male. I've had to try to learn to use those words. And there is the whole 'human' thing. They were just people to me. Why isn't it females' dorm instead of women's dorm?"

He couldn't help but smile back. "I'm unsure. I think that's just what the building was named when we were brought here and it stuck."

"Why are Species called female or male instead of women or men?"

"Mercile referred to us solely as that. They were men and we were less. Just males."

He hated to see her humor fade as sadness invaded her gaze. "Oh. I know about being thought of as less." Her chin lifted. "The guards gave me mean names."

He didn't even want to know what she'd been called. It would piss him off. "I like the name you took."

"The rescue team chose this one for me and I kept it."

"It is very fitting."

She smiled again. "You think I'm attractive?"

Beauty took his breath away and trapped it inside his chest until he forced his lungs to work again. "Yes."

"Good. I think you're attractive too." Her hand left his chest and timidly rose to his hair, her fingertips brushing the ends of it. "Why is it so short?"

"I worked with the task force of humans who work for the NSO. I just returned to Homeland days ago. I lived in the basement at the unit's headquarters. We cut our hair to fit in with the others."

"I hate basements." Her hand lowered to curve around the top of his shoulder and made him very aware of her light touch. "Did you have windows?"

"No."

"I didn't either," she admitted. "I remember the times I was taken out into the sunshine." Her eyes closed as if she clung to the memory so she could picture it vividly in her mind. Her expression validated his guess when she smiled. "It was so warm and bright. Those are some of my best memories of growing up."

"I'm glad you had some good ones."

Her eyes opened and she smiled. "There was a small courtyard with grass and a water fountain. Once a week I was allowed outside for an hour or two. Master didn't like how pale my skin would become and he said I needed a little color."

Shadow wanted to wrap his fingers around the human's throat and choke the living shit out of the one who'd abused Beauty. She was grateful that someone had allowed her time out of her cell because they hadn't liked the way she looked. It also explained why she would run outside during a storm. She had no idea how dangerous it could be.

"Promise me something, Beauty."

"Okay." The instant agreement stunned him a little. She didn't even know what he wanted but granted his request. It reinforced her innocence.

"Stay indoors when there's a storm. You could have been struck by lightning or a tree could have fallen from the wind and rain. It's dangerous to go out in them."

"I know."

"Then why do it?" He frowned, showing his displeasure.

"I just wanted to do something, anything, to break free I guess."

"You are free."

She ran her hand from his shoulder to the center of his chest and she ducked her head, laying her cheek against him. "I'm really not, Shadow."

Her words alarmed him. "What do you mean? You are free. Is someone saying otherwise? Look at me. Tell me."

She hesitated. Had someone at Homeland abused her? Frightened her? Was someone bullying her and ordering her to do things she didn't want? He'd get her to talk and he'd immediately handle the situation. He'd beat on anyone who intimidated her.

"I'm a Gift Female," she whispered.

"Yes. Who has frightened you? Who gives you orders?"

She finally met and held his gaze. "No men are allowed to approach or talk to me. I'm not allowed to work with them the way the bigger women do. We never leave Homeland to visit Reservation." Tears glistened in her eyes and it tugged at his heart instantly.

"It's for your protection."

"Against what? You? Are you going to hurt me?"

"Never!"

"Exactly. Are other Species men going to hurt me?"

"No. They'd never dare."

"I'm..." Her voice died.

"You're what?"

"I'm lonely."

Her tears spilled over and slid down her cheeks. He couldn't resist wiping them away with his thumb. It hurt him to see them. "You're surrounded by females. I'll talk to them and they will spend more time with you. Just tell me what you need and I'll make sure you get it."

"You're the first man who has ever held me, Shadow."

Her words slowly sank into his stunned mind.

"Male. Sorry." She sniffed. "You're holding me. You don't want anything more than to keep me warm and comfort me. I've never sat on

50

someone's lap before or gotten to listen to their heartbeat. Even touched their hair."

He was mute, astounded.

"I listen when men visit my friends but that's never going to happen to me. I'd never have gotten to speak to you if it wasn't for you finding me in the storm and bringing me here to safety. Being a Gift Female is a prison of sorts. Master had sex with me a long time ago but he never held or talked to me. He just did what he did and never even removed all my clothes. I've never been kissed. The other women know all that but I'll never know what it's like." Her attention dropped to his chest. "May I tell you what I always wanted to know the most?"

"What?" He managed to get one word out around the lump in his throat.

"I wonder what it would be like to sleep with someone holding me and have him there in case I woke from a nightmare."

Shadow had never considered what life was like for a Gift Female. They had only females to comfort them and he couldn't imagine being segregated from over half his own kind after knowing freedom. There were fewer females than males. The female officers he dealt with were warm and he always appreciated their touches when they gave out hugs or pats when he worked side by side with them.

"I'll hold you for as long as you want, Beauty."

She sniffed. "Will you sleep with me?"

He was going to get in deep trouble in the morning when he returned her to the women's dorm and had to answer questions. Gift Females were

51

off-limits. Spending a night alone with one was against the rules. He knew that but he couldn't deny her. She gazed at him with hope and longing.

"Yes."

"Thank you."

His dick had softened, all interest in sex gone with her admissions. He was grateful for that. He glanced away. The floor was harder than the long wooden box he sat on. It wasn't going to be comfortable for him but she was all that mattered.

"We'll sleep here until morning and then I'll return you home." He shoved away the thought of what he'd face. Tiger or Fury would wish to speak to him. Worse, he could be taken to Justice. He hadn't been free as long as they had and his motives might come under scrutiny. "You can sleep on top of me. You're safe."

"I know. Thank you." She smiled.

Consequences be damned, he thought, staring at her. "I'll keep you warm and you may listen to my heartbeat if you wish." He glanced at the light. "Do you want it on or off?"

"I don't care."

He just turned—she didn't weigh much at all—and stretched out flat on his back along the bench. His feet hung off the end but Beauty settled down over him, sprawled facing him. Her hands curled at the top of his shoulders and she rested her cheek over his heart. He slowly wrapped his arms around her waist to keep her from sliding off him to the floor.

"Comfortable?"

"Yes. Are you?"

"Yes," he lied.

"Thank you, Shadow."

"Don't ever thank me for this. I'll be here if you have a nightmare. You're protected."

He closed his eyes to block out the soft light from above and forced his body to remain lax. Her breathing against his skin was warm and he knew as time passed that she fell asleep when her own heartbeat slowed. He doubted he'd slumber at all, too worried he might turn over or touch her wrong in his sleep.

Chapter Three

Beauty woke slowly, enjoying the warmth of her bed and the strange noise that somehow seemed comforting. Her eyes opened to stare at something odd hanging from a wall a few feet away. It slowly dawned on her that she was staring at net bags filled with an assortment of balls.

She froze, confused, but then realized the noise she heard was a heartbeat. *Shadow.* Memory returned instantly as her fingers gently dug into firm, hot flesh. In her sleep her hands had lowered to his sides to become trapped between his biceps and ribs.

It was a nice feeling, being so warm and snug on top of a man. She breathed in his scent, enjoying it. The smooth skin under her fingertips tempted her to explore. The thought of running her hands all over his body was hard to resist. The only reason she didn't do it was an uncertainty if it would wake him. He might get angry. That wasn't something she wanted to test. It would ruin the unique moment of waking with someone for the first time in her life.

The room was lighter than it had been the previous night as she gently lifted her head to find the source. A small window at the back of the room allowed in sunlight. Her focus shifted to Shadow's handsome face. He slept peacefully, looking much younger.

His arms rested over her back, a heavy weight she enjoyed. Her legs were stretched down his as she became aware of something else. A firm object was nestled between her slightly parted legs. The silky material of the flags they wore prevented a lot of her skin from touching his but something else was definitely between her thighs.

Beauty gently twisted her head and stared over her shoulder to find the source. Her lips parted when she realized what was poking up. Fear gripped her for a few seconds but she calmed. Shadow was aroused and it was a scary sight. His cock jutted upward between her thighs. The material covered the thick, rounded shape but she knew what it was.

Her legs tensed, unintentionally squeezing his sex with her thighs. He sucked in air, his chest under her expanded, and she turned her head in time to peer down into his blue eyes. They were confused at first as he blinked but it only lasted a heartbeat before his memory must have kicked in. His nose flared and a soft rumble came from his throat. It was almost a soft growl or maybe a moan. She wasn't sure which but she was fascinated by him.

His arms around her waist tightened but then relaxed. His hands rubbed gently, almost a pat to assure her she was safe. She continued to stare into his sexy eyes. They were very attractive and she didn't want to look away. The urge to explore his body with her hands struck again. Would he mind? Get angry? Stop her? She opened her mouth to ask permission but never got the words out.

A faint sound from outside drew her attention to the door. The body under hers seemed to harden all over and she gasped when the arms tightened around her waist. Shadow moved fast for someone who'd just woke. He shifted her quickly, lifted her to the side, and she watched with wide eyes as he crouched on the floor next to her. A deep snarl burst from his throat and his hands clawed against the concrete flooring in preparation to launch an attack. She could see his lips part and he showed his fangs.

The door burst open and Beauty whimpered, terrified at the sight of two big men filling the doorway. She almost slid off the long box in her haste to flee. She ended up huddled on it instead. Her attention shifted to Shadow. He was big and he was defending her against danger. Some of her fear eased.

The two men who stepped inside were in uniform. Shadow slowly rose to his full height. "Hello. I apologize. I heard someone approach and didn't realize it was you."

Beauty stared at the two officers as they watched her. She noticed both of them had paled. The one on the left snarled and rage changed his features into something scary as he glared at Shadow.

"She's Gift. What are you doing with her?"

"I can explain." Shadow growled back.

"Really?" The other man glanced at Shadow's waist. "I see what you were doing."

Beauty realized what the men thought had occurred. Shadow was definitely aroused and the flag tied around his waist did nothing to hold down his erect cock. She tore her attention away from it and slowly uncurled her body to slide off the box and stand.

"It isn't that way," Shadow protested. "I found her running in the storm."

"You thought you'd take advantage of her?" One of the men reached for the radio clipped to his belt, quickly using it to call in for help. "This is

Book. Get a female officer to the park now. We have a Gift Female on scene with a Species male inside the sports equipment building. Code red."

"No." Shadow backed up, his hands raised, palms out. "It isn't a code red."

"Move away from the Gift Female," the man ordered.

"Wait!" Beauty inched closer to Shadow's side.

The two officers ignored her. "Walk forward, outside and do not resist. We are taking you to Security."

"I said wait!" She spoke louder.

"Jericho, you know me," Shadow hissed. "This isn't what it appears. Inhale. I did not share sex with her."

"It doesn't matter. You were alone with her and neither of you are dressed. We located your abandoned cart and have been searching for you. You obviously spent the time with her. You need to explain this."

"Stop!" Beauty yelled, actually stepping in front of Shadow to get between him and the officers. "This isn't...he didn't...just stop!"

"I'm trying to tell you what happened," Shadow spoke at the same time.

One of the officers finally lowered his accusing gaze and it softened when he met hers. "You are safe. A female is on her way. Remain calm and please step away from the male."

"No. I won't." She opened her arms wide and made sure no one would get around her to reach Shadow. "He didn't do anything to me."

"Beauty," Shadow spoke behind her, "move out of the way. I'll go outside with them."

She turned her head to stare at him, more than a little upset that he seemed to be in trouble for spending the night alone with her. "No. You didn't do anything."

His expression became shuttered. "I broke rules when I didn't immediately radio in the situation. You're not helping me. Please step aside and wait for a female to arrive. It will be fine."

She studied him closely but she couldn't tell if he was being honest or not. Her arms dropped to her sides and she faced him, noting that he wasn't aroused anymore since the flag draped smoothly over his thighs.

"It will be fine," he assured her a second time. "It will make it worse if you don't allow me to go."

"Okay."

She didn't know what to do as he bent to retrieve his discarded clothing and boots. The officers stepped outside with him and the door closed after them, leaving her alone inside the equipment building. Beauty darted to her discarded nightgown but it was still wet. She released it and stared at the door, straining to pick up any conversation.

It was too quiet and she wanted to go outside to make sure Shadow wasn't in trouble but hesitated. The other men had seemed really angry and they frightened her a little. She hated not having the courage to march out there and state again that she hadn't been hurt.

Minutes passed before the door opened and dread gripped her when Kit entered, anger forming crinkles around her mouth and eyes. The tall

58

Species woman wore her work uniform. She always intimidated Beauty a little.

The feline sniffed loudly before her gaze swept the room and halted on Beauty. "Are you harmed? Did that male do anything to you?"

"No."

"How did he take you from the dorm?"

"He didn't. I went for a run in the storm and he found me."

"I bet he did."

"He wanted to call for someone right away but I asked him to stay with me. He didn't do anything wrong."

"Sit."

Beauty instantly sat on the edge of the box, the other Species' tone so harsh it made her knees weak.

"I don't smell sex but there are things a male can do to hide the scent. Did he force you to put your mouth on his dick?" She growled the words. "Did he ask you to touch him?"

"No."

"Don't lie for him!"

"I'm not." Tears filled her eyes at the ugly accusations, a reaction she couldn't help. "He didn't do anything wrong. He just stayed with me the way I asked. The storm was bad and we slept here."

Kit stomped closer and gripped Beauty's arm. "Let's go."

Beauty was hauled to her feet and pulled to the door. The rain had stopped when they stepped out into the early morning sunshine. The grass was cold and squishy under her bare feet. It surprised her when she glanced around to find no one else nearby. Shadow and the two officers were gone.

"You need to be trained better," Kit hissed. "Gifts are clueless children and I don't enjoy babysitting you. I keep telling Ellie and Breeze you need to be toughened up and taught to fight but they coddle you. A male would never pull this shit on a female officer." Kit's hand tightened on her as she walked faster, pulling Beauty alongside her through the park.

"Do you know what he could have done to you? Anything. You're weak and wouldn't have been able to stop him. You even allowed him to spend the night with you. That's stupid. Do you know anything about our males? He could have seduced you and you couldn't handle that." She snarled a curse under her breath. "Never mind. Just don't talk at all. I'm furious."

"Shadow is—"

"I said don't talk." Kit came to an abrupt halt and growled, showing fangs. "I was on my way to breakfast when I received the assistance code. I'm hungry and want to eat. Instead I'm taking you home. You're grounded for a week. No privileges. You aren't to leave your room."

Defiance rose inside Beauty and she jerked hard to free her arm from Kit's hold. "I'm not a child!"

Kit growled. "You need a spanking and I might give you one if you don't shut up."

"Shadow didn't do anything wrong and I'm not weak or stupid. I'm an adult and probably almost as old as you are. You can't restrict my privileges and don't threaten to hit me. You should have been a canine mix because you're a bitch."

"What did you say to me?" Kit took a threatening step forward.

Beauty refused to back down. "I don't know what your problem is but you're mean, Kit. I might not be as strong as you or as big but I have something you never will."

"I'm dying to hear this. What would that be?"

"You have been given so much but you don't appreciate it. You're cruel to your own kind when we aren't the enemy."

"I am not."

"I live next door to you." Beauty walked away, determined to distance herself from the angry Species and return to the dorm on her own. She took five steps before Kit's hand clamped down on her shoulder to make her stop. She stared at Kit.

"What does that mean?"

"You think Shadow forced me into that shed. You're the naïve one if you believe I didn't welcome spending time with him. I'd never treat him the way you do our males by using them and tossing them out your door the second you get what you want from them. Release me."

Shock was evident on the feline's features as her eyes widened. No words came from her lips but she did release her. Beauty faced forward and marched through the damp grass, avoiding the muddy puddles.

"Hey, Beauty?"

Her back stiffened but she kept going, refusing to verbally spar with Kit. She'd stood up for herself and said the words that had filled her head. It had felt good despite being terrified the woman would strike out. The fight would be short and Beauty knew she couldn't win if there was actual violence.

"You're growing pretty brave for a primate. Too bad your fangs aren't as sharp as your tongue. Words don't hurt as much as physical pain. Remember that."

Beauty halted and peered over her shoulder to see if Kit was still watching her, wondering if it was a threat. "I wouldn't agree and that statement just proves who is more intelligent between us." She opened her mouth, curled her upper lip back, and hissed at the feline. She had sharp teeth and didn't hesitate to show them for once. "I'm not as weak as you think."

Kit did the unexpected by suddenly grinning. "Get your ass home. I think I actually like you. Breeze is fit to be tied. Good luck with her. You better hope Ellie has arrived at the dorm to handle you instead."

Beauty hurried through the park to the sidewalk. Carts and Jeeps passed her but she kept her head down, refused to glance at them to see if she was being stared at. It wasn't normal for a Gift Female to walk alone. Escorts were usually assigned to them if they left the dorm. Her wearing a flag would also draw a lot of attention.

Dread made her stomach quiver when she reached the front doors and Breeze opened them. The tall Species wore an oversized T-shirt and it was obvious by her messy hair that she'd recently rolled out of bed.

"Are you all right?" Concern etched her features. "Should I take you to Medical?"

"I'm fine." Beauty wanted to flee to her room but the canine had other ideas when she grabbed her hand, holding on to it. It made her stop to stare up at Breeze.

"Security wouldn't tell me his name. I want it or I'm going to sniff you to find out." Her voice deepened into a growl. "I'll take care of him. He'll pay for what he's done."

"He didn't do anything." Beauty hated the way everyone assumed Shadow had done something bad to her. She wiggled her hand free and crossed her arms over her chest. Worry for Shadow made her feel braver than normal. "Leave him alone. Better yet, mind your own business."

Breeze gaped at her in astonishment. "What?"

"I appreciate your concern and the fact that you'd go after a man in retribution for whatever crime you assume he committed but leave him alone."

"Are you running a fever? Feeling ill? Your immune system isn't as tough as ours. Did you catch a cold?"

"No. There's nothing wrong with me. That's the problem. No one seems to be able to realize that. I'm not weak or stupid. I spent the night with a man who held me while I slept. That's all he did and I'm grateful to him. Not grateful that he just held me without trying to have sex with me but that he was there at all. Shadow is wonderful." She spun away and rushed to the stairs, longing to reach her room to get away from everyone.

Breeze caught up with her as she yanked open her apartment door and entered. She almost closed the door on the other Species before she saw her. The door was pushed open and her apartment invaded by a wary canine sporting a frown.

"Beauty? What the hell is going on?"

"Leave me alone." She decided to retreat to her room since there was no way she could physically kick out Breeze.

The door slammed and she jumped, her head snapping around. Breeze hadn't left but instead watched with her dark, intense gaze. "Talk to me. What has gotten into you? Why were you even outside last night? Did he come in here and get you? How did you even meet Shadow? He's one of the newer males. He was assigned to the task force."

Tears welled in her eyes and she hated them. "Why bother to talk? I'm a Gift Female. I know the rules."

Breeze stalked her, moving on bare feet in a way that made her feel a little fear. She was an intimidating woman and had an odd expression on her face. She paused a few feet away.

"I can't help you unless you tell me what is wrong."

Beauty wiped at her tears. "You wouldn't understand. No one does."

"Make me. Talk. What does you being Gift have to do with this and what rules?"

She pondered speaking her mind. She didn't see any anger on Breeze's face though. "I'm not Halfpint or Tiny. They are terrified of men. I love both of them, they are my friends, but they need those rules to protect them. I don't."

Breeze's eyes widened in surprise. She sidestepped to the couch and sat. "Go on."

"I'm lonely. Do you know what it is like for me?"

"No." Breeze's voice softened to almost a whisper. "Tell me."

"I just want what everyone else has."

"We're equal here."

"No. We aren't. Have you stayed out all night with a man before?"

"Of course."

"Did angry security officers take him away? Were you called names and insulted as though you were somehow tricked into being with him? Were you followed to your room to have it invaded by someone who demands answers?"

"Who called you names and insulted you?"

"Kit. She thinks I'm a child and stupid because I wanted to know what it was like to be held by a man. He didn't try to do anything to me sexually but I wish he had. He never will though. I'm Gift. He won't even speak to me again and it's not fair."

"Oh shit," Breeze muttered, understanding dawning. "You went in search of a male?"

"No. I wanted to feel free and alive. I don't here. I ran into the rain to get away from this place and he found me. The hail started and Shadow took me to the small building to protect me from the storm. He tried to leave right away to call for assistance but I just wanted to spend time with him." Hot tears spilled down her cheeks. "Now he's in trouble because I tricked him into staying with me and everyone seems to be angry at him. He did nothing wrong except believe me when I said I'd be terrified if he left me alone. I just wanted to get to know him."

Breeze closed her eyes. Beauty didn't know what the other woman was thinking but she guessed now she would be in trouble for admitting that she'd lied to Shadow. It was a bad trait Species detested, though it was sometimes necessary. Tricking a man into spending the night wasn't for the good of anyone but Beauty. Breeze opened her eyes and gazed at her.

"I'm going to place some calls and make sure Shadow isn't in trouble. Then you and I are going to talk. Don't go anywhere. I'll be right back."

"I know. I'm restricted to my room. Kit grounded me."

"She what?" Breeze rose to her feet with a snarl.

"That's what Gifts are to all of you, right? Children? Why did you bother to save us? It's a prison without abuse but it's still captivity. Sunshine, nicer living conditions, and food aren't enough." Beauty fled to her bedroom and closed the door.

* * * * *

Shadow paced the room, hating that he'd been denied the opportunity to change into his clothing. The flag secured around his hips had made other males laugh when they'd seen him, more than a little amused, until they'd heard why he was being taken to Fury.

The male entered his office with a grim expression. "Shadow."

"Fury."

"That's taking team spirit a bit far."

66

Shadow bit back a snarl. "My uniform was soaked from the storm and this was all that was available. It was better than being naked. Book and Jericho refused to allow me to change."

The corners of Fury's mouth twitched. "It isn't every day you see a male wearing a wolf head wrapped around his waist."

"I didn't do anything to the Gift Female. I spotted her running in the rain. I believed she was a human at first but quickly determined her origins. I only took her to that building to get her out of the hail but she was too terrified for me to leave her alone to radio for help. I only held her to keep her warm."

"I'm aware." All humor fled from Fury. "I just spoke to the males. They didn't pick up the scent of sex."

"She's a Gift Female."

"You know protocol."

"She refused to allow me to leave her alone. I had left my radio in the cart."

The other male raised his hand to his chest. "What is she? This high? Do you expect me to believe she prevented you from doing the right thing?" His palm lowered. "Try again."

Shadow adjusted his stance and crossed his arms over his chest. He felt ridiculous in the flag. "May I speak freely?"

"Always."

"Something upset her enough to make her leave the safety of the dorm. I was concerned and she behaved fine until I intended to call a female officer for assistance. Have you ever looked into Beauty's eyes? I couldn't say no. She wanted to spend the night away from her home and asked me to stay with her. I hoped she'd tell me what was really going on but she didn't."

Fury leaned back against his desk. "Are you implying she's being abused by someone there? That one of our females is harming her? Do you have proof of that?" Anger glinted in his eyes. "I want to get to the bottom of this immediately."

Shadow hesitated. "I don't know. She didn't want to go back, Fury. She nearly panicked when I said I'd leave her to call for assistance."

The door opened and Shadow's mouth opened in astonishment as Breeze stormed into the room wearing just an oversized T-shirt that fell to her thighs, her hair a tangled mess.

Fury straightened. "Hello, Breeze. I would say good morning but it isn't one. What is going on at the women's dorm?"

Breeze studied Shadow from his bare feet upward to his attire and finally held his gaze. "Shadow."

"I didn't do anything to the Gift Female."

She turned to stare at Fury. "We have a problem."

"I'm aware. I left my mate and son at home to be here on my day off. Why was Beauty out in that storm instead of safely inside her apartment? Do you know? And before you tear into the male, I believe him—that he didn't attempt to initiate shared sex with her."

"I'm not here to castrate him. I just left Beauty." Her gaze cut to Shadow. "She defended his actions." She put her hands on her hips as she

68

focused back on Fury. "This is hard to say but we majorly screwed the pooch."

"What?" Fury's eyebrows shot up.

"It's a human saying," Breeze explained. She pointed a thumb at Shadow. "It means we have made a major mistake. Our Beauty resents being classified as a Gift Female and she's curious about him."

"I don't understand."

Shadow was with Fury on that one. He was confused too. "Curious how?"

"Stay out of this, toga boy," Breeze muttered, dismissing Shadow. "Are you hearing what I'm putting down, Fury?"

"No. Could you speak plainly? Not all of us love human slang and I haven't even had coffee or donuts this morning."

"Okay." She nodded. "Here's blunt for you. Beauty is curious about males. As in I think she resents the protective bubble we've formed around her to keep them from offering to share sex. We have a Gift Female who might be ready to experiment a little with having physical contact with males." She jerked her thumb at Shadow again. "Get it? We never thought any of them would want to be touched but we should have."

Shadow felt about as stunned as Fury looked. He hoped his mouth hadn't fallen open the way the other male's had. He sealed his lips tightly together to make sure. His mind began to work again and he forced the air from his lungs.

"She didn't try to initiate sex with me."

Breeze turned her head to stare at him. "Are you sure?"

"I'd have noticed."

She approached him until only inches separated them. "She's not a typical female, toga boy." Her hands suddenly flattened on his chest and dug in enough to make him growl out a warning not to hurt him. "This is how I'd come at you. I'd knock you on your ass if that's what it took to get my point across of what I wanted from you but she's not me." She released him quickly and she spun to face Fury. "Her just asking him to stay with her might be her version of attempting it. They've never dealt with our males. Maybe humans enjoy timid hints and those are the only males she's known. Toga boy here might have missed those hints she might have put down."

"Stop calling me that," Shadow demanded. "She spoke to me and never said anything that implied she was interested in sharing sex."

Breeze looked at him over her shoulder. "What did she talk about?"

"Her captivity." He paused. "She shared some details about the male who had her and her life."

"See?" The canine female threw up her hands. "There you go. Human women babble about their pasts when they are around a hot guy they are interested in. I watch their movies and that's a dead giveaway." She frowned at Fury. "What should we do? Give him to her? It won't be hard for her to unwrap him with the outfit he's wearing."

Shadow staggered a little. "What? Give me to her? No!"

Fury had the audacity to laugh. "True. It's just a little knot at the waist." He ran his fingers through his hair and his expression changed to a grim one as he watched Breeze. "Is that what you suggest? We send him to her to

70

appease her curiosity? I think we should find a male who has a lot of experience with human females. They are vastly different from Species and so are Gifts. He might scare her, and hell, maybe we should consider one of the task force members. Maybe a human would be better in this case. I know a few of them very well and I'll consult with Tiger and Brass. We could find a very mild one whom we could trust to back off if she changes her mind."

The idea of someone from the task force touching Beauty sent anger coursing through Shadow. "Humans abused her and you want to send one to her bed? No!"

"Fury has a good point though," Breeze sighed. "Our males are aggressive. It's not as if we have any Gift males. We could send Smiley to her. He's primate and very mellow. He's also smaller than toga boy and won't crush her. Primates like sex face-to-face too. I'm sure she'd appreciate that over being mounted from behind. I can't see her taking the swelling and locking together afterward very well either. She's little."

"So is my Ellie and she handles me fine." Fury glared.

"I'm not dogging on canine males. Hello! I'm canine too." Breeze rolled her eyes. "I'm just saying she's Gift. She might not appreciate a fully turned-on Species with the canine traits." She glanced at Shadow. "Toga boy is canine. I'd suggest a feline but again—the aggressive traits."

"I said, stop calling me that," Shadow growled, losing his temper. "Are you certain she wants to share sex? She didn't give me that impression and I slept with her on my chest all night."

71

"Maybe he's right. We might be reading too much into this. Talk to her, Breeze. Maybe she's just confused or it's a passing thing." Fury sounded hopeful. "We should investigate this more but if that's the case, I insist on it being a Species male. Shadow has a point. Humans abused her."

"You do that. It's my job to protect my females and see to their needs." Breeze glared at him. "She feels enslaved by our rules regarding Gift Females. She said so. I'm going to do something about this right now."

Fury regarded her warily. "What do you have in mind?"

Breeze turned her head to narrow her gaze at Shadow. He could almost see her mind working, plotting something.

"No." He vehemently shook his head. "I'm not the male you want to use as some experiment to see if she wants to share sex." The idea sent him into a panic. "I was abused too and it's been too long since I shared sex with a female. I avoid it."

"Even better." Breeze smiled. "You won't initiate it and you'd be sensitive to her trauma." She glanced at Fury. "Are you thinking what I am?"

"Shit," Fury groaned. "I think so."

"What?" Shadow glanced between the two Species staring at him with calculated looks. "No. Whatever you are thinking, no!"

Chapter Four

"I refuse." Shadow glared at Brass.

The male watched him silently for long seconds. "Fine. The Gift Female showed an interest in you and you're the only male she's had contact with but I'm sure she'll do fine with a stranger. Is that the stance you're taking? Think about it long and hard."

"Haven't I been used as an experiment enough?"

"She's Gift. Wouldn't you lay down your life to protect her? They are our weakest females and helpless to defend themselves."

"Of course I would die if that's what it took to keep her safe."

"You feel secure that all males would take care with her? You're putting her in someone else's hands if you refuse to escort her to Reservation and live alongside her. What if they don't take her feelings into consideration as much as you would? What if they press her into doing more than she is comfortable with if they become really aroused? You wouldn't do that, would you?"

Shadow glared at his friend, guessing he'd come to Homeland just to be the one to talk him into agreeing to Breeze's plan. "Of course not. You're using guilt tactics?"

Brass shrugged. "She knows you. I'm aware of your history. She's not human so you shouldn't have adverse reactions being near her but you know all about having the will of your body taken from your control. You share that common bond with her. I trust that you would be hypersensitive

73

to her feelings and not pressure her into anything. How many males have that background?"

"We've all been forced to share sex at times due to Mercile attempting to breed children from us."

"You were drugged and strapped to sterile machines while your seed was forced from your body. It was a form of rape. The Gift Female was forced to endure a human putting his hands on her without regard. Neither of you had other Species to comfort you or make those events less traumatic. I read your report about what happened the night you spent with her. She allowed you to hold her and she admitted she'd never been kindly touched. You could have pushed for more physical contact but you didn't. You are perfect for this assignment. She may not wish to share sex but at least she'll feel secure enough with you to attempt it if she does. You're the right male for her."

"I'm not the right male for anyone." Shadow hated to admit weakness. "I'm deeply flawed inside, Brass. I suffer nightmares often, cold sweats, and I'm not prepared to share sex with anyone. I've had females offer but I have refused. I keep having flashbacks to the time I was held inside that warehouse."

"Wrath got past it."

"He's a stronger male than I am."

"Bullshit." Brass softly growled, flashing irritation in his steady gaze. "He is like a brother to you because you're so close and have similar traits. Do I need to call him here to speak to you? He and Lauren are enjoying their first days inside their new home in seclusion. Do you need his words instead of mine to convince you that you should be the one to tend the Gift Female? What would he say?"

"Shit." Shadow knew when he was beaten. "He'd tell me to go because I couldn't live with it if someone else pressured her into doing something she wasn't ready for when I could have prevented it."

"Exactly. You would be less inclined to mistake any signals she sends and be certain of what she wants before you act. Now pack a few weeks of clothing and be ready to fly out in thirty minutes. We're out of here then."

"I haven't taken the time to settle into my apartment yet. I haven't unpacked."

"Good." Brass drew closer. "You are the right male for this, Shadow. I'd worry if another male were to spend time with a Gift Female. This is new territory. We have no idea what to expect but we want them to thrive with freedom the way we do. She's fragile emotionally as well as physically. You won't forget that."

"That is true." He couldn't argue with Brass' logic.

"Just be yourself and all will be fine."

He wasn't so sure of that but the idea of Beauty being secluded with another male to allow her the freedom to pursue possible physical relations with him made Shadow want to snarl. She was too innocent and someone could take advantage of that.

* * * * *

75

"What is Reservation like?" Excitement and worry warred within Beauty as she watched Breeze pack her clothing in a duffle bag. "I've heard there are miles of trees and lots of open space."

"There are both of those things." Breeze grinned, meeting her gaze. "You will enjoy it. You're being sent to a cabin near a river." The smile faded. "You must not wade into the water. Do you understand? The current is strong. There's a small area that is safe. Your escort will show you. It's an inlet where the current doesn't reach and the water is only about waist high."

"Your waist or mine?"

Breeze chuckled. "Mine but you aren't that short. It won't be higher than your breasts."

"I don't know how to swim."

"I guessed that. None of us knew but we learned."

"Will my escort teach me how to swim too?"

"I'm unsure if he knows how. Just stay away from the main body of the river." The taller Species closed the bag. "There you go. You're loaded up with enough outfits to last you a few weeks. Getting away will be good for you and you will know real freedom. The Wild Zone is just the place. The inhabitants were warned to stay away. Not that they'd harm you."

"Do they know I'm Gift?" Beauty hated the idea of being stared upon with pity. She got it a lot when she was in the general population and caught the attention of some of the men who dared glance her way.

"Anyone who sees you knows. Your size gives that away but yes, they are aware and that's why they will stay out of your territory."

76

"Oh." Disappointment hit.

"What is wrong?" Breeze's dark gaze sharpened, not missing anything.

"Nothing."

"Talk to me right now."

"I'd hoped going there would change things. I wanted to speak to men and get to know some of them."

"The Wild Zone is filled with our antisocial Species but they are aware they might be frightening for you if you were to run into them."

"Explain." Beauty perched on her bed.

"Some were considered failures by Mercile Industries. Their facial differences can be more severe than ours."

"I don't understand."

"Their animal traits are more pronounced. They look more animal than human. That's what I'm trying to say." Breeze reached up and rubbed her nose. "Ours are slightly wider than a typical human's but some of the Wild Zone males can have flatter features, their mouths shaped like whatever animal DNA they were mixed with, and their hair texture isn't always as human."

"Are they not allowed to live at Homeland?"

"They can live anywhere they wish but they prefer to keep away from humans entirely. They get stared at and it's uncomfortable for them. They were also treated less kindly at Mercile so they really detest humans. We had it rough but they had it much worse. They aren't prone to wanting to live with others and enjoy their solitude."

"Have you ever met any of them?"

"Of course." Breeze smiled again. "I've spent a lot of time at Reservation. I've even shared sex with one of them."

"What was that like?"

Breeze hoisted the heavy bag to drop the strap on her shoulder. "Interesting. Let me just say that their animal traits are also very close to the surface of their personalities. You have no reason to fear them though. They were spoken to by Valiant and Leo. Both of those males rule the Wild Zone."

"They are like Justice here at Homeland?"

"They are feline mixes but I wouldn't say they are similar to Justice in other ways. Justice is social and gets along well with others. Valiant and Leo are, well, different. Let's just say that when they say something our males listen. Justice earns respect. Valiant and Leo are very frightening."

"Are there any women Wild Zone residents?"

"Just Tammy. She's Valiant's human mate."

"I meant antisocial women with more animalistic traits."

"None of them survived." Breeze looked grim. "If they ever existed at all. None were found when we were freed. Mercile either didn't make what they considered mistakes with females or they had them killed." Breeze spun away to head for the bedroom door. "Sometimes I wish Kit would be sent there. She's a thorn in my side. I'd love for her to be someone else's problem. Let's go."

Beauty slid off the bed to follow. "What is Kit's problem?"

78

"I have no idea. She refuses to talk to me about why she is turning so mean." Breeze paused by the front door and held her gaze. "Are you ready for an adventure? You'll have fun and hopefully you'll enjoy this vacation."

"Who is my escort?"

"Shadow volunteered." Amusement showed on her features. "You know him. Is that all right?"

Her heart raced. "He asked to be the one to go with me? Really?"

"Is that going to be a problem? We figured you'd be comfortable sharing a cabin with him. There are two bedrooms."

"That's fine." Beauty tried to hide her excitement at seeing him again. "He isn't angry at me for getting him into trouble?"

"He was never in trouble. The males were just concerned for your safety. Everyone is aware that he didn't harm you. It's all good." She paused. "Do you want to talk first?"

"About what?"

Breeze lowered the bag to the floor and pressed her back against the door, staring at Beauty. "Sex."

Her cheeks turned really warm. "No."

"You're going away with Shadow. He won't offer to share sex with you but he's still male. I'm going to give you advice whether you ask for it or not. Are you ready?"

Embarrassment filled her that the other woman could read her so well. She nodded sharply, more than willing to listen to anything Breeze had to say.

"Okay. I'll assume you're curious but I'm guessing any sexual experience you've had wasn't enjoyable."

Beauty fought back tears as memories surfaced. "No," she whispered.

Anger glinted in dark-brown eyes. "I wish I could kill that bastard who had you under his thumb but that's another day when we catch him once he returns to the States. It's not that way when you share sex with someone who cares about you and who wants you to enjoy the experience. Our males do both. They are different from humans, which is a good thing. A Species male would never hurt you. They growl and are aggressive but saying no to them means stop. They will. Am I clear? If he's lost in passion then just box his ears. That's opening your hands and hitting his ears on both sides at once. You'll have his attention. A male would never strike you back. Repeat the word 'no' and he'll retreat immediately."

It stunned Beauty, thinking about hitting one of the big men. They were fierce. "Are you sure this ear boxing won't make a man really angry?"

"Oh, it will, but they'd never harm a female. I promise you that. That's another huge difference between our males and the humans you met when you were in captivity. They would never find honor in harming someone they knew would be defenseless against their strength. They will skulk away to calm but return in a better mood." She drew in a deep breath, exhaling slowly. "Shadow won't initiate sex with you but you could go after him. Do you want me to tell you how to go about that?"

Beauty nodded.

"Strip naked. Tell him you wish to share sex. Be blunt. That way he can't mistake it for anything else."

80

"What if he doesn't want me?"

Breeze laughed as all the tension faded from her features. "He's male, hon. You're beautiful. You were given that name for a reason. Shadow isn't a moron or blind. He'll want you. And remember this. It's important."

"Okay."

"He's more afraid of you than you are of him. Trust me on that."

Doubt assailed her. "I believe you're wrong."

"I'm right. For all their macho crap, nothing is scarier to one of our males than someone they think might break under them. You haven't seen any of our males fall for humans but I have. It's some funny shit but don't repeat I ever said it." Breeze sobered. "Shadow was abused while in captivity. Just know that he's got some sexual hang-ups too and he will be sensitive to what you have survived."

It hurt Beauty to be reminded about Shadow's past. "He knows what it's like to be spun around and pinned down while someone hurts him from behind?"

Breeze closed her eyes and breathed heavily for long seconds before she focused her gaze on Beauty. Rage simmered there. "No. His suffering involved drugs and machines. Do me a favor though. Tell Shadow to take you facing him if you decide to share sex with him. Tell him it's important and I said so. Can you do that for me?"

"Yes."

"Good." Breeze pushed away from the door and lifted the bag. "Let's go. The helicopter pilots should be prepared to fly you to Reservation by now. Just tell Shadow if the flying frightens you. I'm sure he'll be more than happy to be comforting. The ride isn't long."

"I've never been conscious before while in the air. They drugged me when I was brought here."

"It will be fine. I've flown lots of times."

The hallway was empty but Beauty wasn't lucky enough to avoid the women when they stepped out of the elevator on the first floor. At least ten of them stood silently waiting, their expressions worried. It was Tiny who spoke first.

"Enjoy your vacation, Beauty. Have fun." Her gaze darted to Breeze. "She'll be safe, right? You promised."

"She will. A very nice male is going to escort her there and he'll keep her safe."

Tiny shuddered a little and Halfpint stepped to her side to hold her hand. She looked nervous but obviously forced a smile. "We will miss you but we know you need some freedom."

Beauty walked over and hugged the duo. They didn't understand why she wanted to leave the safety of the dorm but the fact that they accepted it meant a lot to her. "I'll be back before you notice I'm gone."

They both appeared doubtful of that but they quickly hid their emotions. "I'm sure that's true," Tiny whispered. "Be careful of the male."

"Let's not have any of that," Breeze ordered sternly. "He's a good male and he's Species." She strode toward the front doors. "Come on, Beauty. You have a flight to catch."

82

She released her friends, trying not to allow their worried stares to make her wary of leaving. The concept of seeing and spending time with Shadow excited her a lot. He wasn't angry if he'd agreed to be her escort. She'd be able to get to know the man better. No fear inched up her spine over the thought of living in close quarters with him. He hadn't tried to molest her in any way when they were alone inside the equipment building.

Breeze dumped her bag into the back of a golf cart and took the wheel. "This is going to be great but I put a cell phone in your bag just in case you want to call me on the sly if you get hung up."

"The sly?"

"You know, if you find yourself at a loss in a situation. My number is programmed in. You remember what you were taught about how to use them, right? Dial me if you need advice, okay? Day or night." She threw the small engine in gear and they sped away from the dorm. "I'll keep my phone close, even in the shower. I've got your back."

Beauty grinned. "I'm really glad you're my friend but I'm cool."

Breeze turned the wheel and drove them toward the helicopter pad. "Am I rubbing off on you with my mad human slang?" She chuckled.

"I learned it from my guards. It's Species talk that I find difficult to adjust to and speak."

Breeze slowed the cart to a stop and stared at her. "Like what?"

"Male, female, human, and I have a feeling the term 'share sex' might be a new one I have to learn."

"Don't feel pressured to do anything with Shadow. He doesn't expect it. You know that, right? He probably hopes I'm wrong about you being sexually curious."

Beauty's cheeks heated. "You told him that?"

"I did." There was no regret in Breeze's direct stare. "He had a right to know and it involves him in case you do want to experiment. This will avoid him being shocked or thinking you are having a miscommunication. It happens with our males when you attempt subtlety. That's why I suggested getting naked and telling him exactly what you want. He won't be confused."

Beauty let it sink in that Shadow was aware of her inner turmoil and that he had become the focus of it. She was attracted to him and hoped that something might happen between them. She longed to know what her neighbors experienced when they had visitors. She decided to be direct.

"I'm not like you, Rusty or Kit."

"That's obvious and it's not just your size."

She pondered if that was an insult but saw no distain in Breeze's expression. "I don't want to go from man to man if I do this. I want to only get to know one."

"I respect that. Our males can be dominating. Just remember that and don't allow him to rule you. They are bigger but there's a saying that applies. Remember it—'the bigger they are, the harder they fall'."

Beauty quietly considered her words. She hesitated to get out when they parked, studying her friend. "What if something happens and I want to keep him?"

Breeze grinned. "Get naked and stay that way. He won't leave. They are hard to toss out of bed so if you don't try, I doubt he will go anywhere."

Beauty smiled back. "You make it sound so easy."

"It is." Breeze hoisted her bag. "There he is. He's totally staring. That's a male who notices you. He doesn't have a chance if you take off your clothes. Just wait until you're sure."

"I will," she promised softly, turning her head to gaze around until she found the tall man with short blond hair. He stood in uniform next to the helicopter and appeared as nervous as she felt.

"Gift wrapped," Breeze chuckled.

"What?" Beauty tore her attention from Shadow to glance her way.

"Nothing. Let's go. The blades are starting and the pilots hate wasting fuel."

Chapter Five

The cabin rested in thick woods and Beauty couldn't help but openly stare at all the trees. The tops of them nearly blocked out the blue sky surrounding the small clearing where the two-story structure had been built. She licked her lips as the Jeep halted.

"This is your stop." Jaded, the council member, refused to glance her way. He had spoken only to Shadow since he'd picked them up from the heliport but she knew he wasn't being rude. He meant to avoid frightening her by addressing her directly. "It's been stocked with everything you could possibly need and there's a set of satellite phones inside. We left two in case something happens to one." He paused. "You can get cell phone reception usually but sometimes it is sporadic. Call the Reservation number if you need emergency assistance." His voice lowered. "We have females on duty around the clock just in case."

"In case of what?" Beauty spoke for the first time since Shadow had lifted her inside the helicopter. The ride had terrified her but he had held her hand silently during the flight.

Startling, bright-green eyes flashed her way for a few heartbeats before he glanced at Shadow. "In case you need a female, Beauty."

That translates to "in case I freak out", she guessed. "It will be fine. Shadow won't hurt me. I know I'm safe."

Shadow slid out of the Jeep and reached for her. "Allow me to help you down."

86

She rose from the backseat and his strong hands encircled her hips. He lifted her slowly over the edge until she stood on her feet on the dirt road. He released her immediately to grab their belongings.

"Thank you, Jaded. I am certain we will be fine as long as there is food. I've learned how to cook thanks to the task force. They were very helpful while I lived at their headquarters."

The other man chuckled. "I bet they were. The ones I've met say they married their jobs. Not having access daily to cafeterias such as we have would make them eager to learn to prepare their own meals. They'd starve otherwise." His humor faded. "Call if there're any issues that arise. We're all here to help."

Beauty refused to wince despite the strong urge. She had a sneaking suspicion that everyone at the NSO had been made aware she might be interested in pursuing a physical relationship with Shadow. It was embarrassing and uncomfortable for so many to know what should be private. She ducked her chin to hide the blush on her cheeks and turned to face the cabin.

Jaded left and the sounds of the river could be heard once the engine faded away. Birds sang and the treetops whispered from the wind. It was a peaceful place she looked forward to enjoying for the next two weeks.

"This way." Shadow carried their bags as he led her to the front door.

She rushed after him. "I'll get the door."

He paused and she ignored his frown as she shoved the door open. Shadow jerked his head to indicate she should go first. Curiously, she did just that.

The inside had rustic charm with log walls and what appeared to be handmade furniture created mostly from natural products. She smiled. "How pretty!"

"Brass said the Wild Zone residents made most of this." He stared at the coffee table someone had painstakingly sanded from a thick log cut in half, the insides of it smoothed and flattened to a level surface. "Nice work."

"The couch is nice too." She stepped closer. "More logs with large cushions. How clever."

"The bedrooms should be upstairs. I was told there are two. You should pick which one you want."

She spun around to stare at him. Nerves made her heart flutter. Half of her wished to invite him to share a room with her but she wasn't brave enough to ask. "It doesn't matter."

He shrugged. "I'll give you whichever is nicest. I'll return immediately."

He fled for the stairs and she watched him disappear. She resisted the urge to follow. The bad thing about being segregated from Species men was her lack of knowledge on how to speak to them. She moved through the lower floor to explore the open space. It consisted of a living room divided from the kitchen by a bar with stools. There was a small bathroom with only a toilet and sink.

Shadow returned without their things. He avoided her gaze.

"I am going outside to learn the area. Stay inside until I'm sure it is safe."

"No one will hurt us here."

That got his attention. "You're female and I'm not sure I trust that some of the males won't be curious to see you. Brass told me to do a few things to ensure they know what boundaries not to cross."

"Boundaries?"

"I need to mark the area around the house just to make certain they are aware I am here."

"You brought signs?"

He dropped his gaze to the floor and strode for the door quickly. "Stay inside."

He was gone before she could ask another question. He hadn't been carrying anything. She walked to the window and watched him disappear to the left of the cabin. She spun and rushed up the stairs, hoping for a view from the second floor to see what he was doing.

The bedrooms were small but she barely noted the details as she hurried through the one that would hopefully give her a view of Shadow. The curtains were open and she spotted him walking through trees. He paused at one point with his back to her and her jaw dropped open as he reached for the front of his pants. While she couldn't see him exposed, she guessed he was peeing on a tree.

I need to mark the area. His words sank in and she backed away from the window before he caught her watching him. He'd meant that literally— he was marking the area as an animal would. It floored her.

Species aren't like humans, she reminded herself. Her gaze landed on the bed to see Shadow's bag sitting neatly on the lower end of it. She was inside his room. The bed was a big one with a headboard and footboard made of sturdy branches.

She went to the other bedroom, which had an identical bed to his, and began to unpack, making sure not to get too close to the window in the event Shadow saw her. She didn't want him to know she'd spied.

The dresser had obviously been bought. She neatly stored her clothing inside. The bathroom would be shared by them. It had a door on each side, connecting their rooms. No locks had been placed on either door. He could enter at will.

She stared at the shower with the clear glass doors. There would be no privacy if he walked in on her. It went both ways though. She could catch him while he bathed if they weren't careful to listen before entering to make sure the bathroom wasn't already occupied.

The door downstairs opened and closed. Beauty went in search of him immediately. He was crouched in front of the fireplace when she returned to the lower level, studying it. She knew he was aware of her since the steps creaked slightly under her feet.

"Did you mark the area?"

"Yes." He didn't glance at her. "They will be aware I am here and will stay back from the cabin."

They'll smell him. She didn't say it aloud. "I'm not afraid of them. They are Species."

"They don't see many females unless they venture into the more populated sections of Reservation. I don't want them to be tempted to come here to meet you. Some of them aren't stable."

90

"Would they attack me?"

He rose to his full height and turned toward her. Indecision was clear on his features about giving her an answer. It irritated her. She deserved the truth.

"Please be honest. Do you think I'm in danger from them? I'm primate. Does that make a difference? I've heard most of them are canine and feline. I watch television and have read many books since my release. Are they so untamed that they will wish to hunt me? They have predator instincts, right? I'm aware of the food chain in the animal kingdom."

"You're female."

"And? Does that mean I couldn't stand a chance of surviving if one of them came after me?" She couldn't see winning that fight either since men were so much stronger.

"It means they wouldn't wish to hunt you." He walked away into the kitchen to wash his hands.

She stared at his back and allowed his words to sink in. "Sex?"

He visibly stiffened as he shut off the water. "Yes." He dried his hands on a towel and opened the fridge to inspect the contents. She couldn't see his face. "Don't worry. I'm here and none of them will get close to you. Just don't go outside without me there to protect you in case one of them is brazen enough to cross the boundary lines I set."

"Shadow?" She said his name softly, wishing he'd quit avoiding her.

He slowly closed the door and turned his head until his blue gaze found her. "Yes?"

"You could just tell me that. Are you afraid one of them will seek me out to offer to share sex?"

"No. I'm afraid one of them might try to grab you and take you home with him. I warned Brass that I am not good at tracking. I have a keen sense of smell but I'm not used to the woods. It might take time to find you. Don't go anywhere without me. I want you to promise you'll lock yourself in the cabin if trouble arises. I'll handle it."

"I promise." She didn't want to be kidnapped. "Would they hurt me if that were to happen?"

"They know you're Gift but some of them aren't right in their heads. They wouldn't realize the emotional trauma they caused and might attempt to urge you strongly into sharing sex."

"Seduction?"

His eyebrows rose in surprise. "Yes."

"I told you, I read." She hugged her chest. "I wasn't aware felines or canines did that when they were interested in a woman. Usually they try to impress one by other means instead of carrying her off."

"It's the human in us." He took a step closer but paused. "That's the part that makes us go after and take something if we want it badly enough. You're a temptation to a lonely male." His gaze lowered. "You are attractive. Small. You couldn't fight back well and they'd be eager to protect you."

"Protect or seduce?"

"Both."

92

"What about your instincts? What do you think when you look at me?"

He cleared his throat and turned away. "Are you hungry? I could fix us sandwiches."

"Shadow?"

He opened the fridge. "They really stocked it well. There is enough lunchmeat here to feed an army." He closed it and jerked open the freezer side. "It's mostly full of meat. I'll thaw some steaks for dinner. I'm a good cook. Do you enjoy your meat fully cooked or just seared?"

"Fully cooked. You're not going to answer my question, are you?"

"No. I am not. I'm here to protect you."

"No, you aren't going to answer that question about your instincts or you aren't going to be tempted to seduce me?" She was stunned that she'd spoken her thoughts but didn't regret it. She wanted to know where he stood on the issue.

Shadow smothered a growl. The female should be timid but she acted as if she were a female officer with her blunt questions. They made him feel uncomfortable, though he admired her courage. He slammed the freezer closed and cut his gaze her way as he placed the frozen meat on the counter.

The expression on her face sliced his heart a little. She appeared fragile and a little frightened. "You are safe with me. My instincts are in check."

She squeezed her chest a little tighter—he didn't miss that fact or anything else about her. Her breathing quickened and her eyes were wider.

She appeared ready to bolt and he tried to seem less threatening as he took a step back.

"I know you wouldn't do anything harmful to me."

"Your body language implies otherwise."

"I'm not used to speaking to men. I'm just nervous."

"There's no need." An idea came to him and he sank to his knees. It made them almost eye level. "I give you my word of honor that I'd never do anything to purposely frighten you or cause you alarm. Relax. I hate seeing your defensive stance."

She glanced down her body and dropped her arms to her sides. Her gaze lifted to meet his. "I do that when I'm unsure of a situation. I've always been alone and only had myself to hold when I don't know how to handle something. Why are you on your knees?"

"To show you that we are on the same level. I don't want my size to frighten you."

"I'm actually comforted by it." Her tongue darted out to wet her lips. "You make me feel safe. You could handle anyone who might seek me out, right?"

He hated the way his chest tightened a little over figuring out the root of her fear. "I'd battle any male who came after you to the death. No one would get past me. I am not good at tracking from lack of opportunity but I do know how to fight. That is one skill you can depend on."

She took a hesitant step closer and then another until she paused in front of him. He could have reached out to touch her and was tempted to

94

do just that. He resisted. Her eyes were softer now and all the tension had faded away.

"What else would you do for me?"

"What do you want?" His heart hammered and he hated where his thoughts traveled. Breeze was sure the Gift Female wanted to share sex. His dick reacted by filling with blood as he waited for her answer.

The idea of touching her made him feel a mixture of fear and eagerness. He couldn't deny wanting Beauty. She scented of something sweet and feminine but not of arousal. No fear lingered in the air and he took her word. Gratitude flooded him that she had that much confidence in him. It was a slight miracle in itself after what had been done to her during her captivity. He just wished he trusted himself as much.

Images flashed through his mind of the ordeal he'd suffered. Beauty's features weren't fully Species. Her perky nose and rounded eyes left no doubt that she wasn't canine or feline. The facial anomalies were much slighter than most Species. Her small body was very human. *Fragile. Delicate. Easily bruised.* A cold sweat broke out on his upper lip and forehead while he battled the urge to reach for her. He wasn't sure if he wanted to just hold her to assure her she was safe or if he wanted to do more.

Her lips beckoned. He knew what kissing was and wanted to experience it. The task force males had given him graphic details about how to do it once they'd learned he'd never shared that with a female. The few females who had been brought to him to share sex at Mercile hadn't been with him long enough to want to want that intimacy.

95

"Could you forget that I'm Gift and treat me as though I were just a person?" Longing flashed in her gaze when he forced his focus higher. "That's what I want from you."

She raised her hand and every muscle tightened as it drew closer to his cheek. It hovered so close he could feel the heat of her but she didn't touch him. It dropped away.

"I can do that," he got out.

"Stop being so concerned that you're terrifying me because you don't." She stepped away.

He watched her as she stared out the window. Shadow reached down to tuck his dick farther down his thigh to hide its condition before she noticed and rose to his feet. "I could do that."

"Good." She smiled when she peered at him over her shoulder. "Let's eat and then go see this river. I bet it's pretty."

"We can do that later. We have plenty of time. I'd like to get us settled first and check out the area before I take you for a walk." He fought to keep his voice level. He wanted to growl in frustration that she hadn't asked him to carry her to bed to strip her naked and share sex.

Don't go there, he ordered. *I could harm her with my lack of experience. They should have sent someone else. I'm not the right male to be near her.* Self-disgust flashed through him over the arousal he suffered, knowing it was wrong. "I am going to go out back and carry in firewood first. We'll have a fire tonight. Would you enjoy that?"

"Yes."

"I'll be right back." He darted out the door, closing it behind him, and leaned against it. He had to adjust his dick again and ground his teeth in frustration. He hadn't made it half an hour without wishing to strip her bare.

"Shit." He took a deep breath and pushed away from the cabin. He'd be carrying wood all right. His hand slid down to adjust his stiff shaft to a more comfortable walking position. "Get control," he muttered to himself.

Beauty grinned and hugged her chest. Her gaze returned to the window, surprisingly reflective of the kitchen behind her. She hadn't missed it when Shadow's hand had gone to the front of his pants before he'd risen to his feet. There was only one reason he'd grab that area. He was interested in physical interaction as well but tried to hide it.

Now she just had to figure out how to get him to initiate the sex. Her mind skimmed through everything she'd learned while watching movies and reading romance novels. That knowledge seemed sadly lacking when faced with a flesh-and-blood man, giving her the opportunity to experience good sex firsthand—the teasing, laughter, closeness and soft touches. The joy.

Breeze's suggestion was tempting but she didn't want to risk rejection. It was too brazen for her. She'd have to lure him into suggesting it first. She leaned closer to the window and rose on tiptoe to watch him leave the porch. Her attention locked on his beefy ass encased in tight pants.

She longed to feel it just to see if it was as firm as it looked. The memory of his chest lingered. He had so many muscles she wanted to explore by surfing her hands over each one. It was also unforgettable, waking to discover the state of his body when she'd identified what was nestled between her thighs after the night they'd spent together.

Sex still frightened her a little but she knew deep down that it would be different with Shadow. She'd heard men visit her neighbors often enough that she had no doubt that it would be pleasurable. She felt strange when she looked at Shadow. Her heart always quickened and odd things happened to her belly. Little tingling sensations erupted there at that moment just thinking about it. Of course she wouldn't ask him to leave right after he made those sexy sounds she'd overheard through the walls of her apartment. She'd definitely want his scent on her and her bedding. He smelled wonderful to her.

Scenarios began to play in her thoughts. She could ask him to cuddle with her on the couch to watch the television mounted over the fireplace later when he lit the fire. She wanted to experience that sensation. He might take that for a green light to do more. They could watch a romantic movie. The women in the dorm always loved them. She tossed that idea after considering that men probably didn't enjoy those.

She dropped flat to her feet and paced, deep in thought. It was unlikely that watching guy movies about blowing things up and shooting guns would put him in the mood to offer to share sex. She sighed. It was frustrating wanting something but being unsure of how to accomplish it.

The last romance book she'd read flashed through her mind and she paused. It had worked for the heroine of the book. The man had not only come to her bed but it had initiated their sexual relationship. A plan began to form. Excitement made her laugh.

Chapter Six

It is all going wrong! Beauty blinked back tears of frustration at her lack of success in luring Shadow into carrying her to bed. She'd purposely tripped and fallen against his chest while he'd been preparing their meal in the kitchen. She'd offered to help just to gain the opportunity to set that circumstance in motion. He should have looked down at her, their gazes fused, and then planted a kiss on her. Instead he'd righted her immediately and apologized for being in her way.

Their romantic dinner had turned out to be a bust. He'd avoided looking at her the entire time they'd been seated next to each other at the bar. He'd pulled out a gun magazine, stating it was research. The only conversation they'd shared had been about new security measures the NSO was taking. He'd explained details about their latest monitoring equipment.

Every time she'd tried to steer the topic to romance, Shadow had become flustered. His cheeks had darkened in hue and it had been kind of cute how he'd stuttered his words. Apparently, he wasn't comfortable discussing anything personal. Dinner had ended and she'd known they'd relax in the living room together afterward.

It made Beauty feel inept as a woman. That ability to naturally flirt with men seemed utterly lacking in her case. Self-pity wasn't her style though, regarding her lack of even a semblance of a normal life up until she'd been freed. She'd just have to try harder to figure out how to pique his interest in having sex.

The fire in the hearth was lit but instead of sitting next to her on the couch where she'd left him plenty of space, he sat in a chair across the room.

"You can sit next to me," she hinted, imagining leaning against him and curling up to his side.

"I'm fine here." He yawned. "I am tired and I don't want to fall asleep. The couch is too cushioned for me."

The flames held her stare but not her attention. That was on the man to her left. From the corner of her eye, she saw him cross his ankles. The chunky boots he wore looked uncomfortable. It gave her an idea as she shifted her body to watch him.

"Do you want me to remove your boots? I could do that for you." She'd seen a movie where the wife had done that for her husband when he'd come home from work. He'd kissed her afterward in thanks. "It would be no trouble."

"I am capable of removing them myself. I will take them off before I go to bed." He scowled. "I'm not a weak male."

"I didn't say you were. I just wanted to be nice."

"You are." His head leaned back and he stared at the ceiling.

She followed his gaze, seeing nothing interesting in the wood beams. He seemed fascinated though. The wind outside buffeted the side of the cabin and rattled the windows. Shadow responded by leaping to his feet, instantly alert.

101

"Stay put. I'm going outside to patrol."

"It's nothing." She didn't want him to leave.

He paused by the door, finally meeting her gaze. "It's late. We should prepare for sleep when I return. Go ahead and go to your room. I'll be back soon and put out the fire."

She started to tell him it was too early—just after eight—but he was gone before she could speak. The closing door and a lot of disappointment was all she was left with. She'd have received an F if she'd been graded on her make-a-man-want-her skills.

"Damn it," she muttered, knowing she was reverting to the human talk, though she kept trying to break that habit. "Shit. Fuck. Screw this," she kept going, pacing. Species were hard to deal with. Human guys had always asked her to be nice to them. The guards had always been interested in her but Shadow seemed immune. It confused and confounded her.

She went upstairs to get the phone from her bag. She called Breeze. The Species answered on the first ring.

"Is everything okay?"

"No."

"Did he do something wrong?" A growl resonated over the line. "I'll beat him."

"I fell against him but he just put me back on my feet. I invited him to sit next to me but he chose a seat all the way across the room. Why isn't it working? I don't think he wants me. I was sure those tactics would provoke a response."

The pause was a long one. "You what?"

"I fell against him, believing he'd be tempted to kiss me but he didn't."

"I told you what to do. Remove your clothing and tell him to share sex with you."

"I'm not that bold." Beauty cocked her head, listening for the door downstairs to make certain he didn't return to overhear her conversation. "I don't think he returns my interest."

"He's male and breathing." Breeze chuckled. "He's just clueless about exactly what you want from him. You need to be more aggressive."

"I'm not you." She hated the way it made her feel to admit that, as if she lacked something essential but she couldn't deny being a bit shy. "I freeze up when I even consider something that forward and what if he rejects me? I'd be mortified. I couldn't face him and we're sharing a home."

"Do you want me to call him and tell him for you? I would totally do that. I have the number for his cell phone."

"No! I just wanted advice."

"I gave you that. Strip. Tell him to remove his clothes. That's all it's going to take, Beauty. He won't reject you. He has no female in his life."

"Couldn't you just tell me how to get him interested without me showing him my body first?"

"You could tell him you wish to share sex. That will clear up any confusion."

"I'm searching for a milder approach."

103

"Is this what you learned from humans? It's amazing they ever share sex." Breeze was silent for a moment. "I'm not an expert on this. I attempted to initiate sex with a human and he didn't respond as expected. How about if we pull Shadow and replace him with a task force member? Maybe a human male would be more suited to you."

The concept of allowing anyone but Shadow to touch her killed any desire she had to find out what happened between two consenting people during sex. "No. I want him."

"Are you sure? I could make a few calls."

"I want Shadow."

"He's the only male you've spent time with. You might like another one. I could send a few of them there. We'd have to move you to the hotel though. No way would Valiant handle the residents of Wild Zone if they sniffed humans. I could—"

"Forget I asked. I'll figure this out on my own. Don't send anyone else."

"Fine. Call me any time."

"Thank you."

Beauty ended the call and stashed the phone. She strained to hear the door as she quickly stripped out of her clothes and put on a nightgown. A slight noise below assured her of his return. Her gaze fixed on the open doorway in anticipation of watching him walk up the stairs. It wasn't a long wait.

He paused by her doorway and glanced down her body. She knew the pale-blue sleepshirt wasn't sexy. She didn't own anything that could be considered that by anyone's standards but it did have a low neckline. The

NSO paid for everything she owned and they'd purchased it all online. In this case it was an oversized sleepshirt that fell to her knees, three times too big, and the arms of it were long enough to reach her elbows.

"Good night. I'll be right next door." He looked away. "Do you want this closed?"

"No. I'd prefer the door open."

"You can sleep at ease. Nothing will get inside without me hearing it." He turned, ready to step away.

"Shadow?"

He paused, turned his head and stared at her. "Yes?"

Nerves made her feel a little nauseous. It was on the tip of her tongue to ask him to share her room. Her heart rate increased and a lump seemed to form in the center of her throat, blocking her from speaking.

"Good night, Beauty."

He was gone. She didn't hear his bedroom door close and wondered if he'd left his open as well. Her shoulders slumped over losing her chance to invite him to sleep in her bed. Light came on under the door to the bathroom they shared, letting her know he was in there. Moments later water came on.

She sat on the bed staring at the tiny crack along the bottom of the bathroom door. The shower door creaked. The memory of his mostly naked body concealed only by the flag surfaced. Shadow had a great body, all muscled and beefy. His hair wouldn't take long to wash since it was so short.

The layout of the bathroom replayed in her mind and she focused on the part where he'd be standing under the spray of water. The urge to go join him was strong. Breeze or Rusty would just saunter in there, strip, and step into the stall with him. They'd have the courage to lay their hands on his skin and tell him to do whatever they wanted.

Beauty sat still. She was living alone with a man she wanted but couldn't talk herself into acting bold. It made her feel like a big coward. The water shut off, he opened the shower door and she got to imagine him using a towel to dry off. The light clicked off and silence reigned inside the cabin.

Shadow stretched out on the bed and stared at the ceiling. He'd chosen to sleep in boxer shorts that his human friends from the task force had given him, as opposed to being naked. He hated wearing any clothing when he slept but the open doorway to the hall was lit from Beauty's room. She hadn't turned off her light. It left him wondering what she was doing in there.

It was very quiet in the cabin, no sounds of life besides the wind buffeting the structure occasionally. The dorm he'd recently moved into always held a little noise. Occasional males speaking in the hallways or doors closing somewhere. One of his neighbors enjoyed video games a little loud. It had been welcome after the imposing silence of living in the basement at the task force headquarters. He missed Wrath and wished he could call him.

His best friend and his mate had just moved into a house at Homeland. They needed time to settle in and he didn't want to bother them. It wasn't late so he needn't worry that he'd disturb their sleep but he knew they'd been looking forward to spending time alone. Privacy wasn't something they'd had much of in their previous quarters.

He turned on his side, staring at the hallway. He should be back at Homeland acquainting himself with his new duties. Living amongst so many Species had been pleasant. They welcomed him with open arms and he'd started to make more friends. Then Beauty had decided to run in the rain.

He couldn't regret meeting her but resented the way he'd been manipulated into becoming a test subject. He'd sworn to never allow that to happen again. The fact that it might involve anything sexual really put him in a foul mood. No one had considered his feelings. He didn't want any part of being someone's guinea pig.

That's what I am, he admitted silently. He'd spent many hours familiarizing himself with New Species and their accomplishments during the almost half a year living with the task force. They'd given him access to all the information on his people that he wanted. Gift Females were one of the topics he'd read about. It was deemed that any sexual contact with a male would cause damage to their already frail emotional states. They'd been created weaker on purpose, to make them easier to control and less likely to fight back.

A fine sheen of sweat broke out over his body, although he'd just taken a cool shower. The idea of touching Beauty made him hot. The knowledge that a hundred things could go wrong if she initiated sex didn't cool his

107

blood in the slightest but it did fuel his fears of sharing sex. He could go at her too aggressively because he'd denied his cravings to touch a female.

His dick began to harden just thinking about her under him. The memory of her in that wet nightgown plastered against her skin, which had hidden nothing from him, had been the most enticing thing he'd ever seen. He reached down, fisting his dick through his shorts and adjusted it to a more comfortable position. He paused before releasing it, tempted to tend to the desire to get off. He'd become an expert at masturbation to fulfill his sexual needs.

Do it, he urged. It would curb some of his longing to walk into the next room to seek her company. His fingers stroked his dick and he eyes closed. The feel of cotton rubbing against the head of his cock was a little irritating but was still good. It hardened even more and his balls started to ache.

He pictured Beauty in his mind, her eyes staring at him with trust and he bit back a snarl as he let go of his dick to fist his pillow instead. He'd terrify her if she saw him bare. Worse, patience wasn't his strongest trait. He could take her too fast or too roughly. Knowing that still didn't dull his hunger for her. The ability to face his fears seemed to lesson somewhat in comparison to the hot desire burning through his body.

Guilty, he admitted. He lusted after the delicate female. She'd slept on his chest and he'd held her. Protective instincts were a part of his genetics but he'd felt something much more personal when they'd woken to hear someone approaching the shed. He'd wanted to kill anyone who posed a threat to his Beauty. The half-asleep state of his mind might have accounted for the feelings of possessiveness that had gripped him but he wasn't about to lie to himself. That hadn't been the reason or the cause. She'd given him her trust and he'd wanted to keep her at his side.

That's how you ended up here, he chided. Brass had reminded him that another male might harm her unintentionally and he'd have done anything to prevent that. Even if it meant lying on his side with a hard dick, sweating out his frustration, staring at the light in the hallway while he contemplated what she was doing in the next room.

The light under the bathroom door suddenly came on and he strained to hear her every movement. A smile curved his lips when the sink faucet came on and moments later the toilet flushed. She was shy even about someone knowing when she tended to her needs. That amusement faded. She'd purposely camouflaged going to the bathroom so what would she do if she were naked under a male who was intent on getting much more personally acquainted with her body?

The faucet turned off and the light faded as she left the other room to return to hers. The hallway dimmed as well but she didn't close her door. He'd have heard it if she had. He breathed through his mouth and tried to relax. Tomorrow would be a long day but he'd exercise restraint. It wouldn't be easy. He was already at his limit and they'd only had hours together. *I've signed up for a new torture, wanting what I can't have.*

* * * * *

Beauty gave up on sleep. A good hour must have passed and her restlessness only grew worse. She pushed back the covers and rose, sliding out of bed. She tiptoed across the floor and out of her room where she paused. Her hearing wasn't as good as most Species but it was better than

109

regular people. The sound of slow, steady breathing assured her she hadn't woken Shadow.

The stairs didn't creak as she crept down them and headed toward the back door. The area would be safe and she just wanted to get a little fresh air. The door was easy to unlock by feel and a warm wind blasted her the second she got it open. It was pleasant on her skin as she stepped out onto the porch. She closed the door quietly behind her.

It was a small space with a little roof but she didn't stay there. The three steps took her to a grassy area that was soft under her toes. The river noise was faint, calling to her sense of curiosity.

It wasn't hard to make out the dim shapes of trees as she followed the sound of moving water. The tree density thinned and suddenly she stood on a dirt embankment staring out over the blackness with just a few glints of moonlight reflected. She smiled, proud to have found it by herself. One glance around and she found a nice fallen log to sit on.

A howl startled her. Her heart raced as she stood, instantly fearful. It was really close and she turned, studying the darkness carefully. Something moved to her left, a twig snapped and a low growl rumbled.

"Shadow?" She whispered his name, afraid to speak too loudly. She really hoped it was him. New Species did that when they were angry and she figured he'd be furious if he had woken to find her gone. "Is that you?"

Something else moved to her right and she turned her head in that direction. A dark shape crept closer from behind a tree. It was big but low to the ground. Unless Shadow was on all fours, it wasn't him. She backed up slowly, terrified. Another growl came from her right and she glanced that way to spot another big, low shape moving between two bushes, creeping closer.

"Shadow?" Her voice rose slightly. She wanted to scream his name but fear restricted her lungs.

The smell reached her nose as she began to pant. Fresh blood was what she was picking up if she had to guess. That didn't bode well. Another smell came with it. She identified it from the times she'd petted a few of the guard dogs the Species officers sometimes brought into the women's dorm.

"Good doggies," she crooned, backing up further. She had to be close to the river's edge. "Where are the officers who take you for walks?"

One of them stepped out into the moonlight enough for her to get a good look at it and she whimpered. It wasn't wearing an NSO collar, nor did it look as if it were friendly. It bared its fangs and snarled at her.

"Shit," she breathed, knowing a wolf when she saw one.

The other one prowled closer, coming at her from the side. It snarled too and crouched a little, probably preparing to launch its body at her. They were stalking her and she was their prey. Her instincts screamed it. *Danger.*

No one had warned her about wild wolves running around the woods. She backed up, tottered but regained her balance, glanced back and realized she'd run out of space. She could jump into the water, pray the wolves wouldn't follow her in, but she couldn't swim. The drop to the water wasn't far, perhaps three feet to the dark river, but she had no idea how deep it would be.

"Easy," she crooned, turning to face them. One sharp breath and she tried to steady her shaky voice. "Stay!" The firm tone made her proud.

They inched closer, both growling low and deep. *They are going to attack me.* She could sense the danger as if it were a smell she could inhale. Both of them tensed, their big furry bodies lowering slightly in the front in preparation, but another howl eerily pierced the night.

Both of them turned their heads toward the direction from which it had come from. Beauty allowed her instincts to take over and she sprinted to the right along the river's edge. She ran as fast as she could, ignoring the pain in her bare feet.

They were in pursuit. Their labored breathing and heavy bodies crushing leaves and twigs assured her of that. She wasn't sure in which direction the cabin lay but kept moving as she dodged trees and bushes. One good intake of air and a scream finally burst forth.

The wolves were gaining on her, too fast for her to outrun, despite the advantage of her altered genes. The river wasn't an option but she did see a low-hanging branch ahead. Desperation made her try to jump for it and rough bark tore into her palms. She wasn't strong enough to keep hold of it though and crashed to the ground hard on her belly.

She rolled into a ball, the only thing left to do, waiting for the wolves to tear into her. Her arms covered her face and her palms covered her ears. Something big landed next to her and she whimpered.

"No!" The masculine voice was loud and brutally harsh.

A heavy weight pressed against her ass. Beauty wanted to cry when a hand pinned her shoulder to keep her in position. The snarling wolves were close but Shadow didn't move away from her. He was using his body to shield hers.

"Go," he snarled. "Find rabbits."

One of the wolves whined.

"Go!"

They retreated, crashing through the woods loudly. The hand on her shoulder left and the weight leaning against her ass moved away. He was breathing heavily. Hot tears filled Beauty's eyes and she knew how close she'd come to dying.

"You're safe." The voice came out less animalistic and a new fear shot through her. That wasn't Shadow.

She slowly moved her arms, peeking up, and made out the shape of a man crouching a few feet away. He was big.

"They are gone," he informed her, his tone softening. "Don't fear me." He moved slowly, offering her a hand. "Take it. Let me help you up. You're in no danger."

"Beauty!" Shadow shouted her name.

The guy next to her turned his head and growled.

She gasped in air. "Shadow! I'm here!"

That prompted the man to snap his focus back on her. "He should watch you better. Take my hand. The ground is cold and I want to make sure you weren't hurt. I don't smell your blood. I was following them when they began to act strangely. I just didn't know it was you they wanted to hunt."

He didn't attack so some of the fear eased. "Who are you?"

He lowered his hand. "Torrent. You're the Gift Female. Why are you out here alone? You could have been dinner to that wolf pack."

"I sneaked out," she admitted. "Shadow didn't know. I thought it would be safe if I kept close to the cabin."

"Beauty!" Shadow was really close and seconds later he rushed to her side. He landed inches away in a crouch, snarling at the man. "Get away from her."

Torrent backed up slowly. "I saved her from a wolf pack." He sounded angry. "You need to watch her more closely. It's not just Species residents she needs to be protected from. We have a lot of wild animals running loose. Didn't they warn you?"

"No." Shadow's voice was still rough.

"We have tigers, lions, bears, and wolves roaming the Wild Zone. We offer shelter for them here at Reservation when humans find them too dangerous. We'd rather handle those animals than see them destroyed." The other man crouched too. "I'm Torrent." He paused. "Someone should have told you about them, Shadow." He glanced at Beauty. "She admitted to sneaking out. Prevent that in the future. It's only luck that brought me out tonight. I just returned with a new wolf and discovered the pack sniffing after something. It was her. I tracked them while they hunted to make sure they weren't after one of our other rescued animals."

Beauty sat up, dusting off dirt. Shadow stood and offered her a hand. She took it and was gently pulled to her feet. He kept hold of her.

"You brought a new wolf here?"

114

Torrent sighed. "Humans sometimes take in wild animals, believing to make pets of them. They abandon them or turn them over to shelters when they realize they can't be tamed. We started a program to accept the ones slated for death. The residents needed something to do and enjoy caring for them. I am the one sent out to pick them up and release them here at Reservation. It's my job. Tonight I drove to pick up a wolf cub rescued from an abusive owner. I knew one of the female wolves would take him under her care. He's quite young."

"Thank you." Shadow bowed his head as the other Species straightened. "Beauty will not go out alone again." He turned to stare down at her. "Are you hurt?"

"I'm okay."

He sniffed loudly. "You were terrified."

"They were chasing me. I thought I might have to jump into the river but I don't know how to swim."

"You need to learn." Torrent cleared his throat. "I'll leave you now. I'm going to go check on the cub and make sure the pack has returned to their territory. I'll ask a few of our males to keep a closer watch on them to make sure they don't return to this area while you're visiting." He paused. "Teach her how to swim. All the animals here are too well fed to waste their time wading into the river to fetch their food. She would have been safe from them if she'd gone into the water."

Shadow's hand clasped hers a little tighter. "I don't know how to swim either."

115

Torrent hesitated. "I'll return tomorrow after lunch and teach you both. It's a needed skill." He turned and walked into the darkness. A wolf howled in the distance.

Chapter Seven

The small hand in his reminded Shadow that Beauty waited for him to address her. He watched the Species male leave and didn't miss the dark shapes that trailed him from both sides. The smell of the wolves was strong enough for him to estimate there were at least half a dozen or more.

Shadow fought to control his temper as he forced air in and out of his lungs. Rage was a strong emotion. No one had warned him about the dangerous wildlife that could harm them. Of course that came in second to the fact that the female had left the cabin. Another male had to save her. All the things that could have happened nearly sent him into a fit of temper.

"Shadow?"

Her whispering his name didn't help matters. He'd woken to the sound of a faint scream, knew it was her and she wasn't in the cabin. He'd thrown open the window, slid down the roof and landed on the ground hard. Desperation and fear for her safety had heightened his senses as he'd crashed through the woods following her scent.

His feet were bleeding but he ignored the pain. He spun, glaring down at her. "You are lucky those wolves didn't tear you apart or that male didn't hurt you. Do you understand?"

She paled. "Yes. I didn't know there were any. No one told me. I was only warned about residents and you said you marked the area and it was safe!"

He glanced down her body and stared at her bare legs. The big sleepshirt she wore nearly glowed in the darkness. She may as well have worn a big sign that said "come get me" to any predators for miles.

"Don't talk and don't fear me," he warned before releasing her hand and bending.

She gasped when he grabbed her hips and jerked her forward until her belly bumped his shoulder. He hooked his arm around her waist and he gripped her at the small of her back. He straightened, adjusted her gently where she hung across his body and headed toward the cabin.

"Shadow?"

"Silence," he snarled. "You heard him. Lions, tigers, and bears are out here. You've already attracted the wolves."

He had no problem finding the cabin and set her on the porch. The door was locked. "Stay."

He had to climb up to the roof, enter his open window and rush downstairs to unlock the door. Beauty hadn't moved an inch. He just scooped her into his arms, spun and stomped inside. He kicked the door closed behind them and freed a hand to twist the locks. He refused to look at her face as he carried her up to the bathroom and gently placed her on the counter.

"Don't move." He knew his tone was harsh but he still battled rage. She'd left the cabin without him and he wanted to yell.

"You're bleeding!"

He looked down at the tile floor and noticed the bloody footprints. "That's right. It happens when you leap from a second-story window and rush through the woods at night without shoes." He turned on the shower and just stepped inside with his boxers on. "Don't talk to me right now."

The cold water helped dull the pain as it pooled around his feet, washing away the sweat and stench of his own fear from his body. All he could think about while he'd raced to find her was how he could be too late. A male could have traumatized her or an animal could have torn her apart. Time allowed his emotions to calm and that's when he shut off the shower.

His gaze met hers. Tears flooded her eyes and she still appeared paler than normal. He grabbed a towel and began to dry his skin as best as he could with wet shorts on. He cleared his throat, trying to keep his emotions out of his voice.

"You don't leave the cabin without me." He paused for effect. "Do you understand?"

"Yes."

He didn't want to terrify her but fear was a lot better than death or being forced to confront an aroused male with the mentality of an animal. "Do you realize how small you are? How helpless?"

Her arms crossed over her chest and pushed her breasts together, giving him a good view of the soft mounds beneath the fabric. It pissed him off more.

"Yes."

"I don't think you do."

He threw the towel down and advanced. The way she gasped and shrank away was almost enough to stop him but he had too much

119

adrenaline pumping through his veins to call a halt to his need to teach her something that might save her life. His hands flattened on the counter on each side of her as he leaned in until her head rested against the wall. She had nowhere to go to avoid him while he invaded her space. Fear flashed in her eyes while her breathing increased.

"I could do anything to you, Beauty. You couldn't stop me." He got in her face until their noses brushed. "Hit me. Push me away." His voice deepened. "Do you think you could win?"

"No," she whispered.

He stared deeply into her eyes and felt like a total bastard. She was genuinely afraid. New urges struck that he resisted. He wanted to kiss her and put his hands all over her body. He backed up a few inches.

"You're lucky that male seemed tame. He could have taken off with you. You'd be inside a room with him instead of me. He wouldn't be getting this close to you to prove a point. I might not have been able to find you. Tracking isn't my best strength out here. Do you have any idea what kind of nightmare images flashed through my head while I looked for you? I heard your scream and believed I'd find you dead or not at all."

He breathed in and out until he leashed his desire to take the lesson further just for an excuse to touch her. He wanted to. His dick began to harden but he ignored it despite the wet cotton making it uncomfortably noticeable.

"I'm sorry."

"You are lucky to be safe right now. I trusted you to have the good sense to help me keep you out of danger. I've learned my lesson." He released the counter and backed away. "I hope you've learned yours. Strip and take a shower. I'll get you something clean to wear and place it on your bed. You call me the second you are decent. We're not done."

He spun, stormed into her room and closed the door between them to give her privacy. He paused, listening. Her ragged breathing made him feel worse. He guessed she fought the urge to cry but finally the water turned on.

Her bag was unpacked so he found her things in the dresser. He didn't feel comfortable sorting through her feminine things but he located a gown similar to the one she had worn when they'd first met. It had tiny straps at the shoulders and the soft cotton was very thin. He dropped it on the bed and used the hallway to enter his own room. It only took him seconds to switch the wet boxers for dry ones. He tended to his feet next. The cuts weren't bad but they'd be painful for a few days until they totally healed.

He couldn't allow Beauty to shrug off what she'd done. Next time he might not reach her in time or the male might not be civil enough to be so polite. She needed to understand the dangers. The females at the dorm had coddled her too much but it wasn't her fault. That's how Gift Females were treated.

"Damn," he rasped.

Beauty dried off and checked both her feet. There was a little damage to one heel but she'd gotten off lucky. Shadow couldn't say the same. She used her damp towel to clean up the bloody footprints. She was filled with both regret and shame. He'd gotten hurt because she'd done a thoughtless

121

thing. Worse, he'd seen her cry. The last thing she wanted was to appear weaker than Shadow already believed her to be.

It had seemed so harmless at the time. She'd just wanted to go outside, never thinking it would really be dangerous. Shadow had marked the area and Species didn't hurt other Species. All men avoided her. It was a good thing she'd been wrong about that, considering Torrent had saved her life.

She opened her bedroom door and was in for a shock when Shadow stood facing her. She'd heard him in his room and thought it would be safe to quickly dress. She covered her bare breasts with her hands and twisted away, trying to hide her lower half.

"Shit." He spun around. "Sorry. I didn't think you'd walk out naked."

"I thought you were in your room."

"Your nightgown is on the bed."

She darted to it and yanked it over her head. In her haste the straps didn't want to fit her arms as they tangled with her wet hair. Things couldn't get much worse. He was angry and he'd just seen her naked. She tugged down the nightgown after untangling herself and stared at his broad back.

"I'm decent." Heat still warmed her cheeks when he faced her again. "Sorry." *I don't think this is what Breeze meant when she said to show him my bare body.* No way was she going to ask him to have sex with her now. There was no missing the glint of anger in his eyes when she dared to meet his direct gaze. "I'm really sorry."

"I've been thinking."

Dread gripped her. "You want to return to Homeland? I blew it, didn't I?" She hugged her waist, a habit she hated but couldn't stop.

He glanced down at her chest and then looked away. "No."

The sick feeling grew worse. "You're going to have someone else stay with me?" She wanted him, not a different man living with her.

He shook his head. "I'll sleep on your floor in here. That way you won't be tempted to take any more strolls alone since you'll have to step over me to do it. You aren't to leave my view unless you're showering."

His words sank in and she was torn between hurt and anger. He hadn't offered to share her bed but preferred the floor. That rejection deeply wounded her. The part where he thought she might make the same mistake twice was insulting to her intelligence. She wasn't a total idiot.

She walked to the window to stare out but only saw her own reflection since the light in the room made it impossible to see anything else. Her hair fell in a wet mass over both shoulders. No wonder he didn't want to sleep with her. She looked like a drowned rat. Worse, she felt like a mouse. A frightened, timid one.

"Those are the new rules."

"Are they?" Her anger built. She was tired of being told what to do and what not to do. She was free and wanted the right to do as she pleased, the way all the other Species did. She faced him. "So you've spoken? It's final? No discussion between us first?"

His eyes narrowed. "What does that mean?"

"I said I was sorry. Neither of us knew there were dangerous animals out there. I went outside to get some fresh air but then wanted to see the

123

river. I know you peed on the trees to mark the area to keep other men away. I'm Gift so none of them approach me anyway. I'm a leper in our society or may as well be."

"A what?"

"Don't you read? I do. It's someone with a contagious skin disease. It's called leprosy. That's how I'm treated. It's as if I have it and someone might catch it from me if they come too close."

"Males avoid you out of respect and concern for your well-being."

She was fed up with hearing that. Everyone was trying to be so protective that they may as well wrap her in bubble wrap and lock her inside a room. It wasn't fair and it wasn't right. She wasn't Tiny or Halfpint and she was tired of being lumped in with them.

"That's a crock of shit."

His eyebrows shot up.

"That means bullshit. No one asked me if I wanted to be labeled with that title or treated the way I have been. I just wanted a normal life. I'm entitled to the same things as any Species."

"You've been abused."

Is he kidding? Her anger boiled. "So have you."

He paled slightly. "It's not the same. The things done to me didn't break my spirit."

"I'm not broken either." He was really pissing her off. "Do you think I haven't heard the stories from some of our people? I have. Some of the women were raped by guards while they were at Mercile. Their size and

124

strength saved them sometimes but not always. Only one man hurt me and I know it could have been a lot worse."

"I don't see how."

"I could tell you. Halfpint and Tiny never want to be touched, ever again. They are broken inside to the point that men terrify them. They want to be protected and kept away from everyone who has a dick. I can't even imagine some of the horrible things they've survived. It wasn't a picnic for me but Master wasn't some deviant sex freak."

"He wasn't your master." Shadow snarled. "Don't ever call him that again."

"It's the only name I have to call him. I could call him dickhead or asshole but you get the point. He was an old man and I probably could have fought him off but I knew how much worse things could be if I did."

He frowned. "Explain."

"The guards, Shadow. He was the only thing keeping them from raping me. He paid them to watch me and keep their hands to themselves. Not that they kept their mouths shut. I never had a doubt what they wanted to do to me because they were often vocal about it. They tried to bribe me into allowing them to do sick things to me for more food and a promise I wouldn't tell on them. I've been really hungry in my life but never that much. I had words to use as a weapon. That's all I ever dared have."

"Words?"

"As in threatening to tell on them if they touched me."

"He touched you."

"Yes, he did. It wasn't nice either. I was an object to him instead of a person. I knew it. I felt it. I was something he owned. He'd have me dress in pretty outfits so he could admire how I looked as though I were one of those paintings he had upstairs. I've got emotional scars, sure, but I felt lucky after I spent time with the other Gift Females and heard their horrible stories. And, besides, I grew up there. I didn't know people lived any other way. It was traumatic and scary but that was normal to me. I didn't know anything else existed."

He gaped at her.

"Do you know what Halfpint suffered? The man who owned her showed off his half-animal woman and would let them touch her." Tears filled her eyes just thinking about what a hellish nightmare her friend had suffered. "He'd sit in a chair and watch them do whatever they wanted. There was only one rule. They couldn't bruise or scar her. He liked her looking good."

Shadow snarled.

"Tiny was given to a guy who was into stuff that makes me sick to my stomach. She'll never allow a man to touch her again. She'd rather die. I don't even want to repeat the things she spoke of. It made me feel guilty for feeling sorry for myself. The one who had me only forced me to accept him into my body. It hurt and was emotionless but he didn't beat or humiliate me by doing it in front of others. He didn't make me say I loved the things he did to my body. I was never bound while he forced me to take him into my mouth or…" She grew quiet, trying to rein her raging emotions.

Shadow stared at the floor, his hands fisted at his sides. She calmed.

126

"I refuse to allow my past to ruin my future. I'm not physically as strong as the other women but I'm not broken inside either. I'm healing. I refuse to do anything less. The more I learn, the more I'm grateful for. Do you understand?"

He looked up. "Yes."

"I feel shame sometimes for not fighting." It was her turn to stare at the floor. "I did everything he asked because I was too afraid he'd stop protecting me from the guards. I was terrified that he'd die when he got sick and there would be no stopping them."

Silence stretched between them.

"We should get some sleep." Shadow walked to the doorway. "I'm going to get my pillow to sleep on the floor here in the hallway."

"I thought you were sleeping in my room."

He paused, his back to her. "The hallway is better. It puts me farther from you."

Ouch. "Would you do that if I were Rusty or Kit? Sleep on the floor? I have learned to never leave the cabin without you. I'm aware of all the dangers now. You don't need to babysit me as if I were a child. I'm not."

His gaze dropped to her breasts. "I'm more than aware."

Her heart rate increased. She didn't need to ask him what he meant by that. His attention to her chest made his meaning clear. He presented her with his back but didn't leave.

127

"You can sleep in your room instead of on the floor. I give my word, I will never do anything like that again. I will ask you to take me to the river next time."

"Why would you even do it?" He glanced back.

"Go to the river? I walked outside to get air and heard it. I was curious. I thought you were sleeping and didn't believe it was a big deal. I could make out shapes well enough to believe I could reach it without falling into a hole or into the water."

He combed his fingers through his hair, breaking eye contact. "Fine. I will accept your promise."

"Thank you."

He hesitated. "No, I wouldn't offer to sleep on the floor for the other Species females. You're not them though."

"I'm less, right? Weak? Perhaps useless?" Kit had told her that the men saw Gift Females that way. "Look at me."

He spun around. "What?"

"I'm just a woman, Shadow. I'm getting stronger every day and I refuse to be locked inside a box while you and everyone else tosses away the key. I might not be as physically fit as our women but that doesn't make me less." Her chin rose. "I'm shy and less inclined to be brutally blunt but give me time. I want a normal life and that's something I'm going to have to earn in order to be treated equal around here, isn't it?"

A soft growl rumbled from him. "You want to be treated the way they are?"

"Yes."

His gaze drifted down her slowly, taking in every inch. "You shouldn't say that right now. You don't know much about Species males, do you?"

"What does that mean?"

"I just saw you bare and you're demanding for me to see you as if you are any other Species female." He softly growled. "Be careful what you wish for, Beauty."

Her heart accelerated as they stared at each other. She glanced down his body and noticed for the first time that his shorts were tented from his semi-erect cock. She was surprised at his aroused state. They'd been arguing but it seemed to turn him on. That made no sense to her.

"Good night." He stepped out of her view to return to his room.

Beauty hesitated then rushed after him before she could chicken out. "Shadow?"

He spun, a low growl passing his parted lips. "What?"

"Tell me more about Species men."

His eyes widened and his hands reached up to grip the top of the doorframe of his bedroom. "Not now."

"You said I don't know much about Species men. Tell me what you think I should understand about them."

He seemed to be studying her face before he spoke. "You can't be that innocent."

Her outburst of temper still fueled her courage. "Are you attracted to me?"

"You know I am." He glanced down at the evidence. "It's obvious. There's no hiding it in these boxers."

Beauty followed his gaze and gawked a bit at the sight of Shadow's cock straining against the material. The outline of it was thick, big and intimidating. She wasn't sure how she'd missed noticing his condition until he'd mentioned it. Then again, he had such beautiful eyes that they distracted her. So had his bare chest and broad shoulders. Every breath he took made her appreciate the sight of both. There was just so much about him that she found fascinating.

Shadow wouldn't do any of the things Master had. She was willing to trust him even if he wasn't so sure of her faith. First though she needed to figure out if he was so resistant to them becoming closer because she was a Gift Female or it was a result of his life traumas. His mouth said one thing but his body showed interest.

"Do you want to sleep with me?" She couldn't believe she'd just blurted out that question but it beat staring at the ceiling all night berating herself for being a wimp. "I thought you were angry. I'm confused. I don't understand how you could have that reaction when you don't like me."

"I'm furious." His had a death grip on the wood. "I have all kinds of things going on inside me."

"What kinds of things?"

His chest rose as he sucked in air before exhaling it slowly. "I don't dislike you. That's the problem. You could have been killed by the wolves or taken away by another male. That awakes certain instincts inside me."

"What kind?"

He closed his eyes and turned his head to the side to rest his forehead against his inner arm, frustration pretty clear on his face.

"I'm trying to understand," she explained softly. "It's not my fault I was kept away from Species men and don't know that much about you."

His head snapped back in her direction, his eyes opening. "I'm male, not a man."

"I told you, I'm working on the language thing."

"You did." He released the doorframe and took a few hesitant steps forward as his hands lowered to his sides.

She didn't retreat, though part of her wanted to. He was big and mostly naked but it was Shadow. It surprised her when he suddenly dropped to his knees before her, making their faces almost the same height. He stared deeply into her eyes as he gently encased her hips within his grasp. She had no words despite wanting to know what he was doing.

"I'll explain," he rasped.

She nodded, refusing to look away from him.

"You're mine to protect. I know in my mind that you don't belong to me but my impulses say otherwise. Another male got too close and I know what he could have done to you. It makes me kind of crazy inside."

"What do you think he would have done to me?"

He scowled. "Are you sure you want the truth?"

She nodded sharply.

"He would have stripped you bare and seduced you. He would have mounted you when you were willing to accept him." His voice deepened.

"He would have turned you around and taken you from behind. That means sex."

"Breeze said to tell a man to take me facing him because of my past."

He paled slightly. "Why?"

"That's what..." She paused, remembering he hated the term "master". "The asshole did to me. He always took me from behind so he didn't have to look at me and know it caused me pain."

Shadow hung his head until his forehead almost rested against the top of her nightgown. His hot breath fanned through the thin material right between her breasts. She only hesitated for a second before reaching up and lightly brushing her fingers through his short hair.

"How did it hurt?" His tone was gruff.

"I don't understand."

He kept his head down. "Was it just because you're small and him being inside you was painful or was it because you didn't want him and weren't wet?"

He was blunt enough to stun her. She wanted to be as honest with him. "I don't know. I didn't want him to do that and it just hurt."

He released her hip with one hand and slid an arm around her waist, holding her. "Did it ever feel good? Even once?"

"No." Maybe there was something wrong with her. She hadn't considered that until this moment.

He finally lifted his head and she stared into his eyes again. "Never?"

"No."

"Did he caress you? You said he never kissed you. Did he attempt to arouse you?"

"He would grab my hips and tell me to hold still. That's all."

Anger flashed in his gaze before he looked away. "He just forced you to your hands and knees when he took you?"

"Kind of. He had me bend over the end of the bed and grip the footboard railings. It was a narrow bed."

A snarl made her start. It was a loud, dangerous sound.

"Don't," he rasped, holding her gaze again. "I'm not him."

"I know that."

"Are you curious about sex and want to know how it would feel if a male you want touched you?"

Her cheeks were burning now and she wanted to hide from his intense stare but answered honestly despite it. "Yes."

"Why?"

"I don't understand the question."

"Why would you want a male to touch you after you've been hurt?"

She tried to put her feelings into words. "I didn't at first but then I started hearing the other women who live next door to me when men visited them. They kept inviting more of them to their apartments. I envied them because it sounded so different from what I've known. The sounds were of pleasure, not pain. They enjoyed it. I just want to know how it would feel to have someone touch me that way. I can't explain it any better than that. I liked you holding me the night we spent together."

"I'm not the right male for this."

"You don't want me." It stung. "It's okay."

"I want you. I'm just telling you the truth. I've avoided females."

"Is it because of what was done to you? Does it make you hate women?"

"Not hate, no. I'm afraid I'll lose control if I have a flashback. I suffer nightmares."

"What exactly was done to you?"

He didn't answer and she thought he wouldn't until he took a ragged breath. "They gave me breeding drugs and put things over my eyes to force me to watch video images of human women touching themselves. It made my dick hard because I'm male and the drugs aroused me greatly." Pain flashed in his beautiful eyes. "They hooked my dick to a machine that stimulated me to release my seed."

"To steal your semen to sell." She remembered him telling her that.

"It hurt bad and even after my seed was taken they didn't stop. They had drugged me enough to make me mindless so I suffered. I began to associate pain and humiliation with seeing a female body. I've progressed somewhat since being freed. The feminine form arouses me now but the idea of following through with action makes me hesitate."

Beauty continued to stroke his hair with her fingertips. "Did it make you feel that way when I walked out of the bathroom just now without my towel?"

The arm around her waist tightened slightly. "No."

"How did it make you feel?"

He softly growled and lowered his focus to her chest. "Afraid, but I wanted you."

"How could I possibly frighten you?" It amazed her that he'd say that.

He looked up and held her gaze. "You're smaller than me and I worry I'd be too rough if I put my hands on you."

"You're touching me right now and you're being very gentle." She swallowed hard. "Maybe we could help each other get over our pasts."

"How?"

Her heart hammered with fear but she wanted Shadow. "Come to bed with me."

Chapter Eight

Shadow waged an inner battle while peering at Beauty. It was so tempting to take her up on the offer to share a bed. The condition of his dick would make that a bad idea. He didn't just want to hold her in his arms. He would touch, perhaps lick, and even bite. He glanced down her body. There were a dozen places he'd love to scrape his fangs on her skin. Would she shiver with need for more or would it instill terror?

Memories of being chained up while his body was forced into submission to release his seed had damaged him. Those images of nude human females had been arousing and in turn, he'd grown to hate the sight of them. Beauty wasn't them. His mind knew the difference. His body did as well, judging by its responses. Desire he'd long denied heated his blood. Instead of masturbating just to tend his physical needs, he wanted close intimate contact with the Gift Female.

He thought back to the few times at Mercile that he'd been used in breeding tests. The females hadn't been overly friendly or talkative. Their lives had made them emotionally detached. The feline he'd mounted on three different occasions had walked into his cell, stripped out of just her pants and gotten into position on her hands and knees on his cot. When he'd attempted to arouse her by touching her gently and exploring her sex, she'd snarled, "Just do it. I knew they were bringing me to a male and I prepared my body."

That would account for the smell of her. The rich aroma coming off her had made his dick hard and his animal urges surged. Taking her had been physically pleasurable, no denying that, but the act had been cold. She'd left immediately afterward, asking the technicians to take her away.

She hadn't recognized him when he'd seen her again at Homeland—Kit. That or she had purposely ignored their past association. Seeing her alive had been both a relief that someone he'd met during those brief encounters at Mercile had also survived and an embarrassing reminder of what they'd once been subjected to. He'd heard the females had been taken to a lot of males and it had been several years ago. It was possible that he just hadn't been memorable to her.

The other female was one he'd never seen again. A technician had brought her to him twice during the breeding tests. She'd been canine and aggressive. She'd given his body a once-over, assessing him, and flashed fangs. "Just don't bite me. The last male attempted that."

"I won't harm you," he'd sworn.

She'd nodded. "Proceed."

He'd been at a loss as to what to do. Irritation had flashed in her expression when he'd just stood there waiting for an indication of what she expected. "First time breeding?"

"No."

"Make me wet."

He'd glanced at the water source in his cell. She'd growled, pulling his attention back to her.

"You know nothing, do you?"

137

Shame had burned through him. "I can mount you."

She'd pulled at the seams of her clothing, tearing them off. "Follow me. You'll learn."

He'd watched as she dropped onto his mat, rolled over, and spread her thighs. She pointed at the floor beside her. "Kneel right there. What is your number?"

"I am 358. What is yours?"

"It doesn't matter. This is what you're going to do, 358."

She'd kept talking, explaining in detail what she wanted and how to make her wet. It had involved his mouth on her sex. He'd learned quickly, her moans and growls rewarding his efforts. It was the only real skill he knew when it came to females.

Beauty stepped closer. "Shadow?"

He pushed back his memories to return to the present. Most of his anger had dulled. No one had warned him that Reservation had dangerous animals roaming the Wild Zone. Beauty couldn't have known about them either. He had marked the area and told her it was to keep her safe.

"I'm calmer."

"Do you want to sleep with me?"

Her hopeful tone tugged at his heart and also made his cock twitch. What would she do if he wanted to make her wet? The taste of a female was addictive, something never forgotten...and missed. He glanced down at her hips and imagined those thighs spread open to him. A deep growl built inside his chest but he managed to stifle it. Excitement gripped him full force and the urge to push her back on the bed, lick her and then flip her over to mount was so strong he tensed his body to hold still. He barely managed to keep control. He'd go at her with aggression, his desire too strong.

"I can't."

"Oh."

The rejection hurt her and he felt guilt.

"Now isn't a good time."

"You're still angry with me for going outside. Unbelievable! You're so stubborn."

He glanced down again at his engorged dick then frowned. "I'd want more than to hold you."

She didn't flee or gasp. "We could try."

Beauty had no idea what she was offering but he did. He was too excited, would do something stupid, but he didn't want to share that information with her. Coming in his shorts from just putting his mouth on her would injure his pride and worse, probably horrify her or make her feel sorry for him.

He stood and put space between them. "I'm not angry. I'm tired. Just go to bed. We'll discuss this tomorrow."

He strode into his room and closed the door, reaching down to adjust his wayward cock. Gripping the shaft made him groan. It ached so bad it was a physical pain. He released it and slipped his fingers under the waistband of his boxers to stroke along the crown of his dick.

Shadow admitted to being a mess emotionally as he hooked the waistband with his other hand and shoved down the boxers enough to free his member. It stuck out, swollen and red. He hobbled with the material around his knees to the nightstand, fumbled with the drawer and managed to yank out the bottle of lotion he'd put there. The cold liquid didn't even faze him as he dumped some into his palm, gripped his dick and pumped furiously. He just needed to come so he'd be able to think clearly.

His hips bucked as he threw his head back and sealed his lips together to stay quiet. Pleasure gripped him as he furiously stroked his cock in a tight fist. He was almost there, so close, and just the thought of Beauty naked was enough to send him over to the edge in a pathetically short time. His balls drew up, tightened, and then he was jerking from the explosion of his release.

A soft gasp broke through the haze of ecstasy and he twisted his head to the side, gaping at Beauty. The bathroom door that connected their rooms was cracked open enough to see her big, startled eyes and he followed where she looked. The last of his semen jetted out, splashing across the top of the nightstand. His hand still gripped his swollen dick and horror filled him. He tried to speak as his mind tried to function, to come up with something, anything to say to explain being caught jacking off. No words came forth.

She glanced at his face and then shoved the door closed all the way. It slammed and he winced as his grip loosened on his shaft. Another door slammed a second later—her side of the bathroom—and seconds later, the one in the hallway followed. She'd sealed her room.

"Shit," he snarled. She was probably traumatized and terrified. Disgust welled as he looked down at the proof of his desperate attempt not to go after her.

He stripped off his boxers completely, used them to clean up his spilled semen and walked to the bathroom door. He listened but no sound came from the other room. He entered to wash his hands. The light stayed off since he didn't want to see his own reflection in the mirror.

It was tempting to tap on her door to apologize but he wore nothing. She might mistake his reason for trying to see her as something nefarious instead of just desperation to make sure she was okay. Shadow spun, returned to his room, and put on sweatpants. He strained to hear any noise coming from Beauty's room. Was she all right? Frightened? Appalled?

"This is why I told them I'm not the right male for her," he muttered. His ass landed hard on the edge of the bed, he lowered his head and shook it from side to side. "I have no business being around a female."

Beauty curled up on her bed in the dark, her heart doing a funny dance inside her chest. She'd gone into the bathroom to brush out her hair but strange sounds from Shadow's room had piqued her curiosity. She'd just meant to check on him when she'd realized the door wasn't fully closed. Instead she'd gotten one heck of a surprise.

The side view of Shadow standing next to his bed was something she'd never forget as long as she lived. His boxers had fallen to his knees and muscular thighs led upward to a firm, rounded ass that flexed as his hips rocked. That was just the beginning. His dick was big, as thick as it had

141

appeared when it had been hidden under that thin material. He'd been stroking it with his fist.

Pain dulled the arousal she felt at how sexy the sight had been when Shadow's head was thrown back, the muscles in his arm, his ass, and his torso tensed, defining every one. He'd groaned in a way that made her catch her breath as she'd watched him shake and twitch as he came. It did funny things to her stomach. She became aware of her nipples for some reason and she throbbed between her legs. It wasn't a mystery though, what she was feeling. She had the same reaction when she read steamy sex scenes in romance novels that turned her on.

Shadow had suddenly twisted his head in her direction and she'd forced her focus off the very appealing sight of his cock, which he'd still stroked but in slower motions. He'd looked at her, his expression grim. Instinct and fear gripped her as his mouth opened and his fangs showed. He was displeased in a big way. She bolted, slamming doors between them. She'd invaded his privacy and it wasn't until she was closed inside her room that she calmed.

Shadow wouldn't hurt her. Instincts were a bitch. Sometimes she reacted without thought, only later suffering the consequences. The spider incident in the kitchen a month before at the dorm was a perfect example. The other women still laughed and teased her about leaping up onto the island and shrieking when the tiny thing had landed on her hand when she'd pulled out a baking sheet. It must have built a web under the cabinet and her fingers had brushed through it.

The reasonable side of her knew she'd never been in danger. Not with that eight-legged creature, nor with Shadow. The problem was that some things were just embedded in her DNA. Anything unexpected that made her jump had her bounding away and making that horrible high-pitched sound. She almost wished she were canine or feline. They snarled or growled but acted aggressively when they were put in those situations. Definitely not laughable reactions.

Hurt came after the embarrassment passed. Shadow could have shared her bed and initiated sex but he had gone to his room instead. She rolled over, closing her eyes. She'd offered but he'd refused. He'd even seen her naked earlier, albeit it wasn't intentional. There was nothing more she could do. The hints had been provided, she'd been honest and now the ball was in Shadow's court. It just didn't seem as though it was a game either of them could win. Not that she was playing. She just wanted him to want her as much as she did him. Who better to help her heal than someone who'd suffered too?

"Damn," she whispered. "Why do you have to make this so tough?"

* * * * *

Sleep was hard to come by and Shadow felt as if he'd gotten little to none of it when he finally rolled out of bed after the sun had risen. The cabin was so quiet he feared waking Beauty if he opened the door to go downstairs in search of food. It came as a relief when his cell phone vibrated and he answered the call.

"Are there as many trees outside as I've been told?"

143

"Wrath!" The sound of a masculine voice was never more welcome. "How are you and Lauren?"

"We are very good. Lauren and her cat love the house. I am appreciating every room with her." He chuckled. "That is a sexual reference. I went for a run this morning and imagine my surprise when I heard you'd been assigned to escort a Gift Female to Reservation."

"Um, yes." He sat back down, running his fingers through the short strands of his hair. It annoyed him how quickly it grew since he'd stopped cutting it for the task force. "I was."

"Have you shared sex?"

"No."

"Why not? I was told that was the purpose of sending you both to a cabin. To give you privacy."

Resentment burned. "Mercile no longer controls me."

The silence lengthened into almost half a minute. "You feel pushed into this? You're comparing the NSO to Mercile? That is the way I understand your statement."

"Yes. It's a new breeding experiment without the technicians to handle us and no locks to keep us here. It's still expected for us to share sex."

"Is that how the female feels?"

"I don't think so. She, um..." He wasn't sure how to word it.

"She what?"

"I was told she wanted to be alone with me."

144

"She's interested in you but you don't feel the same? You feel no sexual attraction?"

"I do. She's beautiful." His voice lowered. "Sweet. Innocent. But she's a Gift Female, Wrath. She's small and a primate mix. I feel monstrous in size compared to her."

"You will fit. Take your time. I feared that with Lauren. They stretch down there to accommodate your girth. Just don't go too deep until her body has become accustomed to yours."

"That isn't my fear. I suppose it partly is...but mostly I'm afraid of losing control."

"I understand. I suffered those same anxieties about Lauren. I had to trust myself to know I wouldn't strike out at her if I had a bad moment. You just need to remember she is flesh and blood, not those videos and machines. We're free. Our bodies are no longer harnessed for pain and humiliation while our seed is stolen. You won't forget that while you are touching her. Shed that fear. I know what I'm talking about."

"I know you do. I keep having flashbacks to what was done to us."

"You are unable to get an erection?" Wrath whispered, a hint his mate was nearby and he wanted to protect his friend from the humiliation of anyone else knowing if that was his problem. "There are pills for that. You should discuss it with a doctor. We see commercials for that all the time. They say it's not just physical issues but sometimes emotional ones."

"My dick gets hard all the time. My body reacts to her. It's the fear that cock blocks me."

"I had the same problem."

145

"Yes." He knew Wrath would understand.

"Why didn't you call me?"

"You and Lauren finally have your house and this is the first time you've had real seclusion. I know how much you both looked forward to leaving the task force basement. You stated many times you wanted her to cook for you naked and share sex without fear of someone interrupting you. I didn't want to do that."

"In other words, you were being thick-headed and stubborn? I wanted more stable work hours once I finished my time with the task force instead of someone pounding on our bedroom door at two in the morning with an emergency mission. You're my best friend and I don't consider you an interruption."

Shadow chuckled. "I should have contacted you."

"You should have." Wrath agreed. "Let it happen if you are attracted to each other. I tried to deny my feelings for Lauren. Your imagination of what bad things could happen is far worse than the reality."

"She's been abused."

"So were we. I promise you won't turn into an animal and either go into a rage from flashbacks or somehow lose control by taking things too fast. You care for her?"

"Yes. I'd do anything to avoid hurting Beauty."

"You'll focus on her needs rather than your own. We're stronger than we believe. You need to discover that."

"And trust you."

Wrath laughed again. "Exactly. I'd never steer you wrong."

Shadow grew somber. "She caught me jacking off last night. She fled into her room and slammed the doors between us."

"Are you sure she saw you?"

"Yes." He winced. "The light was on in my room and I was standing not five feet from her."

"It's natural. Explain to her that we're highly sexual and not tending to our needs makes us cranky and mean spirited. Nothing is more irritating than swollen, painful balls."

"No shit." He glanced at the closed door, still not hearing anything to indicate Beauty had woken. "So trust myself?"

"Yes."

"I still resent being ordered to share sex."

"I know you well. You wouldn't be there if you truly didn't want to go. You'd have called Tim or Trey to ask them to bring you back to the task force sooner rather than later. Are you still contemplating returning?"

"I don't know. Things are different."

"Beauty."

"Yes."

"Would you miss her?"

He pondered the question. The idea of not being around if she needed him was disturbing. Other males would hear of her interest in him and might believe they could ask her to share sex if she didn't want to be labeled a Gift Female. Anger flared and his teeth clenched.

147

"I will take that for a yes since you didn't immediately deny it."

"I would."

"You should notify the task force and tell them you're not available anymore."

"Not yet. What if this blows up in my face? What if we do share sex and she wishes to explore it with other males the way our females do?" He'd have to kill every male who touched her but that was beside the point. "I'll wait and see what happens."

Wrath laughed again. "You have it bad."

That described the turmoil of emotions he experienced. "I am glad you called and that you and your mate are doing well."

"Last night was very funny."

"What happened?"

"We had a dinner guest. Tiger came over after a meeting with Justice and Fury. Lauren's cat hissed at him and he hissed back. They didn't like each other. She told them to both behave and they had something in common. Then she revealed that they shared the same name. I almost hurt myself laughing at his expression."

"The cat or Tiger?"

Wrath laughed harder. "The one who understood. He was not amused but I was. Fury agreed. He actually fell over from laughing so hard. Ellie was having a movie night at the women's dorm so we invited him too, for pizza."

"I wish I could have seen Tiger's face."

"He got even."

"How so?"

"This morning we woke to someone at the door. Tiger said someone had found a puppy a few days ago near the front gate at Homeland. He'd retrieved it from Security where they've been caring for it. He said it was a housewarming gift and we couldn't refuse."

"That was nice. Do you and your mate like dogs?"

"She fell in love. It is cute and seems to really love us already. He licks my face and follows me around." He paused. "Tiger told Lauren it was a Species custom to name gifts and to meet little Fury."

The meaning sank in. "Fury is not going to be amused but I am."

"Exactly."

"How is the cat getting along with the puppy?"

"They are adjusting but it will take some—"

The sound of glass breaking carried over the phone made Shadow tensed. "What was that?"

"The cat just jumped on top of the wall unit and knocked over a vase. I said Tiger got even but it wasn't just with Fury." He covered the phone a little. "I'll clean that up."

Lauren could be heard in the background. "Bad Fury! Tiger isn't a ball to chase."

Wrath sighed and spoke directly back into the phone again. "The puppy believes that cat is a toy and the cat seems to think it's under attack. I have a feeling it's going to be a long week."

"They'll become friends," Lauren called out. "We'll just have to invite Fury and Tiger back to dinner so they can see that felines and canines can get along."

"She's planning on getting even too," Wrath whispered. "I'd better go. I don't want Lauren to cut her feet. She's naked and too close to the broken glass. Call me if you need advice. Don't hesitate."

"I won't."

Shadow disconnected the phone and stood. He needed a shower, then he'd cook breakfast. The smell of food should lure Beauty out of her room. At least he hoped it would. They needed to talk before he had to meet with Torrent for the swimming lesson. The thought of leaving her alone for an hour wasn't comforting but he didn't want her around other males.

* * * * *

Beauty stretched out on her stomach and cracked open her eyes. The sun was up and the smell of bacon teased her fully awake. She was hungry and a new day had dawned. At first two weeks had seemed as though it would be a long time to see where her attraction to Shadow led but one of those weeks had already passed and they hadn't made much progress. They lived together but they might as well be roommates. It seemed that actual sexual contact might never happen.

She blamed herself for peeking into Shadow's bedroom. He'd been uncomfortable after the night she'd caught him stroking himself. He wouldn't meet her gaze for longer than a few seconds and found excuses to be outside often. Not that she blamed him. She'd probably avoid him as well if he'd caught her in the same situation.

The one time she'd tried to bring it up, he'd shut her down fast by changing the subject, stuttering his words, and ducking out of the cabin after swearing he'd heard a noise. She hadn't. It had been an excuse to avoid the conversation. Any chance of a romance seemed dim as each day passed. She was tempted to ask Shadow to just return her to Homeland. Her heart wouldn't allow it though.

Her nights hadn't been haunted by the past. Instead it had been the tall, blond Species who'd tormented her dreams. As soon as she'd drift off to sleep, he'd appear, stripped naked and running his hands all over his body but he would step back every time she tried to touch him. The sight of all those muscles, tan skin and him fisting his thick cock left her aroused and frustrated.

The floor outside her door creaked before a knock sounded. "Beauty? Breakfast is ready."

"Okay. I'll be there in a few minutes." It had become routine for him to inform her that food was ready, they'd silently eat together, and then he'd be out the door until the next meal.

"Take your time."

The floor creaked again as he left. She shoved off the covers and glanced at her nightshirt. It was tough to fight the temptation to go downstairs just the way she was. That's *exactly* what she wanted to do. Fight with Shadow. She was a grown woman and he was a man. They were alone and she wanted to experience everything life had to offer, including him. She was tired of the avoidance and the casual discussions on neutral topics.

There were signs that Shadow had showered when she entered the bathroom. A wet towel hanging on the rack confirmed it. It only took seconds to strip and wait for the water to warm. After her shower, she hurried to get ready and dressed in a skirt with a loose tank top. The sight of women's legs was supposed to make men think of sex. She hoped the books had it right. The loose top allowed her to ditch wearing a bra.

She looked down. Her breasts weren't overly large but she wasn't flat chested either. Movement was apparent under the top when she bounced on her bare heels, making them shake. Beauty nodded.

"Don't play fair. Life isn't, so why should I be?"

One deep breath and she went in search of Shadow. He sat in the kitchen at the table with two plates of food. It always touched her that he waited for her arrival before he ate. The atmosphere was still a little tense but she had expected that. She took the seat across from him and peered at his face.

He avoided eye contact, his plate seemingly very interesting.

"This looks delicious. Thank you."

Shoulders barely covered by a black tank top shrugged.

"I appreciate it. I hope you slept well."

Tiny lines around his eyes told her he probably hadn't. "Not really."

Beauty studied him. "I've had enough of this."

"Enough of what? Do you want something else to eat?"

"Enough of whatever is going on between us. I can't take it anymore. I'm so sorry that I saw what I did but the last week of us hardly talking and you taking off for hours has been driving me crazy. We should discuss it."

That drew his attention. "I wanted to apologize." His cheeks darkened, showing his clear mortification. "You shouldn't have seen that."

He was blunt and surprised her by not avoiding discussing what had happened. "I was the one who opened the door. I heard noises and wondered what you were doing."

His eyebrows shot up.

"I found out."

His mouth pressed into a firm line as his expression smoothed out.

"You don't need to apologize but I wish I were more appealing than your hand." *I really said that. Crap!* She hadn't meant to express her thoughts aloud.

"You are." His voice came out deeper.

She had to look away, the moment just a bit too intense. "It hurt my feelings." While she was admitting things, she might as well go for broke. "I offered to sleep with you."

"I didn't want to just sleep."

She met his stare. "I didn't either."

He took a sharp breath and the chair scraped loudly across the floor as he rose quickly and shocked her by stepping around the table. His hands gripped her upper arms and he pulled her to her unsteady feet.

"Don't be afraid."

"Okay." Her heart speeded up.

Her feet left the floor and he spun with her until her ass landed on the counter. They'd gone from barely speaking to being face-to-face level. Shadow softly growled, a sexy sound, and wiggled his hips. She parted her knees to allow him to step closer until they were nearly nose to nose.

"I want you."

His confession was what she wanted but it was happening so fast that she struggled to think. "What do we do?" She reached for him. The skin on his shoulders was extremely warm as her fingers curled around them for something to cling to.

He searched her face, possibly looking for fear. That's not how she felt though. Shadow had her pinned on the counter and was close enough to kiss. She lifted her chin and parted her lips, an invitation to do just that.

He leaned in a little and her eyes closed in anticipation. His breath fanned her face, the smell of coffee nice. She waited but nothing happened. Her eyelids parted to peek at him.

Shadow had pulled his face a few inches away. "Not like this."

"We could go upstairs."

"I…"

"You what?"

"I have to meet Torrent for a swimming lesson. After he teaches me, I'll take you down to the river to learn."

Torrent had called to delay their lesson. An emergency had come up concerning a lion cub located at a human's home and he'd had to leave Reservation. He'd been gone all week but maybe he was back now.

Shadow's hands gripped her hips and he lifted, slowly lowering her to her feet. "You should eat." He seemed rattled. He backed away, letting her go, obviously trying to clear his head. "Yes. Eat. I need to, um, check the perimeter."

He kept putting space between them while they faced each other. She glanced down and clearly saw the outline of his stiff cock poking against the material of his sweatpants.

"Shadow?"

"I, um, need to go. Eat." He spun and fled.

"Damn!" What had she done wrong? Maybe he'd expected her to kiss him and had taken her lack of initiative as rejection. "I don't know how," she whispered. He wasn't there anymore to hear her though.

Chapter Nine

Shadow didn't mind learning new things but swimming in the fast-moving water not only seemed dangerous but it held no interest for him either. Shadow wasn't thrilled that the river was so close to the cabin because it posed a danger to Beauty so he'd learn as soon as Torrent freed his schedule.

Shadow sat on a fallen log, peering across the river to the other side. Movement caught his attention as he spotted a Species male crouch to study something in the water. The male was far away, keeping his distance from the cabin, but the sight of him wasn't comforting. He stood, making his presence known.

They stared at each other across the water. Shadow kept a tense posture, his hands fisted in threat, to make certain the male knew he'd defend the territory perimeter. A smile curved the other Species' lips and one hand raised in a wave.

"I'm staying on this side," he yelled. "Tracking one of my lions."

Shadow had no trouble hearing what was said over the sound of the rushing water. "Good."

The male nodded. "It's a female. She's roaming but I don't think she crossed." He straightened, walked along the bank and then pointed. "She got out of the river here. It's all good."

Wild lions. Shadow shivered a bit. He wasn't opposed to animals but he didn't have much experience with them. Lauren's cat was the only one

156

he'd really spent time with and it was a small pet. The concept of a bigger one with sharp claws and fangs wasn't something he wanted to run into.

The male waved again and turned, disappearing into the thick trees. Shadow's mouth fell open. There was no denying what he'd seen. The Wild Zone male not only had more animalistic features and unusual eye shaping—he had a tail. It hadn't been an overly long one but it had hung from the back of his loose shorts to his bare calves.

There were a lot of things he hated about the life he'd been handed but he'd been spared being what Mercile considered a failure. Those males with their more altered features really had it tough. He'd read the reports about how they'd been treated in the testing facilities. Most had been housed kennel style in actual cages. Some had very little communication skills since technicians didn't speak to them often. They were fed and treated as if they were purely animals and hadn't gotten the benefit of any kind of education. Most Species could read, had been taught at a young age, even if it was only for testing purposes. It was hard to judge drug results if the participant wasn't able to verbally communicate or to read to see if their memory or vision had been adversely affected.

His own abuse seemed minimal compared to others as he sat back down on the log, pondering the life of a Wild Zone resident. They didn't even feel comfortable living amongst their own kind at Homeland. Shadow had been given the opportunity to work closely with humans on the task force. He liked most of them, though there were a few exceptions. They didn't make him feel subhuman but they just weren't overly friendly, preferring to keep emotionally detached from other members. It wasn't personal. They treated everyone that way, whether Species or human.

He glanced up at the sky, judging that he'd been gone from the cabin long enough. He'd left in a hurry when he'd fled from Beauty. The temptation to share sex with her had been nearly overpowering until he realized he had her pinned on a counter. She deserved better than to be taken in the kitchen. Guilt hit hard and fast.

Beauty deserved a bed and a male who knew more about sex to make certain she enjoyed it. That male should know soft, pretty words to speak to her yet he felt as if he was constantly putting his foot in his mouth. She'd wanted him to kiss her. Her head tilting back and her lips parting while she'd closed her eyes had been a good indication. There was only one problem. He'd never kissed a female before.

"Shit."

He got to his feet and started back to the cabin. One way or another, he needed to figure out how to give Beauty what she needed. He wanted to do right by her and more importantly, he just wanted her. Wrath had been right. No one would have been able to force him to escort her to Reservation unless, deep down, he'd wanted it. He wouldn't deny that truth. He might not be the right male for her but he wished he were.

The cabin came into sight and a deep sense of relief settled into him when he saw smoke curling from the chimney.

Beauty sat on the couch, holding a small paperback book when he entered. Her dark eyes lifted and his heart stuttered inside his chest. The urge to go to her, sink to his knees and just touch her gripped him hard.

She'd changed clothes while he was gone—something that showed less skin. He wondered if she'd done it in response to him fleeing earlier.

"Hi." She closed the book after carefully placing a bookmark inside. "You were gone for hours."

"I needed to think."

"Are you leaving? Will they send another officer here to guard me or will we just return to Homeland together?"

"Do you want to return? Do you want another male here with you?" A protest froze on his tongue. He refused to force her to stay with him. He'd do whatever she wanted, even if it killed him.

"No." She leaned forward.

"Good." He stepped into the cabin, closed the door at his back and twisted the lock. "I enjoy being here with you."

Some of the tension left her delicate features. "Really?"

"Yes." He hated feeling as if he were a failure as a male. "I'm attracted to you, Beauty. What I feel is a bit fearsome."

"You're afraid of me?"

"I'm not sure how to handle the emotions I feel when I'm around you. I've never experienced them before."

"Me neither." She patted the couch next to her. "Will you sit?"

He crossed the room and gingerly perched on the edge of the cushion about a foot away from her. The wonderful scent of her made his dick twitch. Why did he always feel sweaty, nervous and highly aroused when she was near? All his confidence fled.

"What are you reading?"

"A romance book."

He glanced at it, amused at the cover of a male and female locked in an embrace. "Are they interesting?"

"Yes. I think so anyway."

"Is that all you read?"

"No. I love horror novels too."

That surprised him. "You do?"

"Yes. Especially the crime ones. Who-done-it types of books." She paused. "I had access to children's mystery books in the basement. I found a box of them stored in a corner behind some furniture. There were only fourteen of them but I knew them by heart from reading them so many times." That was back when she'd been free to roam the entire basement. Later a room had been built to contain her to one area.

"I'm glad you learned to read."

"Me too. One of the guards was nice to me when I was young. I think he pitied me. He had a daughter."

She wasn't going to admit that Master had found out and fired the man. Mentioning Master always soured Shadow's mood. That guard had been the one and only person who'd ever done anything for her without expecting something in return.

"Do you read books?"

"Sometimes. There were long stretches of downtime when I worked for the task force but then we'd have days where it seemed I barely closed my eyes before we were pulling out again."

"Was it exciting?"

"Sometimes."

"Were you ever afraid?"

"We raided buildings and homes looking for ex-Mercile employees. Sometimes they fired back. A lot of times they'd be long gone."

"It sounds frightening but I'm so grateful the task force exists. They found me."

"I know." He gently took her hand. "Are you still having nightmares about the task force member?"

"No." She smiled. "I haven't. Not since I met you."

He pondered what that meant but it didn't matter as long as she slept easier. "Are you hungry? I am."

"Yes." She brightened even more. "I'll make dinner. I know it is a little early but you skipped breakfast and were gone at lunch."

"I'll help."

Shadow followed her into the kitchen, enjoying the view of her from behind. She had a round, full butt for someone her size and it fit a pair of jeans perfectly. The tank top hugged her waist. The scent of her shampoo and soap teased his senses.

They worked together nicely as they prepared hot dogs and chips. It was an easy meal that didn't require them to spend much time in the kitchen. Beauty carried her plate into the living room and patted the couch next to her.

"Do you want to watch a movie while we eat?" She pointed to the wall where DVDs were lined up. "I saw some good action films we might enjoy."

"Sure." He wanted to spend time with her.

It was relaxing and a strange emotion rose in his chest at the domestic scene they painted. He glanced around the cabin, wondering what it would be like if they actually shared a real home. One that the two of them lived in together. Longing struck as his gaze returned to Beauty.

She held up two movies for his inspection. "Which one? I really want to see both of these."

Beauty took his breath away. He had to suck in air to reply. "You pick. We could watch both of them."

Sheer joy lit up her expression. "Awesome!"

Yes, this is, he agreed.

* * * * *

Beauty curled tighter against Shadow's chest. His arm around her waist made her feel safer. They weren't real but the bad guys in the movie were still scary. She fisted his shirt while staring at the television.

"Do you think they'll make it?"

He nodded, his chin rubbing against the top of her head. "The good guys always win."

In movies. "I hope so. I hate that gangster guy. His second-in-command should have shot him."

162

Shadow chuckled. "Then the movie would have ended after ten minutes."

"True." She rubbed her face against the soft material of his shirt. She loved being so close to him. All that reading hadn't hinted that men didn't mind women clinging to them during frightening scenes of a movie. "Oh no. Don't they sense that jerk creeping up behind them?"

"Humans don't have our sense of smell."

"Oh." She nodded. "Right. I just meant, you know, like feel the danger at their backs?"

"It's a movie." He offered her the big bowl he held. "More popcorn?"

"I think I'm ready to pop myself."

"This is our fourth bowl." He leaned forward and placed it on the table.

She wasn't about to mention he'd eaten three of them. Shadow had a big appetite to go along with his big body. She adjusted away to allow him to place the bowl down and curled against him again when he straightened.

The action in the movie got intense as it wrapped up. She noticed the way Shadow rubbed her leg with his now-free hand. It was nice and distracted her from the screen. Not that she minded.

"See? He rescued the female and the bad guys are dead."

"It was good."

She hated seeing the credits roll. It was the last of the two movies and that meant they probably would go to bed. One glance at the clock confirmed it was after nine at night. Shadow liked to get up early, which meant he would be ready to sleep.

163

It had almost been like a date, without the going-out part.

"I'll turn it off."

Beauty sat up and nodded. "Okay. I'll clear the table and take everything into the kitchen."

They parted and she took her time rinsing their dishes. Nerves struck. She wanted to ask Shadow to share her bed but wasn't sure he'd go for it. So far he'd refused. She didn't want a repeat of the previous week. Being told no hurt.

"Need help?"

She started and gasped, swiveling her head. "I didn't hear you enter the kitchen."

"Sorry."

"It's okay. You move quietly for someone so big."

"The water was on."

She liked that he hadn't mentioned her hearing wasn't as good as his. "I was done." She twisted the levers, shutting off the water. "I'm ready for bed."

"I made sure everything is secure." He kept a few feet between them. "Ready?"

"Yes."

He stayed close as they went upstairs and she paused by her door. The temptation to ask him to keep following her into her room was strong. She turned to peer up at him. Shadow stared back, silent and sexy.

Be strong. Just ask. Her lips parted.

"Good night." He gave her a sharp nod before turning around and walking to his door. "Sleep well, Beauty." He disappeared inside.

"Damn," she whispered, facing her open doorway.

Shadow had not only gone into his room but he was now in the bathroom. She stared at the closed door that connected their rooms and wished he'd open it into her room. The light flicked off and she heard him return to his room. The door closing on his side was depressing.

She used the bathroom, brushed her teeth and listened for any sound from Shadow's room. The darkness under the bottom of the door implied he'd immediately gone to bed.

Back inside her room, she shed her clothes and pulled on a nightgown. The sheets were cold when she lay down on the bed after turning off the light. She turned on her side and sighed. She wanted Shadow. Not just to curl up with in sleep—she wanted to touch him. Have him touch her back. The memories of her neighbors and their men kept flashing through her mind.

It was frustrating wanting something when she couldn't have it. Breeze's advice also came to mind but she discarded it. She didn't want Shadow to ever feel as though she'd pressured him into having sex and he might if she stripped naked and just entered his room. Would he even agree to it if she demanded sex?

She shook her head. That definitely wasn't how she wanted him. There was an awareness of her body that seemed unending. It was his fault. All those muscles and sexy sounds he made just made her think of sex with him. She wasn't about to ever forget waking in that shed with his rigid cock nestled between her thighs.

Something tickled her ankle and she shifted her leg. It stopped, probably the sheet lying on her wrong. Her mind wandered back to thoughts of Shadow and how to get him into her bed. The days were ticking down until they'd return to Homeland. Her idea that frolicking with him in the water wearing the tiny bathing suit Breeze had packed might tempt him into sex hadn't been an option yet. He wasn't about to let her near the river again until one of them could swim.

Her eyes flew open as something tickled her foot again. Her heart jumped and her breath froze. Whatever it was moved again. She bolted upright and blindly reached for the light as she jerked her legs up to her chest. The lamp clicked on and she gripped the sheet, throwing it back.

A black spider was all she saw before she reacted. The shriek tore from her before she could stop it and she rolled right off the bed. The spider seemed to follow as her horrified gaze tracked it on the edge of the mattress. A loud thump sounded somewhere in the cabin and a door slammed into a wall. Heavy footfalls fell as she scrambled to put distance between her and the bed.

Her bedroom door flew open and Shadow stormed in. She turned her head, looking up at him. He wore nothing but a pair of boxers and a fierce look. "What is it?" His fingers were flexed into claws, his attention immediately fixing on the window. "Is someone outside?"

"Um, it's a spider." She pointed at the bed.

Shadow's mouth fell open as he gawked at her.

166

"Look at it. It's big. It was on my foot."

"That tiny thing?" He crouched, staring at her instead of the intruder in her bed. "Did you fall out of bed?"

"It's a spider." *Why can't he understand how scary they are? It touched me.*

He glanced at it, then her. "Hell."

He straightened, walked to the bed and picked up the spider. She cringed. The thing could bite. It might be small but anything with eight legs had to have sharp little fangs. It made sense to her. Maybe its little legs had clawed tips. *Eight of them. I hate spiders. The creepy, ugly things.*

Shadow disappeared into the bathroom. She heard the water turn on. He returned and bent, his hands still damp as he lifted her from the floor. He tried to put her back on her bed but she clutched at his hot skin, shaking her head.

"It could have family. Maybe a nest in my bed."

His eyebrows arched as he paused, then turned and carried her into the hallway. He used his elbow to turn on the light before gently settling her on her feet. "Are you okay?"

"It was in my bed. On my foot."

"Now it's outside. I opened the window and put it out there. It won't get back inside."

"Why were your hands wet?"

"I washed them." He gave her a concerned look. "I take it you're terrified of spiders?"

"Yes."

His lips twitched. "It was tiny, Beauty. Not even poisonous. I'm pretty sure about that. Hold on. I'll go check your bed and your room."

She followed him just inside the room and watched as he shook out her sheets, bedspread, and even lifted the bed to peer under it. He swept the room, even opening drawers and pushing furniture around until he finally looked at her.

"No nest and no family." Amusement glinted in his eyes. "It was a hermit spider."

"That's not funny." She calmed though. "I'm sorry. I screamed, didn't I?"

"Yes."

"I really hate them."

"I realize that."

She backed out into the hallway and he followed.

"Are you afraid to return to your room? Do you want me to check it again? We could change rooms. There're no spiders in my bed."

Here was her chance. She could use fear again to talk him into allowing her to sleep with him but she still felt guilty about doing that in the shed. Honesty was best. It was the Species trait she admired most and Shadow deserved that from a woman.

"I'm okay. I know you were thorough in your search and no more critters will bother me."

"Good."

It was impossible not to notice his chest. So broad, so bare and so close. The flat disks of his nipples were mesmerizing but not any more so than the way his stomach muscles tempted her to touch them, trace each one and keep going lower.

"Beauty?"

She realized she was staring at his boxers. Warmth heated her cheeks as she lifted her chin. "Sleep with me. Not because of the spider or because I just had a scare. I want you to hold me because I like it when you do."

He said nothing but he swallowed hard enough for her to see his Adam's apple bob.

She took a step closer, until they nearly touched. "Isn't it time we got beyond our pasts? We're two adults. I'm attracted to you. I think you're attracted to me." She glanced down and saw the way his boxers had filled out. The outline of his cock couldn't be missed. "I know you're attracted to me. Wasn't holding me nice? I liked sleeping on you."

"We should talk," he finally rasped.

"About what?"

"This."

Chapter Ten

Shadow trembled, wanting Beauty so bad he froze up to prevent himself from following through on lifting her into his arms and carrying her to his bed. He wanted nothing more than to strip her out of that nightgown and explore every inch of her with his hands and mouth.

"Slow," he demanded.

"I'm not doing anything."

He was without humor. "I'm talking to myself, aloud."

"You're not doing anything. Why tell yourself that?"

"It's what I want to do." He peered into her eyes, searching for fear, but found none. She was entirely too trusting. It made him feel guilty, as though he were the animal Mercile used to accuse him of being. "You should go to bed alone, Beauty."

"You slept with me before. I want you to hold me and we'll keep talking."

He clenched his teeth to avoid snarling. She was either attempting to provoke him or was just too naïve to identify a male on the edge of losing control. He was aroused and she'd stated she was curious about sex. No way could he just lie next to her and sleep.

"Come into my room."

Her voice was so soft, whispered, as if she were afraid. He didn't see that emotion as he studied her. Her cheeks were a little pink though, hinting that she was embarrassed by her request. She was shy—had admitted to that already—a unique trait amongst Species.

"I won't just sleep with you." He wanted to warn her. "I can't. We should wait until tomorrow night if you just want to be held."

"What does that mean?"

"Tonight I'll touch you and do more."

Her pretty eyes widened slightly and more pinkness bloomed in her cheeks. "Come into my room."

It was an invitation and an acceptance of them sharing sex. He couldn't deny the amount of pressure he suddenly found himself under. It would rest on his shoulders to teach her that males touching her could be a good experience. *Male*, he amended. *One. Me.* The concept of someone else putting their hands on her made him furious.

"I trust you, Shadow."

The sincerity in her tone humbled him. He didn't deserve it. She had no idea of the demons he battled. He would do anything for her, including taking things slowly to make sure he didn't hurt her. She wasn't human although she appeared more so than other Species females. Never had he imagined taking a Gift to bed before meeting Beauty.

He took a deep breath and slowly rose to his feet. It just made him feel big and amplified their differences. She peered up at him nervously. He didn't blame her, feeling the same. It had been a long time since he'd had a female. He'd avoided them because he'd been worried he'd fail to please them or his body would react negatively to the sight of them bare. Losing his erection during the sharing of sex would be humiliating but it happened sometimes when he remembered what had been done to him.

"Let's go to my room." He wanted her in his bed.

"Why yours and not mine?"

He hesitated. "It's a male thing."

"The women at the dorm always have men come to their rooms. I thought maybe it was a Species mating ritual."

He couldn't help but laugh. She was so innocent and cute. "The females insist on using their rooms mostly to help them feel in control and males tend to get territorial when they take females into their homes."

"What does that mean?"

"Females don't want to give males the impression that we can keep them."

Her breathing changed a little, increasing in pace as her eyes widened. "Do you want to keep me?"

"Don't be afraid."

"I'm not. I'm asking a question."

"I would never force you to stay where you didn't want to be. I just want you in my bed."

"I'm not them, you know." She swallowed. "I don't want to have different sexual partners. I'm not opposed to dating you." Her gaze dropped to his chest and stayed there, her embarrassment showing again in her cheeks. "That is, if you want to try out being my boyfriend. I'd prefer to have a monogamous relationship."

172

He released her hip to cup her face. It was so delicate in his hand. She met his gaze.

"I mean," she spoke quickly, anxious. "I don't want anybody else and I would hope you wouldn't, you know, sleep around."

"You really don't know much about Species males." He wanted to pick her up and carry her to his bed so much he actually ached to do it.

"Is it wrong to hope you won't have sex with other women and that maybe we could try to have a real relationship?"

He backed up but kept hold of her, urging her to follow. She did and his dick throbbed, filling with blood. He wanted her so much it hurt.

"You are telling me that I can have and keep you." He winced a little at how deep his voice sounded but hormones raged inside him. "Big turn-on," he admitted, softening his tone. "It makes me want to claim you."

Interest sparked in her gaze. "What does that mean?"

He groaned, wanting to show her instead of vocally detailing it for her. "It means you shouldn't say that to me unless you really mean it. I'd keep you in my bed, Beauty. You don't need to worry about me with other females. I already avoid them. You're the only one who tempts me to the point where I'd face anything to touch you."

They stopped by the bed and her lips parted, her surprise clear. "Really?"

She was so small but she could bring him to his knees. Muscle mass and physical strength had nothing on her when she placed her palm on his lower stomach. Her smooth fingertips rubbed and made him want to howl.

173

Pleasure from such a light touch rushed through his system from his brain to his dick.

"I could be really bad at this, since we're being so honest. I've read books and watched porn on the internet." She blushed again but kept eye contact. "Should I, um, take off your boxers? I know guys enjoy oral sex. I've never actually done that but I know the basics."

It would be a miracle if he didn't die before morning. He was going to have to kill himself with restraint. A memory flashed of one of the videos he'd been shown. It had been a camera angle panning down with a human woman on her knees taking a male inside her mouth. The sight had been appealing and made him release his seed but he'd never had it done to him. He shook his head quickly, terrified of shocking her by his raw animalistic reaction or losing control if she attempted that.

"No." His voice came out as a snarl and he winced. "Let me tend to you." It would be all about her. He swore that.

"Are you angry?" She tried to remove her hand but he covered it with his own, holding it against his stomach.

"No. I'm turned-on. Very much so. My voice deepens and I might make scary sounds. Ignore them."

She nodded. "I have heard those sounds through the walls when the women next door had men over. I expected it but I know you're still upset with me."

"I'm not," he swore, already over her catching him masturbating. Now he was focused on getting her into his bed. "You're going to need to trust me. Can you do that?"

174

"I already do."

Yeah, I'm going to die before morning. Beauty was going to kill him. She was so sweet he just wanted to eat her. He smothered a growl at the mental image of her spread out on his bed with his mouth between those pale thighs, licking her pussy. He released her completely to step away.

"Take off your nightgown and lie on your back in the middle of my bed. There's no need to feel shy. You're beautiful."

Beauty hoped she wouldn't faint. She felt lightheaded and her heart raced so fast it felt as if it might explode from her chest. It wasn't fear she felt but close. Shadow was going to touch her and she'd finally get to understand why the women at the dorm invited men into their rooms.

Shadow was sexy and big, two things she appreciated. He was the kind of man she'd had fantasies about since she'd gained her freedom. He was strong, intelligent, and she knew he'd actually tend to her, just as he said. She wanted to know what that entailed. First though, she'd have to find the courage to remove the nightgown. He'd already seen her naked but that had been an accident.

Her hands shook as she gripped the hem of the thin cotton and pulled it up slowly. His gaze riveted on her thighs and the hungry expression on his face encouraged her to just whisk it off. His tongue darting out to wet his lips implied he liked what he saw as he openly stared at her breasts.

She glanced down, wondering what he was thinking. Her boobs weren't perfect, a little on the small side, and they were currently showing that his room was a bit chilly since the window was open to allow in the

175

evening breeze. She hoped he didn't hate the way they looked puckered up tightly.

It took a lot of restraint not to put a hand down to cover her mound. She had a little hair there, unlike other Species women. *Will that matter? Turn him off?* She hoped not. It embarrassed her slightly when he looked lower, fixing on that fact.

"It's just a little," she whispered. "Should I shave it off?"

He shook his head. "No." His voice came out odd, kind of raspy.

"Are you okay?" Concern over his well-being overrode some of her shyness. He had issues too, something she wasn't about to forget.

"Yes," he replied more firmly, in a slightly deeper tone.

She swallowed hard and stepped closer to his bed. The sheets and blankets were tossed at the end where he'd thrown them when he heard her scream. She had to climb up on it—Species' beds were higher than those she'd slept on before moving to Homeland. Species were tall and they tended to take that into consideration when buying or building furniture. Gift Species just had to make do with hip-high mattresses.

A deep growl from behind her made her pause and look back as she crawled to the center of the bed. Shadow had turned, his intense stare locked on her bent ass. She hated the way her cheeks warmed, knowing he could see everything from that position. He didn't look angry though, just really fixated on her body. She glanced at his boxers and it prompted her to roll over onto her back.

He looked huge down there. His cock was hard, thick, and barely contained inside the material that was pulled taut in the front. The waistband actually wasn't touching his stomach in the center anymore because he was so aroused. Shadow was well hung, a saying she'd learned in romance novels she'd begun to read. A little anxiety arose but she figured it would be okay. Sex books had also been on her reading list. They claimed a woman's vagina would stretch to accommodate a penis, even if it didn't seem possible to her way of thinking.

She settled flat and waited for instructions, peering at him to see what he'd do next. He didn't remove his boxers but instead walked to the end of the bed, put a knee on the mattress and it dipped with his weight.

"Spread your thighs apart and bend your knees up."

A shiver ran down her spine at how he growled the words. It was sexy and kind of wicked, in the best way, showing his animal side. Species men were known for being protective of women and she liked that side of him being more prominent than the human one.

"No kissing first?" She thought that was how sex started.

His gaze lifted to hers. "You said you'd trust me."

Beauty tried to relax but it was difficult. "I do. I'm not turned-on yet and..." She wanted to die from embarrassment. "I, um, I'm not ready for you to go inside me. You're big. I read that the wetter I am, the easier it will happen." Shadow had admitted it had been a while for him so maybe he had forgotten. She wanted to work with him so they could help each other. "You can take off your boxers. You won't scare me." She glanced down his body. "They don't really hide your size anyway and I've seen it."

177

"I'm not going to just mount you from the front immediately." He bent forward and his hands flattened next to her knees until he was over her lower legs. "I want you open for my mouth."

Her eyes widened and she fisted the flat sheet under her. "Oh." She knew he meant oral sex. "Um, are you sure you want to do that?"

One of his eyebrow lifted. "Why wouldn't I?"

Beauty glanced at one of his broad shoulders, unable to keep looking him in the eye. "I've never done that before or had it done. I mean, what if I..." She couldn't say it, sealing her lips.

"You won't enjoy it? I'll make sure you do."

She glanced into his dark, piercing gaze. "What if I don't taste good?" There. She'd said it.

His nose flared as he inhaled and another low growl came from him. "You will. You smell incredible. Sweet. I'm Species."

"What does that mean?"

"I want to. I need to taste you. I crave it." He took a heavy, shuddering breath. "Open up for me and stop thinking. Just feel. Trust me, Beauty."

She hesitated, not sure she could expose herself that intimately. She experienced a new level of vulnerability but that moment was about trust. She wanted to know how it would feel to be touched and it wasn't going to happen if she didn't do as he said.

Shadow reached out and his big hands caressed the tops of her thighs. "Just open them for me. It's that easy. Lift them up and spread your knees apart. Please."

178

His voice held an intensity that made her want to do anything he asked. The soft plea was all she needed to relax and let go of her inhibitions. She bent her knees, drawing her feet out from under him, and pulled them up to her chest. She released the sheet to grip her knees as she spread them. Her eyes closed, unable to stare into his anymore to gauge his reaction. Doubt nagged her. She had a tuft of hair on her mound when others didn't and she was smaller in build. It might turn Shadow off.

The snarl made her start and her eyes flew open to stare at his face. He wasn't holding her gaze though, instead he was staring between her legs where she was completely exposed. He licked his lips and lowered his body until he was flat on the bed with his face directly over her lap. He glanced up and she noticed the color of his irises seemed darker, nearly black. It wasn't her imagination.

"Keep them spread open to me. Don't hold back." Two big hands gently settled on the inside of her thighs, pushing her legs farther apart. "I want to hear your sounds. It will help me learn what you like best."

My sounds. She nodded though, unable to trust her voice to speak. She felt as if a lump had formed inside her throat that might choke her.

His head dipped and she squeezed her eyes closed, tense despite trying to loosen her muscles. Hot breath fanned along the seam of her pussy and she jumped when he nuzzled the lips of her sex. It felt as if his chin had brushed against the top of her mound.

"Soft," he whispered. "I like the hair."

That's good that he likes it, right? She hoped so. It sounded as if he didn't mind. She regretted not shaving it off.

179

His thumbs, at least she thought that's what he used, parted her sex lips and she gasped when a hot tongue gently licked across her clit. It came as a shock to feel someone else touch her there but the fact that he used his mouth really had her heart racing. He did it again slowly and applied a little more pressure. He came at her again, doing it over and over.

A soft moan rose and she let it out through parted lips. Her breathing increased. It nearly hurt but in a good way. It was as though he touched her soul so intensely that she couldn't build a mental shield to block out the sensations that flooded her with each flick of the strong muscle manipulating her lower half. It stripped her bare, heart and essence, until nothing was left but each rasp of his tongue.

He growled and vibrations were added against the bundle of nerves that seemed to become her entire being. There was just Shadow and his mouth. She forgot where they were, forgot her discomfort at being so defenseless under him and only focused on the pleasure that grew brighter and hotter. He felt much better than her own fingertip, which had rubbed that area to find release. The comparison seemed unfair. It became too much until she couldn't take any more, her knees trying to slam together. He was going to kill her if it continued.

His strong hands clamped tighter around her inner thighs, holding her open. His lips sealed around her swollen clit and sucked while still rubbing his tongue back and forth rapidly. Beauty thrashed under him, begging with words she couldn't control or understand. She doubted he could either since they were more whimpers than speech. He was going to kill her.

Something inside her broke free, excruciating pleasure tearing through her, making her buck and scream out Shadow's name. He snarled, tearing his mouth away as she panted. Her body slowly relaxed as she came down from the high of a near-brutal climax. Her eyes opened and she watched as he released her thighs.

Shadow crawled up and over her until he hovered inches above her body. His breathing was harsh as their gazes held. She released the bed and reached for him, wanting to touch him just to feel grounded to life again. Warm flesh and firm muscle met her hands as they opened to grip his shoulders.

He broke eye contact to look between their bodies and she followed his focus. He'd shoved down the boxers to mid-thigh and the sight of his cock stunned her. It was as big and thick as she remembered but she was surprised to discover it was a bit red without him having touched it first. She wondered instantly if that hurt.

"Beauty," his voice sounded gruff. "Tell me yes."

She jerked her focus away from his hips. He watched her with a concentration that was almost frightening. She nodded, unable to speak. Some of the tension left his handsome features as he lowered over her. His cock bumped against her pussy and she realized what she'd just agreed to.

He used his arms to brace his weight to avoid crushing her. His hips were between her thighs, making it possible for him to spread his legs to force hers to move a little higher and hold them open. He didn't use his hands to guide the crown of his cock to her body. It was so stiff that he just had to adjust his hips and push against her.

Flashbacks of pain replayed inside her mind but he didn't just ram his man-part inside her roughly. He gently breached her. The slow sensation of her vaginal walls being stretched by the broad girth of his cock didn't cause pain. She was so wet that he was able to enter her without difficulty, though his sheer size made her very aware of him. Her gaze fixed on his face.

Shadow's eyes were closed and he was the one who seemed to be in pain. His lips were parted and his fangs bit down on his generous lower lip. Sweat beaded his brow as every muscle in his face seemed drawn taut, almost into a grimace. Worry for him hit hard and fast, obliterating her apprehension.

"Shadow?"

He stopped moving, his breathing ragged, and his eyes opened.

Her hands petted him, soothed him with caresses. "It's okay."

"I don't want to hurt you," he growled.

"You aren't." She could say that with honesty.

He moved slowly, withdrew almost totally from her body before applying enough weight to push his cock back inside her a little deeper. It was a tight fit but there wasn't any pain. She glanced away from him to look into the space between their bodies. There seemed a lot more of him for her to take.

She shifted her legs and hiked them higher to wrap around his hips. She held his gaze. He'd made her feel really good and she wanted him to find that with her too. They were physically linked. Her belly quivered as he sank into her deeper, a strange but not distasteful feeling. Beauty watched him close his eyes again and his head tipped back as he growled.

He paused, withdrew, pushed back inside, this time a little faster, and she gasped. It was a good sensation. Strange but she liked it. He stopped and stared at her face.

"Release me. I'll go into the bathroom."

Beauty knew what he would do in there. He'd take care of his own needs but she wanted to be the one to do that for him. Her legs clamped tighter around him and she wiggled her hips. Her soft moan surprised them both when the motion seated him a little deeper inside her and touched something that felt really good. She remained locked around him and repeated the motion. It really felt wonderful and she kept going, squirming just to have him touch her there again and again.

"Beauty," he rumbled her name, his voice thick with desire. "I'm losing control. I want you too bad and I'm so close."

His knees spread a little more and then he began to move in and out, fucking her in a deliberate pace that wasn't quite fast but hit that spot every time. She closed her eyes, concentrating on Shadow. His chest rubbed her sensitive nipples and his cock was so hard it could have been made of stone. He entered her a little deeper, his hips bucked faster, and they both had a difficult time breathing.

"I can't hold back," he snarled, suddenly driving into her deeper as his body began to quake over hers, rough jerks as his muscles seemed to spasm.

Her eyes flew open wide when the first burst of hot heat filled her. His dick seemed to be growing larger and thicker as his thrusts slowed, keeping him buried deep inside her. Another hot stream of heat shot into her and he lowered his face suddenly into the cradle of her throat.

She gasped when pleasure suddenly struck, his harsh, jerky movements sending her over the edge again. His cock hit that wonderful spot inside her and seemed to stay there, a throbbing pulse. Her fingernails dug in as she cried out his name.

He managed to keep his weight braced off her for the most part when it ended. They were both panting, sweat trickling between their bodies. Beauty allowed her cheek to rest against his where he kept his face buried at her throat. Her hands slid from his shoulders to hug him tightly, not wanting to let go. She smiled, understanding finally why other Species women invited men into their rooms.

Shadow tried to catch his breath while he worried about Beauty. She clung to him as if she were terrified. He bit back a snarl of self-loathing. He'd totally lost control once his dick was sheathed inside her hot little pussy. It had been a long time since he'd known the powerful pleasure of sharing sex but he couldn't remember a time when it had ever been so passionate. It was because it was Beauty under him.

The sounds she'd made had urged him on and so had her taste, which lingered on this tongue. She'd been so wet, the aroma of her desire a drug that made him higher than anything Mercile had ever given him. The way her body had received him, fisting him with her pussy, had driven him

184

insane. Every stroke of his cock had nearly undone him by making him come fast and hard. After about a dozen or so times of thrusting inside her, he'd snapped.

He'd shed his humanity while taking her. The animal side of him had manifested and wanted to mark her. He had with his semen and almost with his teeth. He breathed in and out through his nose, assured there was no scent of her blood. He hadn't bitten into her the way he'd longed to do.

His dick was locked inside her or he'd move, release her. Her vaginal muscles twitched and he bit back a groan of pleasure as it milked out more of his seed. She was probably attempting to push him out of her but couldn't. The base of his shaft had developed a lump from the swelling, keeping him there for fear of tearing her if he tried to withdraw.

It wasn't easy to adjust his weight, not wanting to move, but he braced on one arm while managing to reach between them to grip his nuts. He found the area on the underside and massaged it to reduce the swelling at a faster pace. It was a trick he'd learned during the worst of the testing at Mercile. It hurt but he clenched his teeth, continued to rub and the pressure eased until he slowly pulled out of the heaven he'd found inside Beauty's body.

He released his balls and reached behind him, tapping her ankle. "Release me."

She shook her head against him, refusing. He flattened both hands and lifted. It stunned him a bit when she came with him. It left him no choice but to sit back on his legs with her on his lap. Her limbs were locked tight

185

around his hips and shoulders and she gave no indication of letting go any time soon. Her strength astonished him for someone so small.

He hugged her back, slowly rocking her in his arms to soothe her. It just proved his point that he never should have been the male to live with her. No one had heeded his warnings and now he needed to find a way to let Beauty know she was safe. He'd never attempt to share sex with her again.

"I'm sorry," he whispered, brushing his lips against her throat. "I didn't mean to hurt you."

Her arms loosened their hold and she pulled back to look at him. Deep gratitude surfaced that there were no tears. He wasn't sure he could have withstood seeing them, knowing he'd been the cause of her pain.

"You didn't."

"You're being so brave." He wished he could kick his own ass.

"That was wonderful." She smiled.

It was his turn to hug her tightly as the meaning of her words sank in. "You didn't yell my name from pain?" He wanted to make certain.

"No." Pink rose in her cheeks before she dropped her gaze to his lips. "I, um, you know." She glanced up and smiled. "Twice."

Shadow tucked his head again, pulling her close. He was out of practice enough to mistake her body's reactions but he was just grateful he hadn't totally fucked up everything. Her muscles hadn't been constricting trying to get him out of pussy but because she'd climaxed.

186

Thankfully. He began to rock her in his arms once more, ignoring his still-hard dick trapped between his thighs. He wanted her again but he wasn't going to press his luck for a second time in one night.

"Shadow?"

"Yeah, Beauty?"

"May I sleep with you?" She yawned. "I'd like to."

He smiled. "I'd like that. You have to let me go though. I'll turn off the light and then we'll cuddle if you want."

Her arms and legs slackened around him until he gently laid her down again. She peered up at him with trust. He flipped off the light but in seconds he was back, crawling into the bed. She rolled to face him as he pulled her against him. He curled around her to cocoon her inside the safety of his arms.

Her breathing changed so fast it stunned him that she could fall asleep so easily after what they'd shared. She'd been through a lot. He wasn't so quick to join her in slumber.

All the things she'd said circled in his thoughts. She didn't want other males but was interested in a relationship. The mere idea of someone else touching her enraged him. He'd break their fingers if they tried to put their hands on her. He'd tear them apart and rip out their hearts if they dared to lure her from him. He'd kill anyone who tried to mount his Beauty.

Shit. Breathing in her scent cooled the intense rage. *I already think of her as mine.*

Chapter Eleven

Beauty didn't want to move but knew she'd have to soon. Shadow's warm body made her feel safe and protected. She'd turned in the night or he'd repositioned her until he spooned her back. The feel of his hard cock pressed against her butt where it was trapped between her and his stomach wasn't something she could ignore. The urge to use the bathroom finally forced her to wiggle away.

The arm around her waist hauled her back and a deep, masculine growl filled the room. It startled her enough that she turned. His eyes were only partially open as he peeked at her and his lips parted, fangs flashing.

"Don't leave me."

"I'll be right back." She cleared her throat. "Bathroom."

His hold eased. "Okay."

She slid out of bed and tried not to be embarrassed that he saw so much of her in the early morning light spilling through the still-open window of his bedroom. It wasn't logical to be shy about her nakedness after the things he'd done to her. That didn't completely alleviate the bashfulness though.

He sat with the sheet covering his lap when she returned. One leg was bent upward on the side of the bed. She was glad she'd taken the time to wrap a towel around her middle before returning to the room, not comfortable being naked. Shadow looked less fierce just waking from sleep with his expression more open and readable. He smiled tentatively.

"How are you feeling?"

"Good." She wasn't sure if she should get back into bed with him or not.

The smile faded. "What is wrong? Do you regret coming into my room?"

Her teeth sank into her bottom lip as she shook her head. "I don't know what to do." Honesty was best. "None of the men spend the night with the women so I have never overheard the morning-after etiquette. Is there such a thing?"

"What do you want to do?"

She dodged his question. "What do you want to do?"

His leg slid flat on the bed and she gaped a little at the sight of the sheet over his lap. His erection jutted upward instead of lying flat. "Don't ask a male that. This is the answer." He reached up to grip the headboard above him, looking relaxed except for his hard-on. "Will you come back to my bed?"

"I want to," she admitted, happy he wasn't shutting her out.

His hands tightened their hold on the wood enough that his knuckles turned white.

"What is wrong?"

He glanced at his hands before looking at her again. "I'm trying to appear docile, not to frighten you."

She laughed before she could prevent it and tugged at the towel to loosen it.

"What's funny?"

"You're so big and strong. You couldn't pull that off. You just look extremely sexy." Her cheeks warmed. "Should I not tell you that?"

He grinned. "What makes me appealing?"

"The way your arms are up and you're stretched out a little across the pillows. It reminds me of something I read in a romance novel but the leading man wore handcuffs."

"I wouldn't wear those but I'll keep my hands here if it makes me less threatening to you."

The towel hit the floor as she stepped closer to the bed. Shadow's gaze fixed on her breasts. All humor faded from his features, the tense look returning. She could identify that expression now. He wanted her and it filled her with a sense of courage as she climbed on the high mattress near his feet.

"Why wouldn't you wear handcuffs?"

He looked away, not speaking. She froze.

"Did I say something wrong?"

He glanced back. "It would remind me of bad times."

"I'm sorry. I was just curious."

"Come to me," he rasped. "I won't hurt you."

"I know. I'm not afraid of you." She crawled up the bed and surprised them both by straddling his lap. Her ass eased down over his sheet-covered thighs. Both her hands flattened on his chest. "I want to hug you. May I?"

"You can do anything you'd like to me," he stated gruffly, swallowing hard.

"Anything?" The idea did funny things to her stomach, making it flutter.

"Yes."

One deep breath and she inched closer to him. "I want to kiss you."

Surprise registered but he nodded. "Okay."

She studied his mouth. It was full and lush—tempting. "Maybe you should kiss me."

"I haven't done this before. Not mouth to mouth."

"Me neither." She smiled. "We'll learn together."

"Together," he repeated, wetting his lips, focusing on hers. "Open to me."

She closed her eyes, parted her lips and tilted her head slightly. The first brush of contact was almost ticklish. He pressed his lips firmly to hers. They were mouth to mouth. The texture of his lips was unbelievably soft. His tongue licked hers and she melted into him. It took a few seconds but she repeated what he did, tasting him and wanting more. It was amazing, that intimacy, and he growled, deepening the kiss.

Her senses focused entirely on Shadow and everything else faded away. Pleasure and excitement seeped into her slowly, radiating from the point of contact, spreading lower. She moaned and Shadow slowly broke the kiss.

They were both a little out of breath. Beauty liked kissing. Judging by Shadow's heated stare, he did as well. She couldn't wait to do it again.

She leaned forward until her body rested against his and slid her hands up to his shoulders. She pressed her ear over his heart, relaxing. "Will you hold me?"

He hugged her around her waist, pulling her more firmly against him. He shifted his hips, sliding her body closer until his cock was trapped between their bellies with only a sheet as a barrier. She inhaled his masculine scent and a funny noise escaped her—it almost resembled a whine.

His arms loosened immediately and his heart rate jumped. "Don't be afraid."

She turned her head, peering up at him. "I'm not. I don't know why that happened."

"You're primate. What were you feeling when you made that sound?"

She evaluated the moment. "Happy. Safe. Sexually aware of you."

His hold tightened slightly to draw her closer. "I growl or snarl when my emotions are strong. Sometimes my instincts are so close to the surface that they refuse to be ignored. That wasn't a human noise." He watched her intently. "It's okay. You were probably having one of those moments."

She relaxed. "I hissed at Kit but she did it first. I hadn't ever done that before."

"Never?"

"Not that I can remember." Beauty allowed her mind to roam as she relaxed, pressing her ear against Shadow's chest. His heart rate had slowed to normal. "I know when I was young that I made funny noises and got into trouble for it."

His body stiffened. "They abused you for being what you are?"

She knew he was angry without looking up at his face. Her fingertips traced his skin, attempting to calm him. "I learned to be quiet." She refused to share the memories of her childhood. Not many were good. "To always think before I did something."

"You can just *be* now." Shadow rested his chin on the top of her head. "You can do or say anything."

She smiled. "Anything?"

"Yes." There was no hesitation, his voice firm.

She let her hands roam from his shoulders down his chest until they rested over his ribs. "Are you sure?"

"Yes."

Her fingers suddenly dug into his skin firmly and wiggled. She didn't know if Shadow was ticklish but she was about to find out. He gasped before his back arched. He twisted his torso and they were suddenly moving. The rapid motion startled her when he rolled over. It happened so fast she wasn't sure how she ended up flat on her back with her wrists jerked above her head and held firmly by his hands. He came down on her, pinning her with his weight.

Amusement sparkled in his eyes. "You want to play?"

"You are ticklish!" She laughed.

"Very." He glanced down. "Are you?"

"I don't know."

"Don't move." He let go of her wrists and shifted his body until he braced his weight on one elbow. His hand slowly opened while she watched him place it on her stomach.

Her heart pounded as she wondered what he'd do. The raspy texture of his calloused fingertips was pleasant when he slid that hand higher over her rib cage to pause under her breast. He glanced up.

"Does that tickle?"

"No."

He slid it higher and cupped her breast, one thumb lightly rubbing back and forth over the nipple. It instantly responded by puckering. A tingle began there that spread lower to her sex.

"How about that?"

She didn't trust her voice as she licked her lips and shook her head. "It makes it feel heavy."

"My hand?"

"No. My chest."

The sheet was tangled between their lower bodies after Shadow had changed their positions. She kicked free of it with one leg and hooked her heel around the back of his thigh, then higher. She couldn't see his back but she could feel bare skin. The sheet didn't cover his beefy ass. It was right there for her foot to explore.

A deep grumble rumbled from Shadow as she stared into his eyes. "That feels good."

Beauty no longer wanted to tickle him. "Keep touching me."

Passion was an emotion she was quickly learning to identify on his face as his nostrils flared and his eyes narrowed slightly. Shadow's mouth closed and the hand on her boob began to massage, his thumb drawing circles around her taut nipple. He was so sexy with his hair messy despite its short length. If he allowed it to grow out he'd be devastatingly wild in appearance. It made her want him more. An ache began between her legs, making her very sexually aware of him.

"I like that. Do more."

He removed his hand, disappointing her. It only lasted a heartbeat because his head dipped to replace his thumb with the tip of his tongue. Beauty closed her eyes and arched her back to give him better access.

His mouth was really warm when it closed over her nipple but nothing prepared her for when he sucked, using his tongue to tease the tip. She forgot his order to stay still by grabbing his head, her fingers sliding into his hair, clutching him to keep him in place.

"Yes," she whispered.

He growled in response.

Shadow tore away the remaining sheet between them. His big, muscular body settled down on her more firmly and there was no missing his stiff cock pressing against the inside of her thigh. She wished he were higher on her body so she could have him inside her while he played with her, suspecting it would feel incredible. She didn't need experience to guess that would be true.

He released one breast to give the other his attention. She had to refrain from clawing his scalp to force him to keep doing that to her. Sensations overtook everything as pleasure and need filled her. She freed her other leg and hiked it around his ass, hugging him tightly.

He sucked on her breast in strong tugs and growled again, his chest against her belly. The ache radiating between her thighs became painful and her clit throbbed, wanting attention.

"Shadow," she pleaded.

His mouth released her as he lifted his head and peered down at her. "What do you need? Tell me. It's yours."

The way he spoke did funny things to her belly again. His voice was so deep, so raw and animalistic, that it called to something inside her. She let go of his head to grip his face. "You."

He sniffed at her once and groaned, lifting his upper body away.

"No!" She clung to him, refusing to release him. "Don't stop."

He froze, his arms straight but his hips still snug against her. "Do you trust me?"

"Yes."

"I want you to get on your hands and knees in front of me."

He wanted to take her from behind. She quickly pushed back a flash of fear, but he must have noticed.

"I'm not him." His intuition was right on. "I want to make you feel really good. I can touch you everywhere if you're bent over in front of me."

"I trust you." She did. "I can do this." Her legs loosened their hold and she dropped her hands away from his face.

He backed away on his hands and knees but then stopped. "Right here. Just roll over and back up to me."

Beauty didn't hesitate. Her body wanted him, *she* wanted him. This was Shadow, not ever to be mistaken for Master. There was no comparison and it seemed an insult to allow them to even share space inside her mind. She turned over and pushed onto her hands and knees, her ass up.

One look back and she paused to admire Shadow's body. He was so powerful. He could force her to do anything he wanted physically but he held still, the only movement the rise and fall of his chest and his rigid sex growing more firm and thick, proof that he wanted her too. It twitched and she looked away to stare at the headboard as she slowly crawled backward to get closer to him.

His hands gently gripped her hips. "Easy, love," he urged softly. "Nice and slow. I won't hurt you."

"I know."

"Is this too difficult for you?" He stopped her by tightening his hold. "Does it remind you too much of him?" His tone deepened to a snarl.

"No." She twisted her head enough to look at him again. "I just want you." His words sank in and surprise filled her. "You called me love."

The tension eased from his features. He said nothing though to explain why he'd said that, instead just slid one of his hands from her hip to curve under her belly, then lower until his fingertips teased the seam of her pussy. He growled softly as he located her clit, rubbing back and forth until a low moan burst from her parted lips. Her eyes closed as she faced forward, lowered her head and clawed the sheets.

He didn't enter her immediately. One of his knees brushed the inside of her thigh and nudged. She spread them farther apart to give him access. He released her hip and came down over her until his body lightly rested against her curved back. The bed dipped, telling her that he braced his weight with one hand. He shifted until his legs were on the outside of hers and slid up until his cock hung heavy against her inner thigh.

"You are so beautiful," he rasped. "So responsive."

It was almost impossible for Beauty to think while he massaged the bundle of nerves with one talented fingertip. His finger slid lower, finding out how wet and ready she was to receive him, but he still didn't enter her. He traced upward again to continue tormenting her clit. He applied a little more pressure, a little faster, and Beauty rocked her hips. The need to come grew from a steady ache to a gnawing necessity.

"Shadow," she moaned.

Suddenly the crown of his cock pressed against her pussy. She moaned louder, urging him on. He didn't stop playing with her clit as he slowly entered her. She knew her muscles were tense but there was nothing she could do about that since she was right on the edge.

He pressed closer to her back after he was seated inside her a few inches. Shadow braced his hand on the bed in front of her shoulder, pinning her inside the cage of his body. His mouth was hot and wet as he placed kisses along her bare shoulder.

She loved how hard his cock was, how big it felt stretching her vaginal walls as he sank into her a little deeper while still strumming her clit. He moved slowly, breaching her more, and she knew she wasn't going to last. Her body quivered from the strong, intense pleasure and the last push to climax was when he withdrew almost totally from her pussy to drive back in with one powerful thrust. It was all it took.

"Shadow!" She cried out his name as ecstasy tore through her. Her muscles clamped down strongly on his shaft and Beauty threw her head back against his chest. Her body quaked from her forceful release.

He snarled and his hand left her oversensitive, swollen clit to wrap around her waist. He moved then, fucking her frantically, drawing out the climax until she couldn't breathe, couldn't do anything but feel.

His cock felt harder, thicker, and he made sounds that normally would have scared her if it wasn't so sexy. She wondered if it were possible to die from too much pleasure. The climax continued to roll through her, seemingly endless.

A loud howl startled her and she thought for an instant that it was Shadow finding his own release but instead of slowing to pour his semen into her, he suddenly jerked out of her body. It was a shock to be bereft of him but then she was knocked over, his body totally ripped away from hers.

She hit the mattress with enough force to nearly slide off the edge of the bed and was horrified to witness Shadow's body slamming into the wall across the room. The sound of plaster cracking barely registered as he dropped to the floor. Terror gripped Beauty instantly as another figure blocked her view of Shadow. It was the man from the night she'd been chased by the wolves and he snarled, bent, and came up with both his hands firmly wrapped around Shadow's throat.

Her mouth opened to scream but nothing came out. The man threw Shadow and he hit the window, breaking the wood frame, and then he was gone. Horrified, she realized Shadow had just been thrown through the open second-story window.

The man turned, his features twisted with rage, and Beauty whimpered. She hadn't seen him well in the darkness, but she identified Torrent by smell as she panted, terrified. His black hair fell midway down his chest where it had spilled forward over his shoulders. Cold, terrifying blue eyes were fixed on her.

She was naked, vulnerable, but managed to glance away from the dangerous Species to the window. Pieces of the broken frame hung from the top but there was no sign of Shadow and no sound to tell her if he lived. Fright over Shadow's fate suddenly overrode the concern for her own safety.

Is Shadow dead? Did the man kill him? The concept hurt so bad that physical pain stabbed through her chest. Pure rage came next. She snarled deep within her throat and surprised them both. She didn't think before she acted. She had to get to Shadow, had to know if he lived.

Beauty moved before she realized what she'd done and launched herself at the Species. The fact that she was naked didn't factor into it when she hit Torrent's chest. Her hands clawed as she grabbed his throat and her knees slammed into his stomach. Her fangs sank into his shoulder, tearing through fabric and into flesh. The taste of blood filled her mouth as she bit him viciously. He stumbled, howled in pain and then they were both falling.

Beauty released him and jumped, using his body as a springboard to find purchase. She hit the floor next to where he landed, rolled, stumbled to her feet and dashed out of the room. Her palms hurt, her hip too from the impact with the floor, but she ignored them as she rushed downstairs. Panic was an emotion she knew well and she allowed it to jolt full force through her as she fled their attacker. The front door was wide open and she'd almost reached it when Shadow's big form suddenly filled the space.

Beauty couldn't slow in time and twisted, trying to avoid him, but he was too big. Her side slammed into his body hard enough to knock the breath from her lungs. He grunted but his strong arms wrapped around her, lifting her right off her feet, and he staggered backward a few feet on the porch before regaining his balance.

It was tough to suck air into her lungs but she did it, turning her head to stare up at him. He had a cut on his forehead that bled enough to run down the side of his face, small scratches were on his throat, but he didn't look at her. He stared at something inside the cabin and snarled.

She twisted to watch Torrent stomp down the stairs. Blood stained his shirt from where she'd bitten him, the material torn, clearly revealing the wound. His hands were fisted and he snarled, looking furious. He wasn't looking at her though. He was fixated on Shadow instead.

Shadow spun around, lowered her, and let go once she stood on trembling legs. He snarled, facing the other man, keeping her behind him.

He swayed a little on his feet. The other Species suddenly crouched, growling, preparing to attack.

They went at each other before she could grab Shadow's arm to help steady him. Torrent sprang as Shadow entered the cabin. Beauty gasped as she watched them tangle and hit the floor, snarling and growling. Punches were exchanged and she was sickened by the sound of flesh hitting flesh.

"Stop!" Beauty screamed but they ignored her. She rushed inside the living room as they slammed into the coffee table, sending it crashing onto its side. Their big bodies rolled right over the busted piece of furniture that it had been made of logs. The smell of blood penetrated her senses and she frantically looked for a weapon. Shadow was hurt yet still attempted to protect her against the aggressive man whom she assumed had come to snatch her. She just wanted to protect Shadow instead.

The fireplace caught her attention and she scrambled quickly to it and grabbed one of the metal rods sticking up from a small box sitting next to it. It was a good weapon, firm in her hand. She spun in time to see Torrent end up on top of Shadow, pummeling his chest with meaty fists. She rushed forward and swung as hard as she could, nailing the man attacking her Shadow. She tagged him in the back of the head with enough force to hurt her hands.

Torrent snarled as he fell sideways, grabbing his head. He landed hard on his back, cursing loudly but didn't try to get up. Beauty's attention switched to Shadow. She was alarmed to see his eyes were closed. A lot of blood was smeared on his face from the wound on his forehead but now there was more of it around his nose and mouth.

She was terrified and enraged at the same time. She just dropped to her knees. The metal weapon clanked as it hit something when she tossed it aside but she didn't care as she frantically crawled closer to Shadow. Her hands ran over his chest first, feeling it rise and fall. Relieved, she realized he was alive.

Movement from the corner of her eye made her aware that Torrent had begun to recover. She turned, all her rage directed at him, and snarled. She leaned over Shadow's upper body, protecting him as well as her smaller frame could.

"Back off! I'll kill you."

His eyes widened as he sat up, staring back at her after she threatened him.

She hissed at him, flashing her fangs. "Don't touch him again."

He used his heels against the floor to scoot away, putting space between them. One of his hands held the back of his head but his other one opened in front of him. "Easy, female."

Beauty knew she was about to hyperventilate. She couldn't seem to slow her breathing. Too many emotions were crashing in on her. Rage. Worry. Fear. Most of all, she wanted to kill the bastard for hurting her Shadow. Her hand on his chest assured her he breathed but she didn't dare look away from the threat to glance down at him.

Her entire body quivered almost violently and she knew she didn't stand much of a chance at fighting Torrent but she'd die trying to protect Shadow. He was unconscious and hurt. She snarled again, hoping to appear fierce. Torrent's eyes would be her first target if he came at her. She'd claw them, try to blind him, the only plan she could come up with.

"Easy," Torrent repeated. He'd stopped moving away, was just sitting there. "Calm down."

"Fuck you! Get out." She managed to lift her hand and point to the open door. "GO!"

He released the back of his head, both his hands opening in front of him to show his palms. It was only a little satisfying to see blood coating one. She'd managed to hurt him.

"I'm not going to hurt you. I was trying to protect you." He glanced at Shadow. "From him."

Another hot flash of rage rolled through Beauty. "Get out. Go!" She snarled at him again as she hunched down over Shadow's upper chest, blocking his face from the aggressive Species. "I will kill you. I'm not weak." She hoped he would believe the threat because she wasn't really sure her shaky limbs would support her weight much longer, let alone enough to fight him in a physical battle.

Torrent paled and his mouth opened but then closed in a tight line. "Okay." He scooted on his ass when his hands flattened on the floor, then he rolled to a standing position.

She glanced away quickly, located the metal rod a few feet away, needing to know where the weapon had gone. The man didn't spin around though to launch a surprise attack. He stalked through the open door and left the cabin.

Hot tears filled her eyes but she forced her body to move. She ran and grabbed the open door. Torrent had retreated off the porch and walked quickly toward a Jeep parked a little way from the cabin. She slammed the door and her hands shook badly as she locked it. Her knees threatened to give way as she put her back against it, staring at Shadow. He was still out cold and bleeding.

There were weapons in Shadow's room. She'd seen them. Somehow she found the strength to push away from the door and rush up the stairs. It didn't matter that she'd never touched a gun before. She'd figure it out and use it if the man returned to try to take her.

Chapter Twelve

Beauty bit her lip and tried the cell phone again. Her hands shook so much she'd touched the wrong preprogrammed contact number a few times. The gun felt cold and foreign resting on top of her bent thigh. Shadow's head was cushioned on her other one as she sat on the floor of the living room. She faced the door, prepared to shoot anyone who came through it.

The right numbers showed and she put the phone to her ear after pushing the send button. It rang three times before a familiar voice answered. "Hey, Beauty. What's up?"

"Help us," Beauty got out, trying to hold back the sobs.

Breeze was silent for seconds. "Beauty? What did you say? What's wrong?"

"Help us." Her voice came out firmer and she sniffed. "Shadow is hurt. He won't wake. His head is bleeding." Emotion choked her. "I have a gun." She stared at it. "A man attacked. Torrent."

"What the fuck?" Breeze snarled. "Where are you?"

"The cabin." Beauty began to cry, unable to stop. "He attacked. I bit and hit him. He is outside but he didn't leave. He's still out there."

"Calm down," Breeze ordered. "I'm on my way to Control. I'll send help to you."

"You come." Beauty forced her raw emotions back, trying to do as Breeze ordered.

"What happened? I'm running but I can still talk to you."

Beauty took a few deep breaths to push back the tears that threatened to overcome her. "Shadow and I were in bed when Torrent attacked. He threw Shadow out the window from the second floor and hurt him. He won't wake." She stared at his face, her free hand caressing his cheek. "I don't know what to do."

"You!" Breeze yelled at someone. "Give me your radio." Her breathing slowed slightly. "Hang on, Beauty. Stay on the phone with me."

Beauty nodded but she realized her friend couldn't see that. She could hear what was going on over the cell phone.

"Patch me through to Reservation," Breeze ordered. "This is an emergency."

"I have a gun." Beauty wasn't sure if she'd mentioned that fact already or not, disorientated from her fear.

"Shit. Don't touch it," Breeze ordered. "You have never been exposed to one."

That was true enough. She'd seen them on television and some of the officers sported them but it was her first time interacting with a real one. Beauty looked up at the door, sure she'd heard something on the porch. "I think he's coming back."

"Who?"

"Torrent."

Beauty removed her hand from Shadow to carefully grip the heavy gun. Shakily, she lifted it with both hands, pointed it at the front of the cabin, and aimed for the wall by the door. Her ears strained, sure she heard wood creak. She squeezed the trigger.

The sharp noise hurt her ears and was terrifying when the gun jerked painfully in her hold but she hoped the hole that appeared in the wall would scare off the man outside. The ringing in her ears prevented her from knowing if he ran off or not but her hearing recovered quickly. All she could detect as she strained to listen again was her own panting and Shadow's slower, steady breathing.

"Beauty!" Breeze yelled over the phone.

She put it up to her ear again. "I think I might have scared Torrent off."

"Shit! Hang on." Breeze's voice became harsher. "This is Breeze from Homeland. Send a team out to the cabin where the Gift Female was sent. Right now! Torrent attacked them. The male protecting her is down and Beauty needs help." She paused. "No, this isn't a joke or a test. Send the females in first. Understand? She's got a weapon."

Beauty lowered the gun to place it on the floor within easy reach. It was heavy and her wrist ached after firing it. It had been so loud but Shadow hadn't even stirred, which only proved how injured he must be.

She ran her hand over his cheek, wiping at the blood. The smell of it filled her senses. Breeze began talking but not to her.

"That's right. Torrent attacked. Don't ask me why. How would I know? I'm not there. Get my females to that cabin right now to protect Beauty and send medical support with them!" Breeze snarled and her voice grew louder. "Help is coming, Beauty. Do you hear me? They should be with you very soon."

"I want you."

"I'm too far away to quickly reach you. It takes time to call the pilots and get the helicopter prepared but I will come as soon as I can. Our females are on their way to you. Don't shoot them. Just put the gun down before you hurt someone. What happened?"

More tears slipped down her cheeks as she blinked them away to stroke Shadow, not caring that his blood stained his hair when she slipped her fingers into it. She could feel a big bump and it worried her.

"We were in bed and Torrent came from nowhere. He just threw Shadow out the window." She sniffed. "I attacked him." It still stunned her that she'd done that.

"Shadow?"

"Torrent." Her voice broke. "I attacked Torrent. I thought he'd killed Shadow."

"I don't know," Breeze told someone, her voice fainter. "You heard what I said. I need a flight to Reservation right now. Run to Control to tell them what is going on. Have them call Reservation to make sure my orders are being followed." She hissed a curse. "Beauty, is Shadow breathing?"

"Yes."

"You dragged him inside from where he fell?"

"No. I ran down the stairs to reach him but he was coming in the door."

"So Shadow is okay?"

209

"No. He was hurt and then they fought. Shadow could barely stand upright but they were hitting each other and rolling on the floor. I attacked Torrent from behind and struck him in the head. Tell me what to do." Panic flared again. "I locked the door. Then I got the phone and gun from upstairs." She took a ragged breath. "Shadow won't wake but he is breathing."

"I should have gone with you." Beauty could tell Breeze was running again, her heavy panting proof of that. "Our females are coming to you and they'll bring a medic. He or she will help Shadow. I'm going to tear Torrent apart. Did he say why he attacked?"

Memory surfaced. "He said he was protecting me from Shadow."

"What where you two doing when this happened?"

"Having sex."

"Son of a bitch!"

Beauty agreed with that sentiment. More hot tears filled her eyes. It had been wonderful but then everything had become a nightmare. Shadow suddenly stirred and hope soared that he'd be fine. His eyes opened as she leaned over him. The blue of his eyes was a welcome sight but the confusion in them wasn't.

"Beauty?"

"I'm here."

Rage twisted his features and he snarled, sitting up so fast he almost smacked his head into hers. She barely avoided the collision by jerking back. A loud groan came from him and he reached up to his forehead while he swayed a bit.

210

"Easy. We're safe." She gripped his shoulders, trying to steady him, dropping the phone in the process. "Help is coming."

The room spun as Shadow sought the threat. His vision was messed up. His head was too, by the feel of the wetness his fingertips found when he touched the sorest spot and located a painful bump. Knowledge of what had happened crashed through his mind, along with the throbbing pain. Fury gripped him. He'd been so focused on Beauty that he hadn't heard the male sneak up behind him until he'd been attacked.

He turned his head and saw blood on Beauty's delicate mouth. It hadn't been his imagination. When he'd landed hard outside and managed to stagger to his feet to reach Beauty, she'd been naked and rushing toward the open door as he entered, but he'd seen red on her face before she'd slammed into his body. He'd barely kept them both upright. Then Torrent had come after her.

He snarled, forced his gaze away to hunt for the male. "Where is he?"

"He's outside. I locked the door." Her hands stroked his arms then his chest. "Help is coming. Did you hear me?"

The immediate threat wasn't present. He focused on her, twisting on his ass to reach for Beauty. They were both naked but that fact barely registered. He was too worried that she was hurt. He gripped her jaw, searching for the injury, but only saw blood on her lips and chin.

"Open."

"What?"

"Open your mouth. You're bleeding."

211

"It's not my blood."

That stumped him. "Whose is it?"

"I bit him."

She bit Torrent. He snarled. He'd kill the male. "Did he hurt you?" He sniffed loudly but his senses were confused. All he could detect was blood.

She shook her head. "He was too intent on fighting with you." Tears filled her eyes. "I attacked him."

Shadow glanced down her bare body but didn't see any other injuries. He must not only be suffering from slightly impaired vision but he was hearing things too. "What did you say?"

Her chin rose. "I attacked him twice. Upstairs after he threw you out the window and again when he was hitting you."

She glanced away and he followed her gaze. A fire poker lay on the floor a few feet away, the end of it bent slightly. Shocked, he jerked his attention back to her. "You hit him with that?"

She nodded, her hands still roaming his arm and chest. "In the back of the head. Are you okay?" Her voice trembled. "You wouldn't wake."

He probably had a concussion. He wasn't sure if he'd passed out when he'd landed but he knew he'd struck his head on the way out the window or perhaps on the edge of the roof when he'd rolled off it to crash into the hard-packed dirt. Torrent's fists slamming into his face hadn't helped either but he'd been too dizzy to be effective against the male's attack when they'd fought.

Shadow had to allow Beauty's words to really sink in. The image of her fighting with a male was beyond his comprehension. He just couldn't picture it. She was too small to get into a violent confrontation. Gift Females fled from violence instead of initiating it. A horrible thought struck.

"Did he attempt to mount you? Touch you?" His voice deepened into a snarl. He would snap the male's neck if he had.

"No."

"I'm so sorry."

He was grateful she hadn't been sexually touched by the male but he also felt other emotions. Guilt and shame mixed strongly, leaving a taste in his mouth as bitter as the blood from the cut inside his cheek. He'd failed to protect Beauty. He'd gotten distracted by her sexy body and how good she felt while he'd mounted her. His guard had been down enough to allow another male to sneak inside his room. He had not sensed the danger until rough hands had gripped him and he'd been sailing through the air. Then falling.

"For what?" One of her hands left his chest to caress his cheek.

He couldn't look at her anymore so he turned his head away. "It shouldn't have happened."

"The sex?"

The pain in her voice was clear enough to stun him and snap his attention back to her. She definitely appeared emotionally distressed over believing he rejected what they'd shared. "No. I failed you."

"You were amazing."

His eyebrows shot up. "I allowed a male to attack us, to attack you. You were in danger but I couldn't protect you. You had to defend yourself."

"Oh. I thought you were talking about what we did in your bed." She continued to stroke his cheek. "We were both distracted. He is to blame."

The sound of engines penetrated the cabin walls. "Go put on clothes." He openly stared at her breasts. "Now. Help has arrived—more males will come."

"I don't want to leave you."

He growled and jerked away from her touch. Pain lanced through his head at the sharp motion. "Do it." He didn't want anyone to see her bare. She was too tempting and appealing. "I am fine."

He wasn't though and knew it. He'd already be outside hunting Torrent to kill him for endangering Beauty if his legs would carry his weight. Spots danced in front of his eyes and he felt weakened with the agony inside his head. He'd suffered concussions before and knew the signs. Nausea roiled but he refused to get sick in front of Beauty. He wouldn't be able to stand more shame added to the growing list he felt.

Regret and indecision passed over her face but she reluctantly followed his orders by rising to her feet. He watched her go, unable to look away from her perky little ass as she took the stairs two at a time in her haste to return to him. He knew that's why she hurried. Her faith in his ability to provide safety was as damaged as his head.

He looked down his body when she was out of sight and groaned. He had no clothing to cover his nakedness and no strength to stand on his own.

There was no way he'd ask Beauty for more assistance. He'd never forgive himself for allowing the attack to happen.

The voices outside were faint but his keen hearing picked up the words.

"Torrent," a female hissed. "What have you done? Sit or I'll have one of the council members beat you."

"I...uh. Hell. I'm sitting, Creek. Jaded, don't you and Bestial look at me like that. This isn't what it looks like."

"What is going on?" The male sounded furious as he snarled. "You attacked a Gift Female? What the hell were you thinking?"

"I came to teach them how to swim." Torrent paused. "I heard noises and let myself inside the cabin to find out what was going on. Shadow was mounting a Gift Female. What was I supposed to assume? I thought I was saving her but I'm having my doubts now, Jaded."

"They are here to bond." The female sounded less irritated. "Didn't someone tell you that? She's curious about the male. They were sent here to see if she wanted to share sex with him."

"Shit," Torrent groaned. "Nobody told me that. I just saw him on top of her and thought she was being forced."

"She showed an interest in that male and resents being protected from his attention," Bestial announced. "Breeze had the Gift sent here so they could spend some alone time to give them the opportunity to see if they'd like to share sex."

"Everyone was told," Creek protested. "We had a meeting about this when we learned they were visiting."

215

"I wasn't here," Torrent protested. "I had that wolf cub to collect with my team and had to pick up a lion cub. I've been gone a lot."

"Shit," Jaded groaned. "Let Creek handle this. Take the medic inside with you. We'll wait out here."

Shadow struggled to his feet when they stopped talking and staggered a little when the room spun. He stopped, took a few deep breaths and made it to the window by the door. He fisted the curtain, tore it from the rod and wrapped it around his waist.

Someone stepped onto the porch just as he reached the door and unlocked it. He swung it open and had to lean heavily against the frame to stay upright. Torrent hadn't attacked to take Beauty away. That dulled some of his rage but he was still furious over what had taken place.

The tall female wore jeans and a T-shirt instead of NSO Security gear. Her long brown hair was pulled back into a ponytail and her dark gaze swept over him from head to foot. "You poor thing."

Shadow winced. He must look hellish and pathetic to get that response from a female. The human male carrying a medical kit hesitated behind her. Shadow glanced away to take in the scene outside. Four Jeeps were parked in front of the cabin and two council members had arrived with the female and medic. Torrent sat on the grass in front of them. The male's cold blue eyes turned his way and held his attention.

"I'm sorry," Torrent stated. "I thought...well, she's Gift. Nobody told me you were allowed to touch her. You were really upset when I saw you last and I thought you might have snapped."

"What are you talking about? What happened?" Creek put her hands on her hips, glancing between them. "What else has happened here?"

The human cleared his throat. "May I approach him? Is he a Wild Zone resident? Do you need to calm him down before he's treated?" He stepped from behind the female. "I'm here to tend your injuries. You're bleeding. I'm not the enemy or here to hurt you."

"I'm not a resident or feral," Shadow growled but then softened his tone. "Just angry but you may approach. I've worked with humans for a while now." He shot a glare at Torrent. "You could have asked what was going on before you threw me out a window."

The female stepped closer, effectively blocking his view of the male who'd attacked him. She reached toward him and he instantly recoiled, jerking away, and nearly fell on his ass when he slid away from the doorframe. She gasped, backing away. The medic tried to step around her but she gripped his arm.

"What is wrong with you?" She flashed fang, looking wary. "Don't attack."

"You can't touch me." He righted his body by gripping the frame again and waited for the world to stop spinning as his vision adjusted.

"You need to be treated." She inched closer and tried to touch him again.

He growled. "Not you. I don't think Beauty would want another female to put her hands on me."

Her eyes widened in surprise, but then she grinned. "Okay." She stepped aside. "He's all yours, Mike."

217

The medic advanced with determination. "You fell out a window?"

"I was thrown." Shadow backed inside the house and leaned heavily against the wall. "I struck my head on the way down. I was punched a few times in the face too. I'm pretty certain I have a concussion."

"I'm Mike." The human set down his case, bent and opened it. "Can you sit? You're pretty tall and I need to examine you."

Shadow just slid down the wall to sit on the floor, careful to keep the curtain around his waist since he could sense the female hovering in the doorway. He glanced at the stairs as he strained to hear any movement from above. Beauty was still up there. He began to worry. It shouldn't have taken her long to throw something on and return to him. She might be hiding from the human.

He remained quiet as Mike looked him over, only slightly growling when the medic touched his sore head, finding the lump. The medic used a bright little light to look into his eyes to check his pupils' responses next. The male sighed.

"I need to take you to Medical. I think you're right about the concussion but we need a doctor to take some scans to see what's going on inside your skull. Are you dizzy? Nauseous? In pain?"

"All of the above," Shadow admitted softly. "Creek?"

The female stepped farther inside the cabin.

"Can you please go check on Beauty?"

"Is she injured?"

"No." He glanced at Mike, then her. He didn't want to insult the human but he might be the reason Beauty hadn't returned to the lower floor.

She seemed to understand. "Right. He's male and human."

Mike sighed. "Right. She's Gift. I'm taking him to Medical."

"I won't leave Beauty." Shadow shook his head but groaned at the pain it caused.

"I will protect her," Creek swore. "You need treatment. She's safe and two council members are on scene. They will stay outside. You don't need to worry about anything but getting better."

Shadow didn't want to leave but he knew it would be stupid not to see a doctor. His head pounded and he feared he'd throw up.

"Beauty!" He raised his voice. "I will be back really soon. A female is here. Do you want to stay with her or go with me?"

He barely heard her answer. "I'll stay."

His gaze searched the stairs but he didn't see her. She was hiding somewhere near the upper landing though. More guilt stirred inside him. She didn't even trust him to protect her against a human medic.

"I've got this," Creek swore. Sympathy flashed in her eyes, proving she might even be able to read his emotions. "Just go and return when you are able."

He watched the tall female Species slowly walk up the stairs. She paused at the top and he knew where Beauty hid as he tracked Creek's gaze.

Chapter Thirteen

"Hello, Beauty." Creek was a pretty woman with a nice voice. "Are you okay?"

Beauty hated that she couldn't seem to move away from the wall but knowing the medic was downstairs kept her in place. The task team might show up next and with them, Shane. She never wanted to see him again.

"Beauty?" The Species lowered her voice. "Do you need to see the medic?"

"No!" She hated the way fear sounded in her voice.

"Don't worry. He's very nice. You're bleeding."

"It's not my blood. I bit Torrent and some of it is Shadow's." She glanced at her hands.

Creek's eyebrows shot up in astonishment. "You are responsible for some of Torrent's injuries?"

"He attacked Shadow and threw him out the window. I was angry." *And scared.* She wasn't willing to admit that though, despite it being obvious.

"That was brave of you."

She peered up at the taller Species. "You and I both know that wasn't why I did it."

"You panicked and just attacked because your instincts took over?"

"Something like that."

Creek leaned against the opposite wall. "I've been there."

"You have?" That surprised Beauty. "You look strong."

"Not when I was in chains and still under the control of Mercile." She hugged her middle. "You weren't raised inside the testing facilities but the technicians we dealt with were big, burly humans. It was rare to see smaller ones unless they were medical staff." She shrugged. "The technicians were mostly bullies with upgraded titles who enjoyed terrorizing us."

"I'm sorry."

"Me too. That's in the past though. How are you doing?" She cocked her head. "They are taking Shadow to Medical right now. We'll be left alone for a bit. The males will stay outside. Why don't you get cleaned up?"

Beauty skirted around the other Species to enter the bathroom. She washed her hands and one look in the mirror had her cleaning her face and neck as well. Torrent's blood had smeared there. Creek followed but paused at the doorway.

"You look nervous. Relax. No one will enter the house until Shadow returns."

"Are our men afraid I'll freak out if they come in here? Is that why they remain outside?"

"Yes. No one wants to traumatize you more. Breeze ordered all males to keep away from you. I'm going to stay until she arrives. They are preparing a helicopter to fly her here as soon as possible."

"What a mess." Beauty resisted groaning as she turned off the water and used a towel to dry off. "How could things go so wrong?"

"What happened?"

"You heard. You talked to Torrent and Shadow. My hearing is good."

"I want your version."

"Shadow and I were in bed together but suddenly Torrent attacked us."

"You mean he attacked Shadow."

"Yes."

"Did Torrent hurt you?"

She shook her head, calm now that the voices had faded. She couldn't hear anything from below or outside except a vehicle leaving. That would be the medic taking Shadow away to be treated.

"Torrent didn't know Shadow was allowed to touch you."

Anger stirred. "I know."

"Torrent isn't a bad male. He thought he was protecting you."

"I'm so sick of that!" Beauty clenched her teeth and glared at the other woman until she calmed enough to speak again. "That's why I was brought here."

"I know. Breeze filled me in on your situation and how you feel. You resent being labeled Gift."

"Resent is an understatement. This wouldn't have happened if everyone would stop treating me as though I were some weak freak." She paused. "I don't need a babysitter."

"Breeze doesn't want you left alone. It could be hours before Shadow is cleared to return. It could be longer if he sustained a lot of damage. Medical might want to keep him overnight."

Worry ate at her. "He seemed okay to you, didn't he? He was talking and on his feet."

"I'm sure he will be fine. Our males are pretty tough and recover quickly after they fight." Creek smiled. "They do it often here."

"I've never seen you at Homeland."

"I live here full time. I'd already transferred here when you were rescued."

"Why? I thought they rotated all the women every few months."

Creek's smile faded. "I like it at Reservation better and I have excelled at my secretarial skills. The council members assigned here need someone to help them. I volunteered."

"Is there a women's dorm at Reservation?"

"I live at the hotel. It's nice."

"Oh." Beauty stepped forward and Creek retreated then followed her into Shadow's bedroom. "I guess I should clean up the mess before he comes home. I don't want him to feel he needs to do it but he will."

"I'll help."

"I can do it myself."

Creek raised her hands. "I didn't mean to offend you, Beauty. I'm here. What else will I do?"

"You could go home."

"Breeze would have my ass. No thanks. That's one female I never want to disappoint. She gave an order and I'm following it." Creek smiled, her features showing amusement. "You know how she gets."

"She is very protective."

"To you maybe." Creek glanced around, studying the layout of the room. "She's kind of a bear to the rest of us. We are the 'soft padding that keeps our males from tearing each other apart'. That's a quote from her. She expects a lot from us."

"I've never heard her say that. What does that mean?" Beauty paused by the bed, her sad gaze fixed on the broken window frame. "I don't know what to do about that."

Creek crossed the room and just closed the window. "It shuts. That's all that matters. Someone else can fix it later. We have people who do that." She closed the curtains, effectively hiding the damage and turned back. "You never got the lecture from Breeze about our duties to our males?"

"No. I wasn't allowed around them." She decided to make the bed.

"Ah." The Species walked to the other side to help. "Our males are gruff and not the friendliest if you haven't noticed. They intimidate others easily. Their soft sides are hard to find but it's our duty to remind them why they need to become social. Otherwise they'd probably have pissing contests with their fists. There would be so much fighting that not much else would happen."

Beauty paused, staring at Creek. "Why? We're all considered family, aren't we?"

224

"It's their nature. Mercile didn't create them to be feeble. We had a lifetime to grow resentful of authority figures. It's our jobs as females to give them a reason to unite. They work together to give us a home." She smiled, tucking in her side of the comforter. "We allow them to do it. We need to be reminders that there's more to living than seeking revenge on the ones who've harmed us."

"What is your job specifically?" Beauty glanced around the room, not seeing anything else to do. She held Creek's gaze.

"Breeze just expects us to always be supportive of our males."

"Is that why you sleep with so many of them instead of settling down with one? There aren't a lot of us who survived."

Creek grinned. "No." She sat on the end of the bed. "Do you know anything about the breeding experiments they did at Mercile?"

"I've heard a little about it."

"We were taken to males to share sex. Sometimes it would be the same one for a few weeks but mostly they'd take us to different ones. They wanted us to become pregnant and probably thought exposing us to several males would help make it successful. Your heart hardens after a few years of it."

"I don't understand." Beauty perched on the dresser.

Creek's humor fled as she hugged her waist. "We learned not to become attached to anyone. It was a painful mistake to become emotionally involved. They would use us to punish the males or use the males to attempt to force us to do their bidding without protest if they suspected we cared too much about each other. Arguing against whatever they wanted was never a good thing."

"What kind of things did they want you to do?"

Fangs dented Creek's bottom lip. "Bad things. I was taken to a male once who'd been tortured. He was in bad shape and I tended to him instead of sharing sex." Anger deepened Creek's voice. "As if he were in any condition to do that. He'd been severely beaten. I think they wanted to humiliate him."

"By having you share sex?"

"He was so injured he couldn't get up from his mat. They expected me to initiate the sex. You said you don't know much about our males but they are proud. It would have shamed him to be expected to perform but not be able to." Her voice lowered. "I doubt he could have gotten it up." She glanced at her lap, then back at Beauty. "Do you understand?"

"Yes."

"I knew they'd refuse to feed me for a few days as punishment for not stripping and trying to share sex with him but I worried he'd die. The technician mistook my compassion for an attachment for the male when he returned me to my cell. That bastard threatened the male's life if I didn't allow him to mount me." Her jaw clenched and her dark eyes narrowed. "I broke his nose and kicked him in the nuts when he got too close. I hope it hurt like hell. I was never going to submit to being raped without putting up a fight. The other technicians pulled him out of the cell before I could do more damage or I might have killed him." She shrugged. "He never tried that again."

Beauty blinked back tears. "I'm glad you were able to defend yourself."

"Me too. Not all our females were so lucky." Compassion filled Creek's gaze. "Needless to say though, we grew to protect our hearts by not getting too attached to one male. We're enjoying our freedom. We have so many choices now and no one tells us who we have to share sex with anymore." Creek hesitated. "Plus, I think some of us feel it would be unfair to just pick one male when there aren't enough females to go around."

"Do you feel that way?" Beauty studied her closely, spotting the hint of sorrow in her features.

Creek shrugged. "I don't know. Sometimes, I guess. Don't ever repeat that to Breeze. She'd be horrified. That wasn't her intention when we moved into the women's dorm at Homeland. She got us all together to discuss how to help our males with our new lives. It was never implied we should share sex with them but it's our duty to make sure we care for them as much as they do us. They are protective and shield us as much as possible from the harshness we still endure from the outside world. It seems a small price to meet their needs." She laughed. "And it's certainly pleasurable. They take really good care of us in all aspects."

"Is there someone you like more than anyone else?"

"No." Creek stood. "I make sure I never spend too much time around any of the males I've become intimate with. There aren't as many as you'd think. A lot of them here are interested in the humans. We have a lot of interaction with the local town."

"Is that scary?"

"Humans?" Creek grinned. "No." Her smile disappeared and she continued, "I'm sorry for what happened to you. Was it bad? I don't know your history."

"I guess it could have been a lot worse. There was only one man who abused me. He was old and he didn't beat me but he wanted to have sex sometimes. It was a cold and uncomfortable experience but I wasn't brutalized. The guards he hired were always trying to bribe or frighten me into doing things with them though. I never did."

"I'm sorry you had to survive that but you don't need to fear all humans. We have some working here and I've made good friends with two of them. You should meet Zandy and Richard while you're visiting Reservation. I have lunch with them often but not together right now."

"You're friends with human men? Do they fight over you? Is that why they need to be kept apart?"

"No." The question seemed to amuse her. "Zandy is a female mated to Tiger and they have a son. She just had the baby but Richard can't find out she was ever pregnant. We trust him but knowing classified information might put him in danger if anyone suspects. Zandy had to transfer to another job to avoid him and he was told she's at Homeland. They talk by phone since they remained friends but I get to see them separately. The baby is adorable. Have you ever seen one?"

Beauty nodded. "Yes. We have a few of them at Homeland. Ellie brings Salvation to work with her all the time. Fury is his father and the baby looks just like him."

"I want one so bad but it doesn't seem it will ever be possible."

"A baby?"

Creek nodded, glancing around. "Let's go downstairs to clean up that mess."

The topic was over. The Species fled the room. Her stiff posture and the wistful tone of her voice revealed her pain. Beauty placed a hand over her flattened tummy, wondering how it would feel to be pregnant as she slid off the edge of the dresser. So far none of the women Species had been able to conceive.

The idea of someone being totally dependent on Beauty was a scary thought. She could barely face each day on her own without wondering how she'd get through it. She loved Salvation and Forest, the two babies she spent the most time around, but was glad they weren't her responsibility. Children needed parents who were knowledgeable of all things and who could teach them how to survive in the world.

"Creek?"

She paused at the top of the stairs, turning back. "Yes?"

"Why do you want a baby?"

Her features hardened. She was silent for long seconds but then relaxed. "I guess besides the obvious reasons of just wanting to know what it would be like to become a mother, I want someone to love. A child would be safe to open my heart to and share my life with."

Beauty mulled that answer and reached out, wrapping her fingers around the other woman's wrist. "I understand."

"Trisha says not to give up hope and that maybe the experts they've hired can find a way around our genetic engineering so we can conceive."

229

"Would you want a mate if you were able to have a baby?"

"You're full of questions." Creek hesitated. "It's not an option right now so I don't allow myself to think of it often."

"But you do."

She smiled. "I have considered it. I see how happy Zandy and Tiger are. She's his entire world and he is hers. It would be nice to go home after work to find someone excited to see me. Of course I doubt I'd be as understanding as she is of his nature. Humans are more agreeable than Species females."

"I don't understand."

"Our males are pushy. Zandy thinks it's cute when Tiger gets very protective of her. I would be irritated. I'm strong enough to care for myself. I might even feel insulted. We'd butt heads often and aggressively."

"She's not as strong as you are." Beauty studied her from head to foot. "She probably needs his protection."

Creek laughed. "That's true. Zandy is very brave but she isn't exactly physically intimidating."

"I like it that Shadow is protective. A lot scares me but I feel safe with him." It wasn't too bad, admitting that. She felt comfortable with Creek. "I want to keep him in my life."

"You two shared sex. How was that? Were you scared?"

"It was amazing." Her heart raced just remembering it. "He was very sweet and it was so much more than I expected."

"Your expectations had to be low after what you've suffered."

That statement shattered Beauty's happiness. "True."

"I'm sorry. I didn't mean that the way it sounded."

Beauty's hand dropped away. "No. It's true. Anything had to be better than what I've known."

Creek gripped her hand. "I'm really sorry. This discussion has left me feeling a bit defensive and a little gloomy."

"I didn't mean to pry or upset you."

"You didn't. It's natural to be curious. Talking about babies and mates depresses me. I'm glad that you enjoyed the sex with Shadow and that you wish to spend more time with him. He seems very concerned about your safety. He's a good male. I can tell these things."

"All our men are good."

"No." She hesitated. "I've met a few that I avoid. They are damaged inside by hatred and closed to emotions. They would never mistreat a female but they are coldly detached from feeling too much. Shadow is very warm and friendly. He'll be good for you but you should know that the more time you spend with him, the more attached he might grow to you. They tend to want to keep something they believe is theirs. Every time you share sex will give him the impression that he can keep you in his bed."

"I'd like that."

Creek gently squeezed her. "I'm glad for you then. He'll return when Medical clears him."

"It's frightening to allow myself to feel." Beauty clung to her hand. "You should take a chance and allow someone to get close to you, Creek. It is scary but I've come to realize I have nothing to lose. I wasn't living. I was just existing. There's a world of difference. I deserve to be happy and so do you. I was forced to spend my life mostly alone but I have more now. I was locked inside a basement with only the guards to bring me food when they decided to feed me. I was only allowed out when Master wanted me upstairs. I hated it when a day or two would go by without seeing anyone but being taken upstairs was worse."

Creek stared at her for long seconds before she released her hand. "I'll give it some thought." She smiled. "You're pretty brave for a Gift, Beauty. Know that. I'm much stronger but the idea of putting my heart in a male's hands scares the hell out of me. I've been hurt enough."

"I'm really not. I'm scared all the time but I'm more afraid of wasting the life I've been given by never taking chances. I have enough regrets."

* * * * *

Shadow growled at Dr. Harris, the wrinkled, white-haired male who was much older than him. The human frowned.

"Don't take a chunk out of me. No biting, damn it. I'm done giving you stitches."

"I will not bite. It hurt. I make noises when I'm in pain."

"Sorry about that but I'm glad you're not feeling ornery toward me." The doctor snapped off the gloves and tossed them in the trash. "I already got bitten this week." He shoved up his white coat to show a bandage on his arm. "Wild Zone residents aren't the best patients. I had to get four stitches myself. I'm lucky he just tore me a bit."

232

"I don't live there. I was visiting."

"Right." The doctor walked over to the wall to flip on a light and study the scan he'd ordered. "No permanent damage, no fractures to your skull, and no bleeding or swelling on the brain. You guys have hard heads." He flipped off the light and turned around. "Are you still experiencing problems with your vision? Dizziness? Nausea? Any ringing in your ears? Headache?"

"The shot you gave me seems to have worked to stop those symptoms."

"I envy you." The doctor took a seat on the stool. "My joints are killing me. Arthritis is a bitch."

Shadow arched his eyebrows, not sure what that meant.

"Never mind. Your kind don't suffer from it and probably never will. That's the advantage to having your hybrid genetics. They strained out the bad ones." He crossed his arms over his chest. "You're fine. You might feel more aggressive for the next twenty-four hours so watch your temper. No fighting. Stay away from the women too."

"I can't do that. I need to return to Beauty. She's waiting for me at the cabin."

"Oh." Interest sparked in the male's eyes. "You're the one assigned to guard the Gift Female and see if she's interested in sex? How is that going? Do you need any advice?"

"It is fine."

"You wouldn't be here if that were true. Is she the one who pushed you out a window? I was told you were shoved from the second floor of a cabin."

"A male attacked me."

"Huh. I didn't get many details. How did that happen? I thought you two were supposed to be alone out there. Was it a Wild Zone resident? They can be a bit unstable."

"It was Torrent."

"Really?" The doctor's eyes widened. "He doesn't live out there but he deals with the wilder Species often. I guess they are rubbing off on him. I thought he'd be a good example to teach them how to control their instincts but maybe I should have a talk with him about how he shouldn't go around attacking other people."

Irritation flared. "He believed I was harming Beauty."

"Were you?"

"No!" Shadow snarled again, insulted.

"Take it easy, young man. I just asked a question. Are you sure you don't want advice? I give it all the time when you guys try to hook up with women who aren't Species. I've seen Gifts and they are pretty small. Are you worried about being too rough with her?"

"We shared sex. It was fine."

The doctor grinned. "Fine, huh? Maybe you do need some pointers. Sex should be amazing." He chuckled. "I was young once. I would have been doing something wrong if any woman said that after I got done with her. In my day—"

A knock sounded on the door and it opened, interrupting the doctor. Shadow identified the male who poked his head inside and growled again. Torrent held his gaze before entering the room.

"I wanted to apologize." Torrent had changed clothes and his hair was wet from a shower.

Dr. Harris stood. "No fighting in my exam room!" He got between them.

Shadow rose to his feet, glaring at the other male over the shorter human's head. "You had no right to enter the cabin."

"No one told me why you two were there. I just assumed a Gift wanted a little fresh air and to see the woods. I'm really sorry. I heard sounds when I went to knock and thought maybe one of the Wild Zone residents might have gotten inside. They are pretty nosy. I went inside to make sure they weren't causing problems. Then I realized you were mounting the Gift. It is ingrained in me to protect her."

Anger still made his blood boil but he acknowledged the regret in the other male's face. He seemed sincere. Shadow unfurled his fists. He'd learned patience when he'd lived at the task force headquarters. Misunderstandings happened often between Species and humans. He just hadn't expected it from other Species males.

"I would never force myself on a female."

"I'm glad to hear that but I don't know you. I assumed the worst." Torrent lowered his gaze. "Do you want to take a swing at me to make us even?" He glanced up, holding his stare.

"Not in my exam room!" Dr. Harris shook his head. "Take it outside in twenty-four hours." He glared at Torrent. "I gave him a shot to help him heal. He's not doing anything until it wears off."

Shadow decided to forgive the male. He had been attempting to defend Beauty, after all. "You could still teach me to swim. I'm afraid the river being so close will pose a danger. I never learned."

"I would be more than happy to do that. We'll start tomorrow."

"Not Beauty though. You stay away from her. You teach me and I will teach her."

A grin lifted the corners of the other male's lips. "I understand. I doubt I'm her favorite person right now." He reached up and touched his shoulder. A bandage could be seen through the thin material of his shirt. "She bit me."

Shadow smiled back, feeling satisfaction. "I'm the only male she wants."

Chapter Fourteen

Creek tilted her head. "Someone approaches. I hear a Jeep."

Beauty trailed her from the kitchen to the front door. The two council members had remained outside where Creek joined them. Beauty hesitated, glancing around first to be sure none of the human task force members were present too. A Jeep parked and relief swept through her as Shadow slid out of the passenger seat.

The dark-haired Species with bright-green eyes approached Shadow while the other one hung back. "How are you doing?"

"Fine." Shadow's gaze sought Beauty before he glanced at the Species. "You may go."

He tried to step away but the male blocked his path. "Not so fast."

"What's wrong, Jaded?" Creek walked down the porch steps to halt at his side.

"The male had to be given the healing drugs. The symptoms will make him irritable, aggressive, and unstable. Shadow, you should return in the morning once you're feeling more yourself."

"I'm fine." Shadow sidestepped Jaded, his focus locked on Beauty again. "I'd never harm her."

Jaded jumped back into his path again. "Rethink it. I could make it a direct order."

"Don't," the other male spoke, his voice deep. "He won't harm the Gift. They are bonding. This time is important."

"Damn it, Bestial." Jaded turned his head. "Stay out of this."

"They've had enough interference. That's why this happened. No one should have come near them. Allow him to pass and let's go."

"We have no idea how he'll react to the chemicals pumping through his system right now, accelerating the healing process."

The other Species smirked. "I do. That's Shadow, formerly of the human task force. I actually read the reports that come across my desk instead of going to all those charity events you frequent. He's taken them at least two dozen times with no ill side effects and never attacked any of the humans on the team. I'm sure they irritated him plenty. She's safe and we need to leave them alone."

Jaded softly cursed. "Okay." He stared at Shadow. "Call if you need anything at all. We're going to put this area on total lockdown so no one comes here again."

"Breeze is on her way," Creek reminded them. "Are you going to tell her she's banned from checking on her Gift Female? I'm certainly not. That's one order I'll refuse if you try to push that on me."

"Fuck no." Jaded growled. "She'd have my nuts."

"I agreed to allow Torrent to teach me how to swim."

Beauty was stunned by Shadow's admission. It seemed she wasn't alone when the other Species showed surprise as well. Shadow shrugged.

"The male's intensions were good. I need to learn how to swim and he offered to teach me. What if Beauty were to fall into the river? It's my duty to protect her against any danger. We'd both drown."

"Okay." Bestial nodded. "What did you learn from those humans?"

"Mistakes happen but you deal with them and get past it."

Shadow approached Beauty. The bandage on his forehead was small but he walked on steady legs. He looked healthier and no longer pale. She was grateful that he seemed to be recovering from his injuries and that he'd returned so quickly. He came up on the porch and paused to stare down at her.

"How are you?"

"I'm fine."

His eyebrows rose. "Really?"

"I was scared," she whispered, unable to see the others with his body in her way. "How is your head?"

"Not broken." He smiled.

"Let's go and leave them alone," Bestial announced. "You have a charity event to go to, don't you, Jaded? We don't want you to be late."

"Shut up. For the thousandth time, I don't enjoy them. They are a pain in the ass."

"I don't see you turning down any of those invitations."

"They are for good causes and our publicity team said they improve our image."

"You mean your image. Say cheese."

"Boys!" Creek laughed. "No fighting. Stop antagonizing him, Bestial. We don't want him to show up with any bruises if you two start exchanging blows. They always want Jaded to be in the pictures. He can't help it that he's so pretty."

The male snarled. "Screw you both."

"You're not my type," Bestial teased.

"It would be so wrong to fuck my boss." Creek laughed again. They left and Beauty listened to the engine sounds fade away. Shadow waited too until only birds singing nearby could be heard. He took a deep breath and reached out slowly to cup her face with one of his hands.

"Are you really fine? I hated to leave you."

"I know." She believed him. "Did the doctors clear you or should you still be there?" It wouldn't surprise her if he'd refused to stay at Medical even if they'd asked him to.

"They said I could go."

"Okay."

He released her and she backed inside the cabin. His gaze left hers to drift around the room. His mouth tightened into a grim line before he looked back at her. "You cleaned up the destroyed table."

"Creek helped me. I knew you'd do it but I didn't want you to be reminded of what happened."

"That is always going to stay with me. I should have heard him coming."

"We were distracted." Heat rose in her cheeks, remembering what they had been doing and that Torrent had seen them having sex. She cleared her throat. "I'm making us food. Go shower while I finish up. It's just sandwiches. I wasn't sure when you'd return but wanted to keep busy."

He hesitated, closed the door at his back and locked it. "Can I hold you first?"

She nodded, stepping into him. The second his arms encircled her waist and drew her against his long frame, she breathed him in. The stench of antiseptic was strong but she wrapped her arms around his middle, hugging tightly. It didn't matter that he smelled bad, just that he was back.

"I'm so sorry," he stated gruffly. "It won't happen again."

"Don't do that."

He tensed.

"That wasn't your fault. Stop blaming yourself. We're both fine. It was a lesson learned. We never thought anyone would enter the cabin."

He rested his chin on top of her head. "I'm proud of you."

It was her turn to tense. "Why?"

"You bit him." He chuckled. "You fought with a male. I won't forget that. You faced your fears attempting to defend me."

Worry melted into warm sensations as she relaxed in his hold again. "Creek thought your pride would be injured and warned me you might be angry. That wasn't my intention. I just wanted to protect you."

"My pride is bruised for allowing anyone to sneak up on us. I was worried that you'd regret coming here with me. I am probably not the right male for you."

It was an improvement. He'd said probably instead of being certain. "You are perfect," she swore.

He hugged her a little tighter. "I'll shower. I reek from being at Medical."

A small laugh escaped. "I wasn't going to complain."

Shadow nuzzled her again. "I'll hurry. We'll talk."

"Okay." Her hold on him loosened but she didn't want to let go. "You need to eat something."

"I do." They stared at each other as they stepped back and broke physical contact. "Food will help my body process the drugs they gave me."

"Are you really okay?"

He nodded. "I'll heal fast. I've adjusted to the side effects. You're in no danger from me."

"I know that. I trust you." She did, completely.

"Living with the task team wasn't easy but I'm glad for the experiences it gave me."

Beauty watched him jog up the stairs and disappear in the direction of his room. She was tempted to follow him. She'd love to watch him strip and shower. Instead, she entered the kitchen to finish preparing lunch. It gave her a sense of fulfillment to prepare food for her Shadow.

She froze. *My Shadow?* Beauty closed her eyes as her heart stuttered inside her chest. He wasn't really hers, not for certain yet. They'd had sex but that didn't mean they were a real couple. Sleeping in his arms didn't mean he'd want her there every night for the rest of their lives. It hurt thinking about a day that might come when she wasn't welcome there.

* * * * *

Shadow rushed his shower, careful of the bandage on his head. He didn't want to get the stitches wet. That would mean another trip to Medical or acquiring an ugly scar. It usually wouldn't matter to him but now he wanted to be attractive to Beauty.

He reached up to run his fingers through his hair to wash out the soap. He was used to the military hairstyle he'd had to keep while working for the task force. It helped him fit in with the team. It had begun to grow out since he'd returned to Homeland with Wrath but not by much.

Did it bother Beauty that he didn't have the long hair that most Species males had? Insecurity was a new emotion he didn't enjoy. He turned off the water and grabbed a towel. He dried quickly, knowing she waited for him.

They were both damaged by humans. He and Beauty had that common bond but was it enough to bridge the differences? She was soft, timid. He wasn't. She'd been sheltered after her release from her prison while he'd faced humans head-on as a task force member after being given his freedom. She'd hidden while he was being treated. What if he wanted to go back to headquarters and work for Tim Oberto again? Beauty would have to deal with the human males on a daily basis.

The answer came to him instantly. He couldn't go back. He'd returned to live with Species as a vacation, not planning to stay, and he'd enjoyed his time in the outside world, but he'd have to remain at Homeland for good.

Shadow entered his room, grabbed clothes from the dresser and sat on the bed. Beauty's image filled his head when he closed his eyes. Her smile, the way she blushed. Her dark eyes staring intently into his seemed imprinted there forever. She trusted him. He'd been the one she'd chosen to approach for sex. The time they'd spent during that storm had somehow made her pick him.

"Damn," he rasped.

The idea of walking away from her wasn't one that sat well within his heart. It ached just considering saying goodbye. Another male would eventually take his place if he left. She didn't want to be segregated from other Species and obviously enjoyed sex. It meant someone would touch her, kiss her, and put their hands on her lithe body. Rage burned inside until beads of sweat broke out over his skin.

No way in hell. She's mine!

Astonishment replaced his violent show of temper. He hadn't meant to form a bond but it was there. He opened his eyes as he rose to his feet to put on a pair of jeans and a tank top. He didn't bother with shoes and rushed down the stairs in search of her. She sat at the table in the kitchen with two plates of food, waiting for him.

Beauty's smile at seeing him made him want to kiss her. He didn't hesitate to crouch near her chair and slide his fingers into her hair at the base of her neck. Her eyes widened a second before he brushed his lips

244

against hers. They were so soft, welcoming, and they parted when he licked over the seam.

He wanted her. Blood rushed to his dick until his jeans were uncomfortable. He pulled back to stare into her eyes.

She blushed but didn't look away. "What was that for?"

"I missed you."

Surprise, then pleasure showed on her beautiful face. "I missed you too." She rested her hand on his shoulder. "More." Her chin tilted up, offering her mouth again.

"Let's eat first."

The flash of pain wasn't missed. He wanted her to know it wasn't a rejection in any form. "I was given drugs to heal faster. I need food to help my system level out."

"Okay." She let him go.

"You're sleeping in my bed again." He wasn't sure how he'd handle it if she refused. *Not well*, was his guess. The air inside his lungs froze, waiting for her reaction.

"I'd like that."

He breathed again. "Every night." He couldn't help but push for more. It was his nature.

"Okay."

Joy and relief merged as he straightened and took the seat next to her. The desire to stay close was strong. He forced his attention from Beauty to the food. "Thank you."

"You're welcome."

He glanced at her to discover her smile. "This smells really good."

"I know how to prepare meals. I learned how to clean too. I can do laundry." She nibbled on her bottom lip.

Something bothered her. He shifted his weight to stare at her. "What is it?"

"Nothing."

He smothered a growl. "Beauty? You have an expressive face." *Beautiful too. Delicate.* "What are you thinking?"

"It's nothing." Her gaze skirted away.

He growled that time, not holding back his frustration. She appeared startled as her eyes met his.

"Don't lie to me. No deceit should be between us. You have something on your mind, something you want to say. Spit it out."

She didn't smile but instead suddenly took great interest in his tank top.

"Beauty?"

Her shoulders sagged. "It's stupid."

"Everything you say matters."

"Okay. I was just thinking how pathetic you must see me. I made you food and I'm listing off my domestic qualities."

Confused, he forced her head up gently with a firm grip on her chin. "Those are nice skills. I'm bad at laundry." The need to assure her was strong. "Do you want to know what new black uniforms being washed with new white socks does? It turned the socks an ugly gray. The team laughed when they saw them the first time we hit the mats to train. No one told me whites should be separated from dark colors, especially ones that have never seen the inside of a washer before."

"Ellie would never allow us to make that mistake. She's our house mother who teaches us living skills." Humor lit up her features before it faded quickly. "I have nothing else to offer you."

He tried to make sense of what she was saying. He shook his head, at a loss. "I don't ask for anything."

"I live with our women. I know they train with our men and they play sports sometimes. They work together at jobs outside the home. I am not trained for anything but house chores." Color bloomed in her cheeks. "They have a lot of experience with sex too. I don't. I keep thinking that all I can offer in our relationship is to keep a good home if we were to share one and make you meals instead of you having to eat at the cafeteria. We won't be able to share work stories or play rough together the way they do. I know nothing about sports or the hundred other things they could talk to you about to keep your interest."

He struggled to find the right words.

"It's pathetic." She tugged out of his hold but kept eye contact. "You didn't even want to be here."

He hated the way she gasped when he lunged. The last thing he wanted was her fear but he didn't stop. She was light when he just scooped her out of the chair to settle across his lap. He liked her there.

247

"I was afraid I might hurt you but I've wanted you since the moment we met." He hugged her tighter to him. "I'm damaged and was worried that would cripple me when it came to sharing sex." His fingers stroked her arm, glad she relaxed. "There isn't a damn thing pathetic or lacking in you, Beauty." He mentally ticked off her list. "I avoided Species women. It wasn't just my hang-ups but they are kind of scary." He softened his tone, smiling.

"Nothing scares you."

"A lot of things do." He wouldn't lie to her. Pride was a small price to pay when it came to making sure Beauty knew her value. "I used to consider sharing sex with one of them and feared my body wouldn't function. Can you imagine what one of them would do if I couldn't get an erection?" His eyebrows lifted. "It wasn't a pretty situation in my thoughts. What if I froze or had a flashback? They are great females but our males don't seem to have those issues. I imagined them laughing or worse. Pity."

Beauty saw sincerity in his steady gaze. It made her chest hurt as she snuggled into him, putting her arms around his neck. She loved being held so close to him on his lap.

"I wasn't put into the breeding experiments much. They rarely sent a female to my cell at Mercile. Then they took me from there and..." his voice trailed off as he swallowed hard. "Abused me with machines and videos of human females. I don't have that much experience either. It's been years since I had a real female under me. Don't you think I was worried that I wouldn't be good at it anymore? You were abused too. It left me shaking inside thinking I'd remind you of that when I touched you."

248

"You don't. There's no comparison. You're really good at it."

"I'm glad." He grinned. *"Really* glad. You are good at it too. I haven't had a complaint."

A load of concern lifted from her shoulders.

"All those skills you mentioned are wonderful ones. I had to learn how to cook a little, living at the task force headquarters but I'd hate to have to live off the ten things I know how to make for the rest of my life or always need to stand in a line to find a good meal." He nuzzled her cheek with his nose. "I'm not a big fan of sports and I'm glad you don't work with me. I'd be too afraid you'd get hurt to be effective in my duties."

Her joy dimmed. "I'm weak."

"Never." His tone deepened into a scary growl. "You're stronger than you realize. It's not just about size or muscle when it comes to strength. You have so much of it inside. You attacked a male. Did you think you'd win?"

She shook her head. "No."

"But you did it anyway. That's brave."

"It was because he was attacking you. Otherwise I would have fled or hid." She paused. "Maybe completely freaked out."

"I'm honored." He nuzzled her again, kissing her cheek this time. "That means a lot to me."

"Really?" The frail ray of hope shone inside that maybe they had a chance of a future.

"Yes." He suddenly stood, adjusting his hold on her. "Let me show you how much."

Her arms tightened. "What does that mean?"

He chuckled, striding quickly from the kitchen and up the stairs. "You don't believe I really want you, while I'm worried about how I'm going to keep my hands off you now that I've had you under me."

Understanding dawned. "You were hurt."

He chuckled. "Never that badly, love."

Excitement sparked inside Beauty at the idea of what awaited her. Shadow entered his bedroom and closed the door with his foot. He strode to the bed and bent, gently placing her on the mattress. It came as a surprise when he spun away, walked to the dresser and dragged it in front of the door.

"What are you doing?"

He smirked, reaching for the hem of his shirt. "No one is going to sneak up on us this time." He pushed the nightstand against the bathroom door to block it.

She understood. Someone would have to break down the door, plow through a wall, crash through the window or tear through the roof to reach them.

His muscled, tan abs grabbed her attention as he tugged the shirt upward, revealing every glorious inch of Shadow's torso. He had broad shoulders. The thickness of his biceps registered next when his arms lowered to drop the discarded clothing on the floor.

"I love to look at you." She hadn't meant to admit it but the confession was out before she could mute it.

"Good." He gripped the front of the sweats, bending to tear them down his legs. His chin tilted until his gaze held hers. "The feeling is mutual. Take everything off, love. I want you bare so I can touch you everywhere."

Her breathing increased as she shifted her body, going to her knees. She clawed at her clothing, wanting the same thing. There had been a time when she would have been horrified if someone predicted she'd be locked inside a small room with a naked man, eager for him to put his hands on her body. That had been before she'd met Shadow. He'd changed her life. She shed her clothes.

Possibilities were suddenly endless and things she'd never dared to dream of filled her fantasies. The rest of her life didn't have to be a lonely existence. Laughter and love were within her grasp thanks to the sexy man just feet away.

Shadow straightened to his full height, going absolutely still. "Are you okay? We don't have to do this."

Her gaze lowered down his body. He was perfect, magnificent, and aroused. The thickness of his cock as impressive as the length. "I want to."

He inched closer and crouched beside the bed, hiding the lower half his body from her sight. "Are you certain?"

"Oh yeah." She smiled. "I want you, Shadow. I love how you make me feel when we touch."

The tension eased out of his features. "Lie back flat."

So demanding. She liked that about him. It made her feel less shy since he was in charge. He put her back on the mattress.

"Spread your thighs."

She parted her legs and didn't jump when he gripped her ankles, positioning them on the curves of his shoulders. He released them to spread her inner thighs, pushing them farther apart. He growled when his heated gaze lowered to focus on her exposed pussy. His tongue swiped his lips and then he lowered his face.

Beauty threw her head back the second Shadow attacked her senses. She dug her fingers into his hair as his tongue licked her clit, pleasure exploding with each strong flick. It was wild, completely untamed, but it didn't frighten her. This time he wasn't gentle as he manipulated her body—almost a frantic hunger to make her come as fast as possible. She was on board with that plan since jolts of need shot through her rapidly.

"Yes," she moaned, her body tensing, the muscles in her legs shaking as she used her braced feet to lift her hips higher, tighter against his mouth.

Shadow growled low and deep, vibrations adding to the mix. Beauty closed her eyes since the ceiling blurred as the climax slammed into her. A harsh cry passed her parted lips as she jerked from the violent rapture.

He lifted his mouth away from her spread thighs and she barely registered it when he gripped her legs, using them to flip her over onto her stomach. Her face rubbed across the bedspread as she was dragged closer to him until her legs were eased off the bed. Shadow curled around her bent body and she gasped when his thick cock slowly penetrated her. She clawed at anything her fingernails could latch on to as he began to move, fucking her with a frenzy that seemed to be born of pure desperation.

Shadow wanted to howl as he held Beauty's hip and managed to maneuver his hand between her and the bed. Her swollen, sensitive clit was easy to find with a fingertip as he rubbed against it. Her inner muscles clenched, almost fisting his cock in a death grip. Her moans were driving him on, making thought difficult. She was heaven and hell, pure rapture and pure need to him.

"Beauty," he rasped, his lips brushing kisses on her shoulder and the side of her throat when she turned her face his way. He wanted to see her eyes. Needed to. And then her sensual dark gaze met his.

Mine! He saw her need, her pleasure, and it was all directed at him. His heart pounded, sweat broke out over his body and he clenched his teeth to hold back his own release. He wouldn't come without her and he could see she was close. His fingertip pressed a little tighter as his dick drove into her faster.

"Fuck. I can't last. Want you too much."

He was about to lose all control when his shaft hardened to the point that he knew he was done. A tight throb tingled at the base of his shaft when the swelling began, a sure sign. Her muscles suddenly quivered, milking him, and her second climax creamed the tip of his dick with wet warmth. She cried out his name and that was it.

Searing pleasure tore through him as bursts of his semen released. His hips jerked from the force of it, his body seized and her pussy tightened even more. *No, I'm swelling.* He shook from the force of his cock pumping cum inside her, jet after jet of it making him groan and revel in sexual satisfaction. He stilled. He was locked inside her the way only a Species canine could.

"I love sex," she admitted, obviously content to lie there with him curved around her.

"I love sex with *you*," he panted, brushing another kiss on her throat. "Was I too rough?" He worried he might inadvertently harm her frailer body.

"Never."

Even in his frenzy, he'd taken care with her. Some of his confidence returned. *Perhaps I've really grown beyond my past.*

"It was perfect."

"I'm glad." He kissed her again. His cock flexed inside her, almost with the rhythm of a heartbeat as it did it again and again. "Are you up for another round? The swelling is fading." Need and desire for her were a living, breathing thing inside him. He'd never get enough of his Beauty. Touching her, tasting her, being inside her sweet body.

Beauty smiled. "Good."

Everything felt right in his world.

Chapter Fifteen

"You're doing great." Torrent chuckled. "See why they call it dog-paddling? We're good at it."

Shadow wasn't amused. "You could have told me to keep my chin up."

"You're smart. You learned before you swallowed too much of the river." The male moved to shallower water, standing when his feet touched bottom. "I think that's enough for today. You are passably skilled and won't drown. It's good that you pick things up quickly."

"Beauty's life is in my hands."

Torrent nodded. "We do what we must to protect our females."

"My female."

Torrent shoved his wet hair out of his face. "It will score you points with impressing her. Maybe I should give Beauty lessons now."

The snarl was instant. Shadow glared at the male. "Don't speak of her or go near her again."

"Fine. I apologized. No one gave me the heads-up that you two were bonding. I guess it's serious?"

Shadow swam to shallower water and stood. "I need to get back to her." He strode out of the water, stripped out of his wet shorts and picked up a towel to dry his body.

"How are things going?"

Shadow faced him when he came out of the river too. "That's none of your business."

"She's like a human, isn't she?"

"Again, none of your business."

"I've spent time with them. Do you want some advice?"

"No."

A grin split the other male's lips. "Take things slow. We're scary to them."

"Drop it. Thank you for the swim lesson."

"You need to learn more. You won't drown but you aren't too skilled just yet. I think giving you both lessons would be safer. I won't flirt with her but I'd hate to think of something bad happening if it comes down to a worst-case scenario."

Shadow decided to be blunt. "I don't want you near her."

"That's why you met me away from the cabin?"

"She's fragile."

The male grabbed the other towel and rubbed water from his face and chest. "I wouldn't say that in front of her. She might take offense."

"She's not typical of our females."

"No shit." Torrent chuckled. "I got that immediately when I found her in the woods that night. They would have had those wolves running for their lives instead of the other way around. She also attacked me."

That reminder didn't amuse Shadow. "How much danger lurks here?"

"Besides the wolves, bears, lions and tigers I already mentioned?" He paused, the towel over his chest. "A few cougars, we've taken in some pit bulls that humans found too difficult to tame, and then there're the residents. Some are okay but some you shouldn't turn your back on." He tapped his head. "They aren't all there."

"Insanity?"

"In spades. They were tortured and in some cases, had no interaction with anyone but the assholes who abused them. Freedom is a concept some refuse to believe. All humans are considered threats to them."

"Beauty isn't human. She's Species."

"She is small and appears more human than most. They may take issue with her. Valiant has warned them sternly to avoid this area. He keeps them in control for the most part. Leo is also good with intimidation. He's a wild bastard though."

"Who is Leo? Is he a danger?"

"Another feline. He won't come after the Gift. I'd worry more about him playing pranks but he's got heart. He's sane but doesn't follow rules. He enjoys giving the officers headaches."

"What about Vengeance?" He remembered how the male had gone after Wrath's female. "Is he still here?"

"Yeah." Torrent tossed his towel down and grabbed a pair of cargo pants. "He has a habit of going after any female he feels might mate with him. He won't come near your female though."

"I'll kill him if he comes after Beauty." Shadow meant it. He'd seen how terrified Lauren had been after her attack at headquarters. Vengeance had

257

tried to force mate the human. He'd never give that bald Species a chance to put his hands on Beauty. "He is lucky to be breathing."

"You're referring to what happened with Wrath's mate." Torrent nodded. "I heard about that. Tiger wasn't much of a fan of Ven's either after he went after Zandy once. They worked it out though. Ven has...issues."

"I don't care. He better not go after my female."

"He's being kept busy while you're at Reservation. Humans abandoned a litter of puppies at our gates so Tiger and Valiant decided to give him that assignment. They need around-the-clock care due to their very young age." Torrent laughed. "Ven's pleased with the task. No way would he leave them to come after your Gift."

"Good. He'll live."

A phone rang. Torrent grimaced, yanking the cell from a pocket of his pants. "Yeah?" He paused. "Shit. How bad was the attack at the gates? Is anyone hurt?" Torrent listened and snarled as the details were given.

Shadow tensed. Someone had attacked the gates? That wasn't good.

"Where?" The male's gaze hardened as he met Shadow's interested stare. "I'll warn them." He closed the phone. "One of our males was shot at the front gate by a sniper but it wasn't with a bullet. They seemed to have tranquilized him. Security called ten minutes ago to inform us we've been put on lockdown but we were in the water. A report just came in from an officer patrolling this side of Reservation. We have intruders. They think Moon and other officers were shot at to pull our resources to that location. Moon was the first one hit so the others took cover."

Shadow's senses went on alert instantly. "Where were the intruders detected?"

"A few miles from here. An officer scented at least four different humans in the Wild Zone near one of our walls. Return to your cabin while I meet Security to search for them." He threw back his head and howled. "Warning to the residents." He took off in a flash, racing away.

Shadow spun, not bothering to dress or grab his discarded clothing. Beauty's safety came first. She wasn't alone but that didn't matter. She was his to protect.

* * * * *

Beauty smiled. "You don't have to babysit me, Breeze. I'm okay. I was just really upset yesterday when I called. I appreciate you dropping everything to come."

"I'm here now." The Species grinned. "Am I cramping your style? Don't worry. I'm going to stay at the hotel once toga boy returns so you two can continue what I interrupted. I figure it will be a nice break if I stick around a few days to spend time with the females on assignment here."

"Why do you call Shadow that?"

"Toga boy? It annoys him. Plus," she laughed, "I'll never forget what he looked like wearing that flag. It was kind of hot."

Jealousy surged inside Beauty. "He's mine."

Breeze grinned. "Feeling possessive? You just hissed at me."

"I'm sorry." Beauty was surprised by her unexpected strong reaction.

"He's all yours. I can look but won't touch. All our males are impressive, if I say so myself, and I do. Is he feeling possessive of you as well?" She grinned. "Never mind. He will. It's who they are."

"I feel things for him."

"How is the sex?"

Beauty hesitated but then answered. "Amazing!" She blushed but refused to look away. "It's so much better than I ever suspected."

"Score points for toga boy!" Breeze chuckled. "I'm glad."

"Please don't call him that. You have to notice how that muscle in his jaw twitches every time you say it."

"I know. It's cute, isn't it?" Breeze stood. "It's good for males to be teased. It reminds them not to be serious all the time. What do you have to eat around here?"

Beauty followed her into the kitchen. "I really am sorry for asking you to come here yesterday. You have a busy life."

"It was good to get away." Breeze waved it off. "No problem. I'm just sorry I got delayed until this morning."

"Is everything okay?"

"Yeah. Creek called me to say you were holding up well after the initial shock and then Justice called an emergency meeting."

"I hope it wasn't over me." The idea that her ordeal had caused their leader to hold a meeting made her feel a little sick.

"No. It wasn't about you. We got some high-priority incoming threats at Homeland. It happens but these jerks sounded authentic enough to be

260

alarming and the calls were traced to a few blocks away. They said bombs had been planted and a few were set to go off at midnight so the task force brought in their sniffing dogs just to be sure."

The idea terrified Beauty. "Was anyone hurt?"

"They were full of shit. There weren't any explosives. We'd have found them. Justice had us on lockdown though. Nobody is going to forget we've already had one helicopter shot down. I was allowed to leave once we were sure it was safe." She pulled lunchmeat from the refrigerator and turned. "So, how amazing was the sex? What was the best part in your mind? Did he take you facing him?"

Beauty opened her mouth but then a loud sound distracted her, making her heart race as something large seemed to land on the porch. A second later the front door was thrown open in the other room and hit the wall.

"Beauty?" The snarl was recognizable.

Beauty rushed into the living room to gape at Shadow. He was naked, his body tense, every muscle from his shoulders to his thighs defined. He sniffed, his head jerked her way and he stepped completely inside the cabin. The door slammed with one forceful shove of his hand, he locked it and revealed his fangs.

"Go upstairs to my bedroom."

"Holy shit," Breeze mumbled. "Impressive. I guess the sex was amazing. He wants you bad."

Shadow's furious expression changed to confusion, before glancing down his body. "Shit." He cupped his semi-erect cock, attempting to hide it

261

with one hand, frowning. His gaze shifted from Beauty to Breeze. "Human intruders have been scented a few miles from here inside the Wild Zone." He glanced at Beauty. "Go upstairs, stay away from the windows and toss me down some pants." He took a deep breath. "Please."

He spun away, marching toward the closet, revealing his beefy ass. "There's a shotgun and ammo in the kitchen above the fridge, Breeze. Secure that area."

"I'm on it." Breeze dropped the lunchmeat package aside and jerked her head toward the stairs at Beauty. "Move it. Get him some pants and avoid the windows." She spun away and jerked open the cabinet that stored the weapon. "How many, Shadow? Are they armed?"

"At least four, possibly more." Shadow yanked open the closet and withdrew a duffle bag. "Officers are hunting them but that's all we know."

Beauty rushed up the stairs. Her hands shook as she yanked open dresser drawers to find a pair of sweats and then darted out of Shadow's room. "Here." She tossed them over the balcony so they landed on the floor below.

Shadow appeared in seconds, a handgun gripped in his fist. He tilted his head to look directly at her. "I want you inside the bathroom, curled into a ball in the tub. You'll be safe from stray gunfire."

She wanted to protest. "I could fight with you if they come."

His horrified expression hurt. "No. Go where it is safe. Now, Beauty."

He put the gun on the table and bent to tug the sweatpants up his legs. Breeze appeared gripping the shotgun and paused by his side. A box of ammunition showed under her shirt where she'd stuffed it to keep her hands free to use the weapon.

"The door in the kitchen is locked and I shoved the table in front of it. We'll hear them if they attempt to enter the cabin that way." She glanced at the front door. "Do you want to cover the front or the back?"

"You take the front and I'll take the back. Humans tend to be sneaky and think we're stupid. They would choose to attack us from behind if their intent is to steal the Gift."

Shadow's words stunned Beauty. "Why would they come for me?"

Breeze glanced up, anger clear on her face. "You heard Shadow. Get inside that tub and stay down!"

They think I'm useless. It stung as Beauty backed out of their sight but she stayed close enough to hear their conversation.

"Do you think they are really after her?" Breeze lowered her voice. "How would they know where to find her?"

"There were meetings about us coming to Reservation, weren't there?" He growled his words, obviously still furious. "Why else would they suddenly breach this area? It's less protected than Homeland. Someone must know she's here."

"I don't know." The shotgun pumped—a distinctive sound. "The humans really are curious about Species females. Justice and the council have purposely avoided our pictures being publicized by using victim laws to protect our privacy. They might just want to take pictures. Humans would know she couldn't put up much of a fight. She'd be the perfect target in that case. They might also be after her for ransom if we do have another

263

leak of information. Gifts are our weakest members and they think we'd pay the most for them."

Shadow hesitated. "The asshole who owned her wants her back. I know I'd do anything to retrieve her if she were taken from me. I made it my business to learn about him after I met Beauty. The few guards captured when she was rescued stated the human was obsessed with her. They feared death by him for allowing her to be taken."

"Son of a bitch," Breeze snarled. "I didn't think of that. He was one of the rich Mercile investors. He'd have the resources to send humans after her and he was never caught."

"It won't happen," he swore viciously. "No one is taking her from me."

Master. Beauty's knees gave out and she sank to the carpet as memories assaulted her. He would do anything to get her back if he felt he could. Just the thought of returning to her old life made her feel sick to her stomach. She'd be locked back inside a dark basement, only being brought out when he wanted to dress her up like the doll he thought her to be. Guards would taunt her again, terrify her and attempt to starve her into submission.

She wrapped her arms tightly around her waist, hugging hard as the chills hit. Worse, the men hired to come after her would have to kill Shadow and Breeze to be able to take her from Reservation. No way would either Species allow her to be returned to the monster who'd held her captive all her life as long as they were breathing. That bit of knowledge drove the terror back.

264

It's not happening. No! Anger surged as she climbed to her unsteady legs and entered Shadow's room. He kept weapons there too. She wasn't going back to that hell. Never again would she be forced to suffer the touch of a man she hated. No guards would call her cruel names while they tormented her with threats of rape and molestation. She'd rather die first.

Shadow's bag held at least six weapons of different sizes. She removed one of the smallest handguns, testing it in her hand. It was heavy and cold. It should have a safety. She located it, making sure it was off and kept the muzzle pointed away from her body. It wouldn't do if she accidently shot herself.

She crept toward the closed window and peeked outside at the woods. There was no movement except for signs that it was a little windy. For once she wished she had the extremely heightened Species sense of smell— primate wasn't as keen as canine or feline.

Her heart rate remained unsteady, part fear, part anger. Shadow and Breeze were in danger. No way would she curl up and hide in a metal tub while they fought, if it came down to it. They might think her useless but she didn't agree. No one had ever really given her the chance to prove she wasn't defenseless but she'd managed to attack Torrent.

Time crawled as the occasional whisper could be heard from below. Breeze and Shadow talked too low for her to pick up the words but she tensed when one of them growled. It had to mean they'd seen or sensed something they didn't like.

"Fuck," Breeze said louder. "Tree trunks don't move but that's what I just saw. They are wearing expensive camouflage clothing. I've got motion in two locations."

"Three on this side," Shadow snarled. "There are more than four."

"I'm calling it in on my cell phone." There was a pause. "I have no signal."

"There should be."

Beauty had to agree. She'd called Breeze from her cell phone without trouble.

"They must have taken out the antenna that boosts the signal this far out." Breeze's voice deepened in rage. "Do you have a satellite phone? They can't stop us from using one of those."

"It's upstairs."

"I'm on it," Beauty called out, happy to do something.

"I told you to get inside the tub," Shadow snarled loudly.

She ignored him. She'd seen one of the phones in the top drawer and pulled it out. It took her a few seconds to figure out how to turn it on. The Reservation number was programmed into the memory. She couldn't get a signal.

"Oh no. It doesn't work."

"Bring it down," Breeze snapped, her hearing keen.

"No," Shadow protested. "Stay up there where it is safer."

"We need help." Breeze's tone lowered. "They are approaching slowly but I see them. Bring it to me, Beauty. Hurry."

Beauty put the gun down in case they got angry at her for having one and rushed downstairs. She handed the phone to the Species. Breeze rested the shotgun against her chest, cradled in one arm, and tried to use it. A shocked expression paled her features.

"This can't be happening," she whispered. "No signal is registering. How is that possible? We were assured these would work no matter what."

"They must be jamming the entire area." Shadow growled. "These aren't typical humans."

"What does that mean?" Beauty glanced between them.

"The task force had jamming equipment that could choke all airways." He looked grim. "Military grade and it's not cheap or easy to come by."

"Do you think they are members of your team?" Breeze paled. "Would they betray us this way?"

Shadow shook his head. "No. It's not the task force out there. I'm just saying, if they got their hands on that equipment, then they aren't a standard group of humans. They have money and contacts." His gaze slid to Beauty. "Get upstairs."

"You think Master sent them after me?"

He growled. "I told you to stop calling him that."

"That's what you think, isn't it?"

He nodded sharply. "He is rich and could hire the best mercenaries. Go upstairs."

"Where are our males? Where is Torrent? He's supposed to be hunting them." Breeze passed the phone back. "Do as he says, Beauty. Stay in the tub. I'm sure they are armed. The gunfire will at least draw some of the residents here if they don't pick up the scent of humans on the wind first."

"Two more," Shadow growled. "That's seven in all unless you have spotted more."

"Eight," Breeze hissed. "One is in the trees. I just saw a glint reflect off something. He's probably using binoculars to check us out." She hugged the wall tighter, trying to hide. "We're greatly outnumbered." She released the shotgun with one hand and used her knuckle to tap the wall. "Not good. Bullets are going to slice right through the wood. This is one of the original cabins that was already here, not the better-quality ones we built."

"We have to assume the worst." Shadow spoke calmly but he looked furious. "There are more of them than Torrent knew of. Security wasn't aware of it either or they would have given him more accurate information."

"You want to assume Torrent and the officers in this area are dead?" Breeze grimly met his gaze.

"Yes."

"We would have heard it if they shot our males. They couldn't take out a Species in a hand-to-hand fight. They are human."

"Silencers." Shadow looked out the window. "We wouldn't have heard anything either if they have snipers taking them out from a distance. Our males wouldn't have even spotted them until it was too late. They could fire before their scents were picked up."

Breeze paled but focused her attention out the window too. "What do we do?"

"Beauty? Get upstairs." Shadow sounded calm when he spoke.

She hesitated, watching them. Fear and dread raged inside her. Her friend and the man she loved were in danger because of her past. Shadow had admitted they were outnumbered and she had spotted fear lurking in Breeze's eyes before she'd looked away. She was the most fearless woman she knew.

"I could go out there and surrender to them."

Shadow's head whipped in her direction and his gaze filled with fury. "What?"

"They'll leave with me. Both of you will be safe." It was a sacrifice she was willing to make. She held Shadow's gaze. "You'll find me again with the task force. I know you will. You have to live to be able to do that. Master won't kill me. He obviously wants me back pretty bad to hire those men." She hugged her waist. "I can't let you die."

He snarled. "Get upstairs. Don't call that bastard 'Master' again and no way will I allow you to be returned to him."

At one time she would have run from his harsh tone but she knew Shadow now. Beauty held her ground and kept eye contact with him. "It makes sense. You'll die trying to protect me but they'll still retrieve me in the end. This is the only way to avoid that." She glanced at Breeze. "Tell him I'm right. You both need to survive. Those men out there need me alive to get paid. I know the man who used to own me." She carefully avoided his name. "He just wants me back. The task force will find me the way they did before."

Breeze's mouth opened, then closed. Tears filled her eyes but she blinked them back. "What makes you think we'll lose? I'm so proud of you right now for being brave enough to offer your life for ours but it's not happening." Her features tensed. "Now get your ass upstairs and in that bathtub. We're Species. We fight. No way are we just sending you out there to be returned to a prison."

Beauty's shoulders slumped in defeat. "You know I'm right."

"We're stubborn by nature." Breeze suddenly grinned. "And we love a good fight."

"Get upstairs," Shadow ordered.

She met his gaze. He was still enraged. No amount of talking would change their minds.

"Do it before I tie you up and put you there," he rasped. "I'll do anything to protect you, even that."

She spun and jogged up the stairs. The handgun felt a little better in her hand when she retrieved it from the dresser top. The safety was off and she entered the bathroom. One glance at the bathtub made her turn and go into her bedroom instead. She peeked out the window, looking for signs of the men Master must have sent after her.

She was Species and she'd fight too.

Chapter Sixteen

Shadow fumed. Beauty had dared offer to give herself up to those humans to be returned to the male who had abused her. The idea was insulting and outrageous.

"Calm," Breeze whispered. "I'm almost choking on the scent of your rage from across the room."

He didn't spare her a glance. "She was willing to give up."

"I heard." She sighed. "It was sweet."

He growled. He'd rather face an army of heavily armed humans than allow Beauty to be captured.

"Her heart was in the right place."

"No, it wasn't." Her heart belonged with him.

"Damn, Shadow. Give her a break. She's putting us before herself. Do you really think she misses the bastard who held her captive? I was there when she was brought to us. There's no way she wants to go back. It proves how much we matter to her."

His temper cooled slightly. "They are holding their positions. What are they waiting for?"

"I don't know but it beats them opening fire on us."

"They don't want to risk shooting Beauty if that's who they are after. That's why I wanted her in the tub. It might help hide her if they can look for heat signatures. It depends on what they are using. Her size is going to make it easy for them to distinguish her from us if they can see through the walls."

"Like in the movies?"

"Yes."

"Working with the task force taught you a lot."

He didn't deny it. The technology the task force had at its disposal was impressive. "How many Wild Zone residents are out here?"

"About forty in all." Breeze paused. "They were specifically told not to venture into this area but I'm hoping the stench of human intruders prompts them to ignore the order."

"Me too." A little help would be good but it might just get some of them killed. He didn't want that. "I wonder what is going on at the gates. Maybe they launched another attack there to keep Security busy."

"Another attack?"

He grimaced, realizing he hadn't filled her in on all the information. He told Breeze about Moon being tranquilized. "It had to be a diversion."

"A good one," she agreed. "We're screwed. Security would have ordered all available officers to the gates to assist there. General protocol is to take all the officers assigned to ground patrol to the hot spot while the ones on the walls keep their posts. They wouldn't dare leave their positions for fear of a wall breach. Somehow the humans got past them."

"It's not over." He refused to lose hope. "There are eight of them but humans are weak. We have a chance."

"Not a good one," she whispered. "What the hell though, right? It's a beautiful day to kill some bad humans. Some of them are going out with me. I figure I'm on borrowed time anyway." She paused, her voice lowering. "I always figured I'd die at Mercile."

Shadow hoped the mercenaries would decide it was too risky to rush the cabin. Time wasn't in their favor. The longer they were on NSO land, the less chance they had of fulfilling their mission. Species officers would eventually swarm the area.

Movement drew him from his musings. Part of a tree trunk separated and took on a human shape. It lunged forward to another tree.

"They are coming."

"I was about to tell you that. Two of them just darted closer."

"Don't shoot until you're sure you have a target. There's open space between the cabin and the woods. They'll be exposed when they attempt to reach us."

Breeze took an unsteady breath. "I guess I should tell you that I'm not a really good shot. I'm better at fighting with my hands but I've passed my training. I won't shoot my own foot."

He clenched his teeth. "Shoot them in the feet instead. It will slow them down."

"I can do that."

"Avoid chest shots. They'll be wearing vests. Target their legs or heads. Just get off as many shots as you can."

"Got it." Determination sounded in Breeze's voice.

273

Shadow took a deep breath, tracking the movements in the woods around them. One human darted closer and he almost reached where the trees had been cut back from the cabin. He was close enough that the black markings of paint on his face were visible. These were definitely not typical humans. *Skilled mercenaries.*

He wanted to keep them at a distance. He lifted the rifle from the weapons he had laid out, hit a panel of glass, and shattered it with the butt. The sound carried and he watched the human disappear behind the tree trunk.

"We're well armed," he bluffed. "Security is on the way. Your time is up. Leave while you can. My people won't allow you to live."

Silence. A full minute passed before a male voice responded from the far right, out of his sight.

"Send out Mud. She is the small New Species with brown hair and eyes. We'll allow you to live if you do."

Rage gripped him and his heart accelerated. *Mud? I'm going to kill the bastard who named her that.* He'd assumed they were there for Beauty and now his suspicions were confirmed. It took a lot of effort to get his emotions in check. New Species had been given numbers when they were test subjects but she'd been tagged with a derogatory title.

"Fuck," Breeze hissed.

Shadow had bad words to say too but calmer ones came out of his mouth. He was careful to speak clearly instead of snarling. "We don't know who you're talking about. No one is here by that name."

"Don't play games, Shadow. We know who you are. It's you and Mud in there."

His absorbed that information. They knew his name, which had to mean someone had betrayed the NSO. The tub worked at hiding Beauty's body temperature if they were using thermal scanning if they were mistaking Breeze for her. The other option was they couldn't see inside. Their intel hadn't warned them that another Species female would be present. Either way the humans obviously only expected to come up against him.

"Son of a bitch," Breeze whispered. "We do have a leak. I'm going to find out who it is and rip off his nuts."

He softly growled to silence her. They'd deal with that later. Right now they needed to stall for time. He decided to bluff by laughing loud enough for it to carry. "I'm Torrent. You are at the wrong cabin, humans. You paid for bad directions. I hope it cost you a small fortune to get screwed over."

"Bullshit." It was another human male who called out. "We've got a lock on your signal. You're Shadow."

The air in his lungs froze while his brain tried to work fast. How would they have a signal? He would have had to either carry something on his person or inside one of his bags. He mentally went over the list of items he'd packed and what he'd worn on the trip to Reservation. The other bag contained weapons. A dozen possibilities of when he might have been tagged with a tracker filled his head. They were small enough to hide in clothing, his boots, or even on the bags. The only people who'd had access to him or his belongings had been his task force team and the few Species he'd come into contact with at Homeland. Of course anyone could have sneaked inside his room at the dorm. Only Species had access though.

"I'm Torrent," he repeated. "I don't know what signal you think you tracked but you're wrong. Shadow is at another location."

"Bullshit." The same human responded, probably the one in charge, and it was coming straight ahead from behind a large rock. "Stop wasting time and send out Mud. Her owner wants her back."

His fangs flashed as he fought the urge to howl. *No one owns Beauty.*

The human spoke again. "It's your coin, jackass. Every team member has them and carries them at all times. Stop stalling and send her out. We haven't opened fire because she's worth a lot of money alive but that's all our orders were." He paused. "Alive. It doesn't mean we can't return her injured. We have a medic to patch her up. It's your choice. Either way we'll come in there to get her or you live by having her walk out of that cabin to us. Those are the only options you have."

Shadow turned his head and caught Breeze gawking at him. "Coin?" She gave him a baffled look.

"Task force," he rasped. "Someone on the team betrayed me." He glanced up at the ceiling, then back at her. "It's still inside my bag. We all keep them, usually on us, in case a member is taken. Only Tim and three other members know the codes to activate the trackers inside them."

Her eyes narrowed. "I understand."

That narrowed down the leak. Shadow silently swore revenge on the team member who'd betrayed him. "I have some of Shadow's things but

276

he's not here." He decided to keep bluffing. Every second could count. It might stall the mercenaries.

"We're coming in. I know what you're hoping for and it isn't going to work. We have at least half an hour before our location is compromised. I have snipers in the trees surrounding the area. Any Species spotted coming this way are being shot. No help is going to reach you."

Fuck! Shadow calmed his rage enough to aim his rifle, watching the location of the human who'd come the closest. He'd shoot the second the male moved. Maybe a few dead bodies would persuade them to rethink rushing the cabin. He doubted it though. Mercenaries were known to be single-minded and vicious. They probably calculated some losses amongst their ranks before agreeing to the mission.

"Kill anyone who enters the open area," he ordered Breeze softly.

"Understood."

Beauty tiptoed away from the hallway, having heard most of what Shadow and Breeze had said. Eight humans were out there willing to kill to take her back to Master. Shadow had shown her how to really live. Breeze had given her friendship. Neither of them deserved to die for those wonderful things.

The thought of Shadow dying left a gaping wound in her soul. She wasn't about to allow that to happen. She'd fight too. Three against eight were better odds. The bag inside Shadow's room was heavy when she lifted it and carried it to her bedroom. They'd target him since he stood in their way. Her bedroom was on the back of the cabin, above where Shadow stood.

She pulled out weapons the way he had, laying them out on the carpet so they were at the ready. It took a few minutes to figure out where to put her fingers on each weapon. *Point and shoot. How hard can it be?* She might not hit much but the extra firepower could surprise those men out there enough to give the two Species downstairs a better chance at survival.

She was careful not to make noise as she dragged a heavy chest in front of the window. She opened the lid, staring inside at the spare bedding. She turned, her gaze sweeping the room. The hardback books lining the shelves by the door caught her attention. They would help prevent bullets from tearing all the way through the wood chest to strike her if those men returned fire. Every step was taken carefully in case she alerted Shadow that she wasn't in the tub as she packed the chest.

She knelt and shifted the curtain enough to peek out the window, watching for any sign of movement. It took a few sweeps but she saw one man right on the edge of the woods. Another was two trees behind him to the right. She didn't spot any more of them but she had targets at least.

It was too risky to crack the window open. She'd have to move the curtain out of the way and be seen if she lifted it up. It would be stupid to give her location away. She could just fire through the glass. Beauty took a few calming breaths trying to slow her rapidly beating heart. *I can do this.* She repeated that a few times. *For Shadow.*

The first bullet fired wasn't loud. It was a dull sound that reminded her of a firecracker coming from a distance but glass shattered somewhere on the first floor.

"Get down," Shadow yelled. "Incoming!"

"Oh God." *It's begun.* Shadow was alive though. She'd heard his voice.

The man closest to the house suddenly lunged from behind the tree into the open, something fisted in his hand. His arm arced back as if to toss a ball but the sound of bullets exploded from the first floor. Beauty watched in horrified fascination as the guy jerked while his clothes seemed to tear open in places. Blood bloomed across his arms, then legs, before he fell back.

BOOM! The sound registered about the same instant the fallen man seemed to blow apart near his head. Blood and gore flew in all directions, mostly splattering across the tree trunk. Bile rose in her throat but Beauty fought it down. The son of a bitch had been about to chuck a grenade at Shadow. It could have been him in pieces below if he hadn't shot the man before he was able to throw it into the cabin.

The second man she'd seen lifted a long gun and opened fire. It was rapid and glass shattered—a muted sound over the noisy weapon. Beauty's hands shook but she pointed at him. Her finger pulled the trigger. The glass broke, a ragged hole appearing, and she kept firing. She missed the first three times and the guy seemed unaware of it until he jerked back. He stopped firing and looked down. She did too, pausing to watch him. He lifted his boot, frowning. She spotted a small defect along the edge.

279

"Shit," she cursed. She seemed to have hit him but not drawn blood. She aimed and fired again.

This time she hit him in the leg just under his knee. He threw himself back out of sight and she ducked behind the chest, waiting for return fire as she grabbed a bigger gun. The handgun didn't fire fast enough.

"Beauty!" Shadow roared her name.

She winced. He'd just realized she wasn't cowering in the bathtub but she at least knew he was still alive. He yelled something else but she couldn't make it out as more gunfire erupted below. It came from the front of the cabin. Breeze must have engaged the men too.

Beauty wrapped her hands around the largest weapon. It looked like one she'd seen in a video game the women played at the dorm. It was chunky with a metal clip inserted in the bottom and was heavy. She was sure it was some kind of assault rifle. She cradled it, found the trigger and rose to her knees. She rested the weapon on the chest and peered through the broken glass at the bottom of the window.

Two men rushed forward while she aimed and squeezed the trigger. Rapid shots blasted out of it. The thing knocked her back and bullets tore up the window to the ceiling before she could ease up on the trigger. She gaped at the damage from flat on her back where she'd landed. The glass in the window was totally gone now and holes were ugly scars on the wall and ceiling where bullets had ripped through them. She struggled to her knees again.

Now that she knew what to expect, she braced her knees apart, tensed her arms and aimed again. Her finger hesitated this time, hoping the kick of the weapon wouldn't send her to the floor once more. The men had taken refuge behind a tree but one darted out to rush the cabin. Someone fired from below, probably Shadow. The guy didn't make it six feet into the cleared area before he went down. He stayed that way, not moving. Blood leaked onto the dirt.

The loud sounds from below assured her both Species were firing weapons. Something struck the top of the mirror over the dresser, breaking the glass. She turned her head to glance back, seeing holes in it and at the top of the wall. It took her a second to realize someone had shot back at her. She ducked.

Heart racing, she leaned back up over the chest and opened fire. Her arms hurt from the strength it took to keep the muzzle down and the gun deafened her but she managed to keep it trained at the forest. She turned the barrel, spraying bullets in a wide arc, not even sure what she was firing at. It didn't matter. The enemy was out there and the people she cared about were inside. The weapon began to click instead of sending out bullets. It was empty.

She threw it aside and grabbed one that was just a little smaller. Fear no longer hindered her. There was no time to think. Bullets were tearing apart the cabin—most of them had to be aimed at Shadow since she could hear the damage being done directly below where she knelt. She opened fire again, wildly shooting into the woods.

Breeze shouted something but the words were lost to Beauty. It was chaos. She didn't understand why help hadn't arrived. The noise from the gun battle had to have been heard for miles. There were officers posted all over the place at Homeland.

The weapon stopped spitting out bullets and she dumped it, grabbing another. She didn't know how to reload, hating the concept of running out of guns but knowing she'd fight as long as she was able.

It came as a shock when brutal hands suddenly gripped her shoulders and she was thrown sideways. The gun was knocked from her grip when she hit the floor with enough force to cause pain along her right side. A big body suddenly slammed down on top of her. She was wrenched onto her back and pinned down flat. A human face, smeared with black paint, was all she could see as she struggled to breathe under the weight crushing her chest.

His eyes appeared dead, chilling as they stared into hers. He shifted and pain exploded in the side of her face when he clocked her with his fist. It came as a shock and blackness threatened to take her but she'd been hit plenty of times before by angry guards. She fought the urge to escape into unconsciousness.

He grunted in satisfaction as he used the hand he'd hit her with to retrieve and then speak into a radio. "I've got the bitch. She was the one on the second level. Clear me a path."

He rolled off her but Beauty couldn't move, still reeling from the blow he'd dealt. She felt sick, as if she'd throw up, and spots blinded her while she continued to struggle to avoid passing out. Her cheek felt broken, throbbed in agony, and her neck hurt too from being hit so hard.

His rough hands dug under her and she was hoisted up, then shifted. He tossed her effortlessly over his shoulder. She hung there limply while his arm pinned her to him behind her thighs. As he walked, the swaying motion made everything worse. She saw guns strapped to his thighs but her hands refused to grab them when her mind urged them to do just that. Instead her arms hung uselessly.

He entered Shadow's room and another voice spoke. "Eyes got it right. Good thing he caught sight of her with his scope and we didn't level the second floor the way we thought we'd have to."

"You want to take her down, or me?"

"You. She's not big, is she?"

"Nope. Doesn't weigh shit either." He stepped up and turned. "Follow me."

Beauty stared down, realizing the man holding her stood on the windowsill of Shadow's bedroom. It was a long drop to the ground below. She felt a flash of fear as he released the back of her thighs. Would he just let her fall? It was a horrifying concept.

Instead both his arms rose, trapping her hips between his neck and biceps on one side. He jumped. They fell about five feet, but then his boots hit the side of the cabin when their momentum slowed. He rappelled the rest of the way down with two more jumps until he roughly hit the ground. Gunfire was loud, the battle still raging. He hesitated a moment while the second man left the cabin and then the arm hooked back around her thighs. He ran into the woods, carrying her with him.

"No!" She tried to scream but it came out more of a ragged hiss.

283

"Shut the fuck up," he panted. "You're a lot of trouble but you're worth a hell of a lot of money, Mud."

No. NO! Her mind yelled when her voice refused. They were going to return her to Master and the life she'd once led. He kept running, taking her farther away from the cabin.

The gunfire suddenly ceased and another fear struck. Did that mean Shadow and Breeze were dead? She couldn't hear anything but the panting of the men as they ran.

"She was more trouble than I thought she'd be."

"Yup," the one holding her replied.

"She doesn't look like a million bucks to me."

"The customer is always right." He slowed to a fast walk. "When is our helicopter coming?"

"Three minutes out. We have to make the clearing. You want me to take her yet?"

"Nope. She is fine and we're close."

Once they got her into a helicopter, it was over. She'd disappear. There was a chance the NSO would locate her again but she didn't believe in luck. Being freed once had been a miracle. She licked her lips and closed her eyes, trying to get control of her body. She was hurt but she was Species. Tough. Her jaw clenched and she opened her eyes.

The guns on the man's thighs were unsecured for easy access and the holster straps flopped with every step. She stared at one and clenched her hands. It had to be done fast. Keeping her body limp was key to making him think she wasn't a threat.

The guy next to them moved slightly ahead and some bushes separated them a little. It was probably the only opportunity she'd have. She lunged and grabbed at the butt of the weapon. Her finger somehow found the trigger and she squeezed as she twisted it slightly. The gun went off, loud, and then the one holding her cried out.

He staggered, blood pouring from the wound where she'd shot him. He went down, crashing to his knees. She managed to tear the gun from the holster as she was thrown away from him. Her back hit the grass but she was prepared to have the air knocked out of her lungs this time.

She lifted the gun and fired at the other man. He threw his body to the side, falling into a bush to avoid the bullet. She was already twisting, struggling to get to her feet.

"Fuck!"

She swayed on her feet but ran. It didn't matter where she went, she just had to get away. Shadow and Breeze needed help too. She might be able to find some of those Wild Zone residents.

Something crashed after her and she knew the other guy chased her. She didn't dare glance at him, afraid of running into a tree or tripping on something in her path.

Run! She urged her legs to move faster. If there was one instinct she was familiar with, it was terror. She let it take her, submerged all her thoughts and only focused on survival.

Chapter Seventeen

Shadow shoved up from the floor where he'd dived to avoid the last splatter of bullets that had ripped open more of the walls. He saw Breeze crawl away from the fireplace. He could smell blood but wasn't sure whose it was since they were both suffering from cuts from flying debris. The walls were destroyed from the massive amount of bullets that had ripped them apart.

He raised his arm, just firing blindly from behind the two thick log end tables he'd sandwiched together on their sides to make them thicker. It wasn't safe anymore to try to target the enemy by searching for them. That would mean revealing his face, something a sniper would hit.

"Shit," Breeze growled. "What is holding up the cabin?"

He didn't have an answer. Enough sunlight poured through all the holes that they might as well have been outside. The enemy had massive firepower and, in his estimation, the only thing that had saved them was the rock trim along the outside. It was low to the ground so it had probably kept them from being shot as they were driven to the floor every time the enemy opened fire.

He could only pray Beauty was safe. It was an older cabin and he was sure the tub was made of cast iron. Bullets hopefully wouldn't penetrate the sides of it. He glanced up but the ceiling had a few holes from ricochets.

"You good?"

Breeze hesitated. "I was hit but it's not bad. Through and through to my side."

It was a wonder they were both still alive. Thousands of bullets must have been aimed at them since the attack had started. He was going to yell at Beauty when this was over. He'd heard her firing one of his handguns at the start of it but was sure she had retreated to the bathroom when he yelled at her. After that it had been impossible to tell where the gunfire had come from. His ears were still ringing.

The break in active gunfire was disturbing. He tensed, waiting for return fire. Seconds passed and nothing happened. He frowned and glanced at Breeze. She was hunkered down, weapon in hand. She met his questioning gaze, a frown on her face as well.

"Do you think they are going to rush us?" Her eyebrow arched in question.

He fired another bullet to make sure the mercenaries knew they were still alive. That should keep them from entering the cabin. Breeze fired a bullet from the other side of the cabin, not looking out either. She'd almost had her face taken off by a bullet and had yelled a warning to him. They'd both stayed down ever since.

No one fired back. More seconds ticked by. Breeze shrugged, one hand going to her waist to hold her wound. He spotted the blood soaking her shirt. It didn't look too bad but he worried.

Hope softened her features. "Maybe help has arrived and they took off. Maybe we should actually stop firing. I'd hate to hit one of ours by mistake."

287

He strained to hear but was still having difficulty because a slight ringing noise remained. The bad thing about having oversensitive hearing was loud noises hurt. Breeze made a keening noise.

"What was that?"

"A distress call. Our males will respond if they are nearby."

They both listened. Shadow watched Breeze. Her hearing might not be as disrupted as his. She shook her head, worry returning. *Shit*, she mouthed.

He had to agree. A howl suddenly rent the air and both of them felt relief. Breeze lowered her gun and grinned. "We've got help."

He hesitated to rise from the floor, not sure if it was safe yet. Minutes passed before something crashed through the bullet-hole riddled door. The male was barely dressed in only a pair of cutoff shorts with a mass of hair that honestly reminded Shadow of a lion's mane.

"Leo." Breeze grinned.

The male glanced around and held Shadow's gaze for a second before rushing to Breeze. He knelt, sniffing at her, and gently removed her hand from the wound. He threw back his head, roaring.

Shadow winced. There was no doubt the male was part feline even without seeing his eyes and facial features. He recognized him as the male he'd seen at the river hunting a female lion. Shadow got to his feet and charged toward the stairs to check on Beauty.

"Are the humans all dead?" Shadow hoped so.

"They ran away. We were being shot at or we would have reached you sooner." Leo forced Breeze down to lay flat on her back, growling when she protested. "Stay still, female! You're bleeding."

Another Species male rushed inside the room before Shadow could get upstairs. Blood ran down his neck. The sight stopped Shadow in his tracks. "Are you okay?"

Torrent turned his head, shoving back his hair to show a bloody ear. "A sniper nearly took off my head. They had a few of them perched in the treetops that kept us pinned inside a ravine about a mile from here. Once they moved, we came this way and I sent a few of the males to get help." He glanced at Breeze, concerned. "Are you okay?"

"Through and through," she responded. "Don't touch my breast, Leo. The wound is down here."

"Just checking them," the male countered and chuckled.

Flesh smacking flesh sounded.

"Stop molesting me." Breeze growled.

Shadow spun away and rushed up the stairs. "Beauty!"

She didn't answer. Panic hit that she'd been shot too. The bathtub was empty so he rushed into her room. Discarded weapons were on the floor, some still lined up as if they hadn't been used. The window was shattered, curtains torn, and there were holes in the wall and ceiling above it. He spun and rushed toward his room. Torrent was in the hallway blocking his path. He just pushed the male out of the way.

The sight of the window kicked out and a rope swaying in the open space made him snarl. He lunged forward, grabbed it and looked down.

289

Beauty was gone. He threw back his head, howling. He was out the window before he even checked to make sure the rope could take his weight. Someone had stolen Beauty. That's why they'd stopped attacking. The mercenaries had taken her from the cabin.

He landed on his feet hard, pain shot up both legs but he swept the ground with his gaze, hunting for sign as he released the rope. Heavy footprints were easy to spot, two sets, one deeper than the other. No smaller tracks were visible. One of them had to be carrying Beauty. He barely registered the fact that Torrent dropped next to him, also using the rope to soften his landing.

"They took her."

"I know," Shadow snarled. "They won't get far."

A gunshot cracked from the south. Shadow's heart stopped. That single shot could mean a lot of bad things. One being that the mercenaries had been given orders to murder Beauty. They'd want to do it in person, perhaps video it for their client or take the head from her body as proof of assassination. The human who'd owned her might want her dead to prevent her from ever identifying him if he were brought to Justice.

He sprinted in that direction, rage spurring him on. He didn't care if the mercenaries outnumbered him or how heavily they were armed. He just needed to reach Beauty. Alive or dead, they weren't taking any part of her near the human who'd abused her.

Torrent followed. He heard the male's harsh breathing as they lunged past trees, jumped over rocks, and sniffed the air, trying to pick up her scent. He caught it, barely, and kept going. The stench of fresh blood made him snarl as he rushed around a grouping of bushes.

A mercenary lay on the ground, holding his thigh with both hands. Blood soaked his leg and the ground as the male groaned in pain. Shadow registered the wound and the missing gun from an empty holster, hope flaring instantly that Beauty had been the one to shoot the son of a bitch.

He dropped to the ground near the guy, disarming him quickly, and just shoved aside the male's hands. The mercenary's expression, hazed with agony, met his. Rage burned brighter as Shadow gripped the wound, purposely using his thumb to dig into it. The male screamed.

"Where is she?" Shadow snarled, ready to tear the male apart. He could smell her on the guy.

The mercenary writhed on the ground but managed to point. Shadow was on his feet and moving in the next breath. "Kill the fucker if he moves," he ordered Torrent over his shoulder.

He spotted a broken stem where Beauty had fled. Heavy tracks marred the softer ones she'd made. Someone had chased her. He was close. Her terrified, sweet scent lingered in the air. He was grateful it wasn't windy as he followed her more by scent than by the tracks on the ground.

Beauty knew the man was gaining ground. His ragged breathing seemed right at her back. Her leg muscles burned and she was tiring fast. She spun, lifted the gun, and tried to aim. He was so close she actually hit him with it. She pulled the trigger, gasping, too out of breath to scream.

The loud shot missed him but he spun away, slamming into a bush, falling. She almost went down too but caught her balance. The river noises drew her, the only way to make sure she wasn't running in circles. She broke from the trees and nearly fell into the moving water.

She spun, looking for escape, but there was nowhere to go. Motion to her left made her whimper. Another man dressed in fatigues barreled at her. Something caught her attention out of the corner of her eye. A third man rushed her way. She was trapped as they slowed, knowing they had her.

"Put down the gun." The one she'd almost shot trained a gun at her.

"I can't swim," she warned them. "You shoot me and I fall in." She aimed the gun, shifting it to point at each of them in turn, keeping the barrel moving. "Master wants me alive, doesn't he? I'll purposely stay under until I drown. I'd rather die than go back to him."

Uneasiness skidded across their features. They believed her and the drop into the water had to be eight feet. She stood at a curve in the river where the earth had eroded the bank. It looked deep too.

"I'll be gone once I hit the water. The current is strong. You blink, I'm gone."

They froze but two more of them pointed guns at her.

"Drop the gun," one of them demanded. "We're not going to hurt you. Our boss wants you alive. Drowning is a horrible way to go."

She laughed bitterly. "And being returned to Master is better?" Her heart rate began to slow now that she wasn't running for her life. "I'd rather die."

They glanced at each other, obviously not expecting that.

"Do you not get paid if I'm dead?" She could guess money was the only reason they'd come after her. It would have to be a lot for them to enter NSO lands, beyond suicidal to attempt such a thing. Species weren't known for being kind to trespassers. "Back away from me."

"She will struggle when she hits the water. It's instinct," one of them muttered. "She'll surface and we'll grab her."

Beauty twisted her wrist, pointing the gun at her chest. "Will I survive a bullet to the heart? One shot and it's over. You'll have done all of this for nothing. I'm not going back." She hoped they believed her bluff. "Get away from me."

"Goddamn crazy bitch," one of them swore. "You won't shoot yourself." He looked unsure though.

"I was caged and chained, kept in the dark and only brought out when Master wanted to see me." She raised her chin as she inched a little closer to the edge near the water, her gaze darting around for an escape. There wasn't one. "They kept me weak from lack of food and water, bathed only when Master decided I should be clean when he put his hands on me." Rage deepened her voice into a soft growl. "Do you think I won't prefer to die before being sent back to him?" She paused. "A bullet is kinder and faster than suffering that fate."

A low branch kept drawing her attention. She kicked off her shoes and the men frowned.

"What are you doing?" One of them stepped closer.

She reacted by jerking the gun away from her chest and firing at him. It didn't matter if she hit them or not. He dived out of the way but so did the other two, the way she'd hoped. She shoved the warm gun into her pants and jumped at the branch, her feet hitting the tree trunk. She was a primate and hoped instinct gave her a strong ability to climb.

She scrambled faster than she'd thought possible, getting higher as her hands curled around the branches, moving as fast as she could. The bottoms of her feet burned a little from the rough bark but she didn't care. She was in a tree!

"Get down here," one of them yelled. "Fuck! Climb after her, Bob."

"She moves fast," he complained. "Damn, look how high she's going."

"I don't give a fuck," the first one snapped. "Go after her!"

"What is she? A monkey?"

"She kinda looks like a chimp," one of them stated. "Did you see her eyes and nose? She's small for a woman too."

She kept climbing until she couldn't get any higher without fear of the thinning branches snapping from her weight. The one she hugged swayed when the wind blew. A sick feeling gripped her stomach as she looked down. She had to be fifty or so feet in the air. All three men stared up at her.

"Get down!" The one in charge pointed a finger at her. "Right now! We don't have time for this."

"The chopper is incoming," Bob announced. "It's about to land."

She looked out to see if she could spot it but too many trees blocked her view even from that height. She listened and heard the noise then, probably too focused on the men to notice before. She turned her head and spotted it. It was flying low, just over the treetops, and coming closer.

She climbed down the trunk slightly until she sat on a lower limb and hugged it tightly, fearful they would try to snatch her from above. She glanced down, instantly sorry. Bob had started climbing after her.

She pulled out the gun, her belly aching from where she was sure she'd been burned from the warm barrel after firing it, and she aimed. He looked up and froze.

"Stay away from me."

"How many bullets are left?" The one in charge spoke softly but she heard.

"I don't know, Dillon." Bob answered. "She's discharged three but that's a Glock 9. I don't know how many were fired off before she stole it and it might have a big mag. Could be a lot left."

She frantically looked for an escape. The other trees were too far away to safely transfer. Some primates were known for jumping from branch to branch but she wasn't willing to risk falling to her death. Her hand shook slightly as she aimed the gun at the man drawing closer.

"I'll shoot you. Stop!"

He climbed to the other side of the wide trunk, out of sight. She shifted forward, trying to keep him in view. Thick branches protected him. She glanced around again, praying help would arrive.

It was as if Shadow heard her silent plea. He suddenly rushed out of the foliage behind the two on the ground. She watched in utter amazement as he grabbed both mercenaries by the backs of their necks, lifted, and threw them. One hit the dirt under the tree, while the second one wasn't so lucky. He slammed into the trunk. The enraged Species wasn't done.

He tore their weapons off them, flinging them into the river. The man in the dirt put up a struggle but one punch from Shadow kept him down. The one who'd hit the trunk recovered a lot slower. Shadow's head snapped up and their gazes caught and held for an instant before he looked at the third one in the tree. He howled.

Startled, Bob lost his hold on the tree and fell about ten feet into thick bushes. Shadow went after him, dragged the groaning man out by his boot and disarmed him. Guns and knives were tossed into the river. Beauty watched in rapt fascination as Shadow centered himself in the middle of the three mercenaries.

"You thought you could take her from me? Fight *me*. You are cowards for going after a small female. Lie there whimpering as you die. I. Don't. Care. I'll attack either way."

Beauty kept silent despite being tempted to warn the humans that fighting an enraged Species would be stupid. Shadow clearly wanted to beat on them and they complied when they attacked. Of course he left them with no choice, his threat to kill them as loud as his snarled words. They probably thought their three-to-one odds boded well against Shadow but he'd made certain they could only fight with their bodies. She lowered the gun, afraid it would accidently discharge and hit Shadow.

Her gaze ran over Shadow. He wasn't bleeding much. His arms and face had scratches but nothing serious that she could spot from her high perch. He moved as if he were unharmed as he dodged a fist aimed at his face and threw his own. She picked up a slight crunching noise before Bob screamed, stumbling back as blood poured from his smashed nose and mouth, landing hard on his ass.

Shadow's foot shot out as the leader of the mercenaries tried to come at him. The scream that came out of Dillon was horrifying when the heel slammed into his groin area. Beauty winced as the injured mercenary just dropped, rolling into a ball. Shadow wasn't fighting nice but he was inflicting pain. He showed no sympathy for his opponents. They had tried to kill two Species and had come to return her to a hellish existence.

The third man hesitated before he launched himself at Shadow's back. Shadow must have sensed it though and dodged, bent a little, and the guy landed in the dirt instead. Shadow came down on his torso, knees first, probably breaking his ribs in the process. Fists pummeled the human as the Species nailed him. Beauty glanced away but then forced her attention back. She wasn't weak stomached. Not anymore.

Bob tried to crawl to the river, probably attempting to escape. Shadow rose from his bloodied opponent and stomped on the back of Bob's leg. A snarl tore from his mouth as the fallen man screamed in agony, suffering a broken leg to match his nose. Shadow reached down, fisted his hair and said something she couldn't hear. Bob sobbed, begging for his life, but Shadow just slammed his head down hard into the earth.

"Beauty?" Shadow's head snapped upward. "Are you hurt?"

"I'm okay." Her voice came out shaky.

"Come down here. Can you do that or do you need me to climb to you?"

"I can do it." Her hands trembled slightly as she shoved the gun back into her waistband and began the descent. It was tougher than climbing up had been. It might have just seemed that way since blind panic no longer gripped her so she did it more slowly.

Shadow held utterly still until she reached the lowest branch and then both his arms rose. She bent forward enough for him to grip her hips. She braced her arms on his shoulders and fell into him. She had absolute trust he'd catch her and he did.

He hugged her so tightly it was hard to breathe. She didn't complain about that or him refusing to put her on her feet. They'd survived and he'd come after her. She'd been sure it wouldn't end so well.

"Look at me, love," he rasped.

She pulled her head back enough to see his face. Small cuts had left one cheek bloody, probably from flying glass inside the cabin when it had been torn apart by bullets. A gash was on his forehead was no longer bleeding, but blood smeared back into his hairline. He let go her waist with one arm and his finger gently touched her cheek.

"Ouch!" She flinched away.

Rage narrowed his eyes. "Who did this to you?"

"It's okay. I'm okay," she promised. She'd been hit before, lots of times. It wasn't anything serious. Now wasn't the time to mention that though. It would only incense Shadow to be reminded of the past abuse she'd suffered.

"Who struck you? Which one? Point him out." His voice came out animalistic and scary.

"I shot him in the thigh and ran away from him."

He studied the men on the ground before he eased her down and jerked his head in the direction she'd come from. "Go. You shouldn't see this."

"See what?" She was hesitant to let go of him and clung to his arms.

The muscles in his jaw clenched. "Go, Beauty."

He was going to kill them. It wasn't just an idle threat to scare them when he wanted the mercenaries to fight him hand to hand. He was seriously pissed and wanted more than blood.

"You don't have to do that. Arrest them. We have laws."

He stepped closer, peering down at her. "Go." His nose flared. "More Species are coming. You're safe. Just walk out of sight and wait for me."

She shook her head. "You could get into trouble if you kill them. Don't do this for me."

He took a deep, shuddering breath, possibly attempting to get control of his rage. "They came to steal you. A message has to be sent and I'm sending it. No one survives if they get near you. I never want this to happen again. The one who paid them might attempt to hire others but word will spread to mercenaries when these ones disappear. They will know death awaits them if they accept this job. Now go."

Shadow was willing to die and kill for her. That was the message he was giving her. Strong emotions welled inside Beauty, almost overwhelming her. Gratitude for the lengths he'd go to keep her safe, appreciation for the self-sacrifices he was willing to make because she didn't believe he could kill without care, but most of all, she felt love.

I'm in love with him, she realized. How it had happened so fast wasn't really a mystery. Attraction, trust, the laughs, the intense discussions they'd shared, and finally the physical bonding had united them in an intricate bond. She also realized she had a choice to make.

"Is this what you really feel you must do or are you just doing it for me?"

"Both."

"Will you sleep better at night knowing they are dead or lie awake being haunted by more blood on your hands?"

Her question seemed to surprise him by his expression.

"I don't want you to kill them if you're going to suffer for it. They aren't worth that. I know Justice will never allow them to go free." She licked her lips, searching for the right words. "I don't want you to look at me and remember death. Don't do that to us."

His head snapped up to peer at something behind her. She followed his gaze and barely suppressed a gasp. Two huge Species had stepped out of the woods, both only wearing loincloths. Their faces were typical of Wild Zone residents. There was no mistaking the more animal-like features they had or the untamed look in their striking eyes.

"The others are dead," one of them rasped. He stared at Beauty with open curiosity but then shifted his gaze up. "These are the only ones left except for the shot one on the ground with Torrent."

"What about the helicopter?"

A big man wearing cut-off shorts stepped out of the woods. His catlike eyes were stunning and so was his unusual nose, a trait he must have inherited from the lion or other large feline genes with which he'd been infused. He waved his hands at the other two, indicating they should go back into the thick trees. They disappeared without a word.

"I'm Leo." He smiled at Beauty. "I'm glad you're safe." His focus fixed on Shadow. "Officers dragged the two humans out of the loud flying vehicle and have them on the ground. Torrent sent me after you to see if you needed help." He bent, grabbing one of the mercenaries by his hair. "Come on, human. Fight and I will hurt you more." He growled low, a terrifying warning. "The officers want you." He grabbed the other mercenary still curled into a ball from being kicked in the nuts. "You too, whiner. Walk or be dragged."

Relief washed through Beauty. It seemed Shadow wouldn't have to kill for her after all. The decision had been taken out of his hands, something she was grateful for. There had been enough bloodshed during his lifetime, in her opinion, and she didn't want to be the reason to add more.

An emotion that closely resembled disappointment flashed across his handsome features before he sighed. "Walk ahead of me but stay in sight. I smell a lot of the residents nearby. I'll take this one and Justice can decide his fate."

"Thank you."

She watched silently as Shadow grabbed the man and hoisted him up roughly. The human moaned in pain but he was alive. He might regret that once he faced their laws. New Species had no mercy for enemies. She walked, keeping close to Shadow.

There was no fear when she noticed a few solitary figures in the woods. They were Wild Zone residents who'd come to help. She smiled at a few of them in thanks, but they kept their distance. Some of their features were shocking, more animal than human. Her heart went out to them. It would be tough for them to fit in at Homeland and the reason for Reservation became apparent.

The first glimpse of the cabin made Beauty's knees go weak. The entire first level was bullet-ridden, all the windows shot out, and holes of various sizes were ugly reminders of the attack. It stunned her that the structure didn't just collapse. Part of the deck had been blown apart, probably from a grenade. She halted in her tracks, not even aware of doing it or the fact that over a dozen Species milled in the yard.

Breeze walked out of the broken front door, helped by a tall Species. Blood soaked her shirt and pants along one side, the red stain bright. She'd been shot or stabbed to cause that wound.

"Oh no." Tears blinded Beauty.

"I'm fine," Breeze swore firmly, hearing her. "It is just a graze."

The man helping her walk growled in response. "That would imply you don't have a hole going through you. Shut up and allow me to carry you to the Jeep."

"No. You shut up." Breeze punched him in the side where they were touching, one of his arms around her waist. It wasn't a hard hit, more of a playful tag with her fist. Her smile appeared forced though. "It's not bad at all, Beauty. You look about to faint. Don't. It's just a scratch."

Something fell heavily to the ground with a grunt and Beauty jumped, jerking her head in that direction. Shadow had dumped the mercenary he'd been carrying and stepped closer, anger still etched on his face. He reached her in long strides and wiped the blood from his hands onto his sweats before clasping her hips.

"I've got you. Climb up me and I'll carry you."

She glanced around at all the Species men silently watching them. They seemed fascinated to see what she'd do. Shadow lifted her without any further warning and she ended up plastered against his chest. He adjusted his hold to cradle her in his arms but she didn't protest.

There was nowhere else she'd rather be. His chin rested on the top of her head. "You're safe. It's going to be fine."

She hoped he was right. Her gaze drifted back to the destroyed cabin and she inwardly winced. *Some vacation.* She had a bad feeling it was over and her time with Shadow might come to an end too. Her arms wound around his neck, holding him tightly. She didn't ever want to let go.

Chapter Eighteen

Medical had turned into a buzz of activity since Shadow had left the day before. Officers were grimly waiting to be seen by the overworked staff. Shadow carried Beauty inside, walked to the front counter, and growled at the human male nurse behind it.

"She was hit and needs to be seen."

"Take a number," the harried male sighed, glancing at Beauty. "She looks okay to me besides the bruise. Both doctors are really busy right now. They are patching up those mercenaries and we have injured officers."

Shadow snarled. "She's more important than the humans who attacked us."

The nurse's eyes widened as he stepped back. "I understand and agree with you but we're in triage mode. It means the most critical are seen first."

Another male walked up behind the counter, a Species wearing blue scrubs, and waited for Shadow to meet his gaze. "I'm Destiny. I was just transferred here from Homeland." He glanced at Beauty. "Hi, Beauty. Are you okay?"

She nodded. It alarmed Shadow a little that the male knew her name. He didn't like it and stepped back when the other male attempted to touch her. He snarled in warning, daring him to attempt it again.

Destiny raised his hands, palms showing. "Easy. I'm a nurse. I trained at Homeland and I'm familiar with all the females, her included. I just wanted to move Beauty's hair away from her cheek to see the damage. The doctors are busy but I could examine her."

Shadow debated it. "I want a doctor. Tell one of them to stop working on a human to tend to her. She's a priority."

"I agree." Destiny lowered his hands to his side.

"I'm okay," Beauty protested.

"Silence," Shadow ordered softly. "Get a doctor, Destiny. She was struck in the face by a human with a closed fist. Her bones are fragile and there's swelling. He might have broken something."

"I'm sure I'm okay," she whispered. "It's fine, Shadow. I can wait. I smell a lot of blood in here."

"That's true. We had a Species shot with a tranquilizer dart and then some of the protesters decided to take advantage of the confusion. They threw bottles and rocks at the officers. A few were hit." Destiny stepped closer. "One of the Wild Zone residents was shot and he's in surgery."

"Clear a hole! I brought two medics to help," a male shouted as the doors were shoved open behind him. Shadow knew that voice and turned his head, surprised to watch some of the task force members enter the building. "Go help," Tim Oberto ordered two task force members. "Do whatever you can."

Shadow swung back around and nodded at Destiny. "Take us to a room." He made sure he didn't bump into anyone while he got Beauty away from all humans. They frightened her and she'd been exposed enough to them. The task force posed a danger right now since a traitor was amongst them.

He ducked his head, hoping to avoid his old boss for the moment. Destiny led them down a hallway to an empty exam room. Shadow glanced around and gently settled Beauty on the bed. He released her and marched to the attached bathroom, making sure no one hid inside. It was clear and he approached Beauty again.

"Do you feel safe with this male?" He indicated the Species nurse.

She nodded. "Yes. I know him. I get regular checkups and he's there often."

He spun around to glare at the male. "You protect her. Don't leave her side. Do you understand? Anything happens to her and you'll die a slow and painful death. I have to go talk to someone but I'll hurry back."

Destiny calmly regarded him. "Everything I'll need is in this room. She'll be safe."

It angered Shadow to have to trust someone he didn't know but he had little choice unless he brought Tim into the room. Beauty had been traumatized enough. "She better be." He left the room, closing the door behind him.

It was easy to find the human task force leader. He stood on a chair in reception, barking out orders to more of the task force on scene. "Sit down, damn it, if you're bleeding." Tim pointed to Mark, one of his team. "Go grab bandages and wet rags. Clean some of them up so it's easier for the medical staff to assess them." He pointed to another member. "Cory, man the damn phones. That incessant ringing is giving me a headache."

Shadow paused behind Tim and growled. The male turned his head and peered down at him. "Shadow. I'm glad you're here. You look banged up, but good. Go to Security and give them a report. We have a second team arriving in ten minutes but we need to know what happened. We're holding an emergency briefing as soon as the helicopter lands."

"The human piece of shit who once held Beauty prisoner hired mercenaries to steal her." He stepped around the chair to face the male. "Someone on the team gave them access to my emergency transmitter."

Tim paled. "What?"

"They knew about my coin and that's how they located the cabin." He wanted to howl in rage. "They admitted it, before you ask how I'm certain. Bragged about it. Someone betrayed me."

Tim stepped off the chair. "Shit." He grabbed his cell phone, dialing. "Someone betrayed all of us but I'm on it. I'll have the son of a bitch by his balls before he can say 'fucked'."

"I want his head," Shadow demanded.

Tim nodded grimly. "Patch me through to Trey, private headset," he ordered whomever he spoke to. He put his hand over the phone. "I'm on with one of the pilots of the helicopter. There're only two possible suspects. I'm going to have Trey arrest them until we can narrow down which one of them it was. They are assigned to his team today."

"How do you know you can trust Trey? I know he has the access codes."

Tim snorted, some of his anger fading from his features. "That boy is the son I never had and he's as loyal as they come. I once thought he'd be good married to my daughter so I checked him out. But then she met Brawn. It wasn't Trey who sold you out. I'd bet my pension on it."

Shadow wasn't sure what a pension was but he did trust Tim. The male wasn't likeable at all times but he had honor. He took pride in his work and his team. His daughter was also mated to a council member. He'd privately shown pictures to his Species team members of his grandson, Kismet. The love he felt for the child was always apparent. Tim would never betray his extended family—the Species.

"Trey!" Tim covered his other ear to hear better. "We have a situation. Glance around and signal all the men on your team to remove their headsets right now just in case the pilot forgot to make this a private conversation." He paused. "They all down?" He paused again. "Good. Just listen to me. Shadow's emergency tracker was activated and that's how those bastards who attacked Reservation found the Gift. You understand what that means. It wasn't me or you so we know who is left. Arrest them both the moment you land and haul their asses to Security. We'll figure it out later but I'll be damned if we're screwed a second time." He held Shadow's gaze while he quietly listened to the response, nodded and hung up. "Trey is on it. He's pissed."

"So am I."

Tim shoved his phone inside his pocket. "We'll figure out which one of them it was."

"I want to be there."

Tim hesitated. "Let's figure out who it is first and then I'll personally leave you alone in the room with the son of a bitch." He glanced around and lowered his voice. "Do you know how many times I wanted to tell the other guys on the team about my grandson but wasn't allowed to? Thank

God." He clenched his teeth. "He could have sold that information as well. I thought the NSO was being paranoid by not allowing humans to know but they weren't." He shoved his fists on his hips. "Just leave enough of him intact for me to get a piece."

Shadow wasn't about to make promises he wasn't sure he could keep. "I need to return to Beauty. This information couldn't wait. I know you've got it under control right now."

"You need to get to Security for debriefing. You were on scene."

"The mercenaries were hired by the wealthy human who bought Beauty from Mercile. Find him to make sure he's never able to attempt it again. She needs me." He stomped away before Tim could respond.

Beauty and Destiny both turned when he entered the room. The male stood too close to her but he just held an ice pack to her injured cheek. He glanced around, sniffed, and knew no one else had entered the room while he'd been gone.

"Thank you for protecting her." He nodded at the nurse. "How is she?"

"Nothing seems broken and she's not exhibiting any symptoms of a concussion. I've ordered a scan to make certain though. She's Gift. It's better to be safe than sorry. Her bones aren't as dense as our other females'. I was going to take her as soon as you returned. Is it all right to move your female now?"

Shadow inched around him and scooped Beauty into his arms. He liked that the male knew who she belonged to. "Lead the way."

"I can walk," she muttered.

"I know you can." He just didn't want her to. She still appeared a little pale and she'd been through a lot. "Let me care for you." As if he'd give her a choice but it was polite to at least allow her to think she had one.

"Thanks, Shadow." Her uninjured cheek nuzzled the wall of his chest as she rested her head there, her arms wrapping around his shoulders.

Destiny opened the door wide and he followed the nurse farther down the hall to whatever tests would assure them Beauty had no serious damage. Shadow stewed, wanting to go to Security to personally show his displeasure at one of his fellow task force members but that would mean leaving her.

Beauty was his first priority.

* * * * *

Beauty didn't complain as she waited for Destiny to return. Shadow hovered at her side and she was grateful. He'd even demanded food to be brought to her while they'd waited for the results. Her stomach was full.

"I was told the scans were clear," the nurse stated when he walked back into the room. "You're fine. Not even a fracture and the bruise only makes you prettier." He winked and smiled.

Shadow snarled. "Don't flirt."

"It's called having a good bedside manner." Destiny stiffened. "I wanted her to smile by giving her a compliment. I'm not offering to share sex with your female. Do you think I'm blind or my nose isn't working? Your scent is all over her and your name is very accurate at the moment."

Beauty frowned. "His name is accurate?"

310

"He's your 'Shadow'." Destiny suddenly chuckled. "That was a good one, wasn't it? He's right next to you."

She smiled. "Thank you for caring for me."

Shadow growled again, drawing her gaze.

"What?" She didn't know why he looked angry.

"It's his job to treat you. I am taking care of you."

"Okay." She began to wonder if Shadow was more hurt than he'd let on. He was unusually irritable and perhaps a bit irrational to make such a slight distinction. "Will you allow Destiny to look at your cuts? I'd feel better. You don't want me to worry about you, do you? I will."

"I'm fine." His stubborn streak reared its head. "None of my injuries require his assistance."

"He is fine," Destiny agreed. "I've been eyeing his wounds and the way he's moving. He's got some bruising but the cuts aren't bad. Just disinfect them the first chance you get and slap some bandages on the worst ones. We fight infection easily but why take the chance?" He turned, opened a cupboard and removed a small box. "Here. It's a mini med kit. It's got everything you'll need."

"Thank you."

The door opened behind them and a human walked in. She remembered him from when she was rescued. Beauty tensed until Shadow stepped between them. His body completely shielded her from the sight of the other man.

"I wanted you to know both suspects are being detained and AI is all over their bank accounts, phone records, and tracking their movements for the past twenty-four hours. We'll figure out which one it is."

"Thank you, Tim." Shadow softly growled. "I still want his head."

"I have a feeling there isn't going to be much of this ass left by the time he's taken apart by our team. He broke the code. Never screw over your brothers. We're sending one of the helicopters back to Homeland. Justice called and wants you to escort the Gift back. She's too exposed here and I have to agree. She needs tighter security."

"Understood."

"Blades up in twenty. I'll have a few of the guys cover you there."

"I'll have officers drive us."

The man hesitated. "Just because we had one bad apple doesn't screw the entire pie, Shadow. I don't want this to sour you on the task force."

"I trust the team but I know the officers wish to speak to me. It will give them the opportunity."

"Sure."

Shadow shook the man's hand and Tim left. He grimly regarded her. "Let's go. I have to give a debriefing before we meet that helicopter."

"So we are going back to Homeland." She didn't really need to say the words but it was better than what she really wanted to blurt out. What was that going to do to their budding relationship?

"We are. You're safer there. There's too much open land here for them to breach and miles of walls that they obviously were able to sneak across."

A knock sounded at the door and it opened, admitting Jaded, the council member. He glanced at Beauty and jerked his thumb at Destiny to leave before addressing Shadow. "You look good after what you suffered."

Jaded kept by the door while he spoke, far from her. She did notice that Shadow didn't step between them. He must trust him.

"Thank you."

Bright-green, catlike eyes narrowed. "Great job. Breeze will be fine. The female is too stubborn to be harmed enough to keep her down for more than a few hours while she undergoes the cleaning of the wound and stitches. She's already made one of the Drs. Harris threaten to quit." He chuckled. "It was the younger one. He'll learn to be as grouchy as his father when dealing with us. Self-defense."

"I'm glad to hear she will be well."

Beauty was too. She kept silent though, not comfortable with someone she didn't know.

"Justice wants a full report when you land at Homeland. You're to take Beauty home. The task force is giving you a lift in about twenty minutes. They have both their helicopters here."

"Tim just told me."

Jaded hesitated, glanced at Beauty and cleared his throat. "Perhaps we should speak in the hall."

Shadow didn't budge. "What is it? Do you no longer trust the team? I know those males. It would be rare for one to betray the others. My faith isn't shaken."

"That's not it." Jaded lifted a hand and ran tan fingers through his short black hair. "We have a problem. Moon was hit by a sniper with a tranquilizer dart."

"Torrent informed me. I was with him when he got the call."

"We believed it was just a distraction to draw our officers toward the front gates so they could gain access to the Wild Zone. But he woke feral. It wasn't a sleeping drug he was exposed to. I'm certain they shot him for that purpose but the result is much worse."

Beauty didn't like the uncomfortable silence that suddenly blanketed the room. "What does that mean?"

Jaded actually looked at her for more than a few seconds before glancing at Shadow. "Are you sure you don't want to take this away from her? It might be upsetting."

"I'm not leaving her alone." Shadow crossed his arms over his chest. "She's stronger than you know. She was almost killed, yet she's calm."

"Understood." Jaded stepped closer, lowering his voice. "Moon is completely feral. He doesn't know us, won't or can't speak and is exhibiting violent behavior to the extreme. The older Dr. Harris ran blood tests after six of our males had to restrain Moon when he attempted to kill them. It will take time to get official results but some of our males sniffed the dart to compare against known drugs. Our senses are faster than running them through machines to identify. The drug is unknown to any of us." His gaze drifted to Beauty, then back. "There's a connection between Douglas Miller and Mercile. They may be working together on this. Who else could come up with a drug that could do something that would send one of ours into a

314

murderous rage? Mercile is the only one who could pull this off with their knowledge of our biology. Moon is one of our most easygoing males. I know him well but that's a stranger I faced inside his room. Complete and total personality reversal."

Shadow's fists clenched at his side. "That would mean this was planned far in advance. They must have been working on a drug that would harm us."

"Or they already possessed it but none of our surviving people ever experienced it."

"There is a Mercile doctor involved in this."

"That's what we're assuming at this point. Douglas Miller may have been waiting for an opportunity. He has the money to support the employees still running from us. I pulled the file on Miller and while we were able to have his accounts frozen in this country, he had vast holdings outside the reach of the US. The bastard even had a human working for him inside the task force headquarters to monitor all movement. Some humans are vindictive. He may have set this into motion as soon as he realized we'd taken back what he held. He finally saw his chance to retrieve…what he wants."

"Who is Douglas Miller?" Beauty was trying to follow their conversation. "What does he want? Is he one of the owners of Mercile?"

Shadow turned and stepped closer, peering into her eyes. His hand was warm when he gently cupped her cheek on the side that wasn't bruised. "Douglas Miller is the human who imprisoned you."

315

Master. It was an emotional slap but she kept her chin up, resisting curling into a ball to protect herself from the pain washing through her system. Not once had she asked to learn more about the human who'd reared and kept her. Getting beyond what had been done to her seemed more important than focusing on the details of who and why.

The conversation between Shadow and the council member suddenly made horrifying sense. She was glad to be sitting down. Shadow softly growled, his thumb stroking her skin in comfort.

"This isn't your fault."

"It is in a way. He is after me. He wants me returned." She pulled away from his touch to lean to the side enough to see Jaded behind him. "You think this…" she had to pause and swallow down the bile that rose. She couldn't get his real name past her lips. "Bastard is working with Mercile to hurt Species in revenge for my rescue?"

Jaded hesitated, glancing at Shadow.

Shadow stepped to her side. "Tell her the truth. She deserves that."

Beauty was grateful for his support and almost reached over to take the hand he'd lowered to his side. She resisted, afraid to look weaker in the eyes of the council member than he probably assumed she was. "Please tell me."

"Mercile is broke and the employees who fled are too. We cut off their money and seized everything they owned with the help of the president. Douglas Miller had a lot of money in foreign countries that we couldn't touch. He's a wanted man who can't return to the States or any country that would extradite him." Sympathy softened Jaded's features. "We know

316

he hired the humans to come after you and we do believe he's responsible for Moon's unstable condition."

Jaded took a deep breath, exhaling slowly. "In no way is this your fault. It's just tied together. Miller and some of the Mercile doctors must be working together to achieve similar goals. He's got the money to hide and help them if he wishes. Mercile made a previous attempt against one of our males with a drug they hoped would make him commit murder. It would have backed their stance that we're dangerous and don't deserve human rights if Fury had murdered his human mate. It would have been a major victory to sway world opinion that they were justified in using Species as laboratory rats for their experiments."

Shadow drew her attention. "A human nurse was assigned to Fury after he was shot in an assassination attempt by other humans against his mate. The drug she exposed him to made him aggressive and violent." He looked at Jaded. "Was it the same drug?"

"Not according to the sniff test. It's something else that appears far worse than the symptoms Fury suffered. Moon is completely violent and unresponsive to anyone or anything. He's either in so much pain he is beyond thought or they damaged his mind so extensively that his personality has devolved to basic survival of his animal genetics. That's what we're assessing right now but it's early. There's always hope the drug will wear off the way it did in Fury's case. We've sent for specialists. They will be arriving within the next few hours."

Guilt ate at Beauty. "Why couldn't he have just died?"

317

Jaded's green eyes flashed anger. "Moon is my friend. I hate to see him this way but I'm grateful he survived."

"I meant the bastard. Not your friend." She suddenly wished she were alone with Shadow. "He got sick and he's old. That's what I meant. This would be over if he had died. He wouldn't be around to come after me or hurt our people."

She didn't mention aloud that she wouldn't be alive either if he had died while she'd been his prisoner. The guards wouldn't have had anyone to stop them from hurting her any way they wished. They would have destroyed the evidence and burned her body to ash, the way she'd overheard them plotting at times.

"I understand." Jaded calmed. "Some humans wish to hurt us anyway. They are afraid of us or refuse to accept what we are. Don't take this personally. If it wasn't Douglas Miller, it would be someone else."

He spoke to Shadow next. "I'll leave now. I wanted you informed of all we know so far. We'll have more solid facts by the time you reach Homeland to meet with Justice." His catlike eyes turned to Beauty. "I meant what I said. This isn't your fault. We're different and sometimes that's reason enough to draw hatred from others. You are in no way responsible for Douglas Miller or his actions."

She was left alone with Shadow. Tears threatened to spill but she fought them back. "I do feel guilty."

"You shouldn't." He brushed his fingertips over her arm, caressing lightly.

"You and Breeze were hurt protecting me. Other Species were hurt. I saw all those men out there in need of medical help."

"Most of the injured were mercenaries." He smiled in an attempt at humor.

The effort didn't work. "Don't make light of this. Please?" She reached out, his chest warm and firm under her palm. It soothed her, just touching any part of his body. "You seemed to already know his name. How?"

"Douglas Miller?"

She nodded.

"I had to review all the files when I was assigned to the task force. He is a fugitive, one of the many we plan to hunt down and capture. I reviewed the files of humans we'd retrieved Gift Females from after you told me your story. The task force doesn't put the names of victims in those files but the clues you gave were enough to pinpoint him and the details of the operation that rescued you. That's how I know what happened with Fury and Ellie as well. They keep the team up to speed on unclosed cases. The human nurse had outside help and we were still tracking down some of her known associates from Mercile."

"Fury was not permanently damaged by the drug. I see him all the time with Ellie. He'd never hurt her." It made her feel hope for Moon. "Their love is beautiful."

Shadow glanced at the clock. "We need to go, love. The helicopter will leave soon."

"Okay."

"It will be fine."

319

She hoped so.

Chapter Nineteen

Beauty's worst-case scenario happened. She wished a hole would open up under her and make her disappear when they reached the helicopter landing area. The tall task force member she spotted spoke to another one but then Shane turned his head. Recognition flared across his features as he smiled.

No, she silently begged, dropping her gaze. *Don't try to talk to me. Please!*

She glanced at the ground, her hands, even her shirt. Shadow had gone to speak to the pilot, leaving her standing alone. Military boots approached until they stopped about four feet away. She knew it was Shane. Her heart did a panicked number inside her chest.

"Beauty? Wow! You look fantastic. Well, except for the bruise on your face."

She had to look up but dreaded it. The lump inside her throat felt large but she had to speak. Otherwise he'd probably pity her after the trauma she'd suffered. It was important to show him that she wasn't the terrified, frail woman he'd helped save. Her gaze lifted to stare up at a face she'd wished to never see again.

"Hello, Shane."

"You remembered my name?" Color flushed his cheeks. "That means a lot to me. We always hope it's a two-way street but it's so traumatic when we go in. We kind of figure we're just a blur of memory."

321

"I don't understand."

"You know, every Species we free is a triumph to us. Giving someone their life back makes this job worth all the bad stuff we deal with. We remember every one but we aren't sure if the ones rescued remember us."

She wished she could forget at least one part of that awful night. "It's something we always remember too."

His gaze swept up and down her body. "You really look good." He blushed more. "I don't mean that the way it sounds. I just meant you're healthy now. You've put on some weight. Not that I'm saying you're fat or anything." He rushed his words. "Dang. My sisters would kick my butt. I'm putting my foot in my mouth. I'm just saying you look good and healthy. Perfect. Yeah. Okay, I'm done. Taking foot out of mouth."

She almost laughed. He seemed more nervous than she was and it made her relax a little. A smile played at her lips. "I didn't take offense. I knew what you meant. It's amazing what some food and baths will do to make someone look better."

"Yeah. You were so thin." He grew serious. "You doing good? I mean, besides what happened here? We all know about the mercenaries coming in to grab you. Are you happy at the NSO and are they taking good care of you?"

"I am and they are." She swallowed. "Um, there's something I need to say."

He shifted his stance. "Sure. Okay."

It took a few seconds to work up the courage but she did it. "I'm really sorry for, um, you know…" She tried to say it but failed to get all the words out. "For what I did or tried to do the night…" *I made a fool of myself when I almost begged you to have sex with me, thinking you'd be a better master and protect me from my old one.*

He blushed again and glanced down before meeting her gaze. "I don't know what you're talking about. You have nothing to be sorry about." Understanding shone in his gaze though. "Nothing at all. I don't even know what you're referring to."

Tears threatened to spill. He was being so nice to her. She blinked rapidly. Maybe apologizing to him would stop the nightmares. At the very least she could earn her dignity back. "I didn't know any better but I do now. Thank you for what you did that night and for protecting me from my own ignorance. You could have taken advantage but you didn't."

He slowly touched her arm, carefully watching her first to make sure she didn't flinch away. His warm fingers gently squeezed her upper arm. "Hey, no worries. It was an honest mistake after all you'd been through and you have nothing to apologize for." He nodded. "Ever. Okay? I'm just glad we got you out of there and I'm sorry I stuck you with a needle. I felt bad about that."

"You had no choice. I freaked out. It was the right thing to do."

"Thanks."

"Get your hand off her," Shadow snarled.

Beauty spun and was barely able to jump into his path as he attempted to lunge at Shane. She feared he'd just plow her over in his haste to attack the other man. His face twisted in a mask of rage. If the scary tone of his voice wasn't clue enough of his intent, the fangs he revealed in threat were.

323

"Stop!"

"Shane was touching you." Shadow didn't even glance at her, instead he continued to glare at the task force member. "You don't do that," he warned, no longer speaking to her. "I'll rip your hand off and feed it to you."

Beauty gently pushed at his broad chest, attempting to get him to step back. "Shadow! Stop it!"

He looked down then. "He isn't allowed to touch you. He was!"

"This is the man who protected me from the sniper bullets the night I was freed."

Shadow's head snapped up and he snarled, trying to reach his target again. Beauty got dragged and might have fallen over if she hadn't been gripping him so tightly. He stopped trying to walk forward when he couldn't get free without hurting her. She knew Shadow remembered her shameful story about what she'd done to Shane that night. The angry Species seemed intent on beating Shane.

"Shadow!" She used her sternest voice.

"What?" he snarled, his eyes narrowing on her.

"Calm down." Her tone softened. "We were talking until you rudely interrupted. I was apologizing for mistaking his intentions and he was graciously not allowing me to take any blame. He was just comforting me. It wasn't how you think."

Shadow blinked and some of the anger faded. "He shouldn't touch you." He glared at Shane. "Tim would have your ass for breaking the rules."

Her hands loosened their death grip on him. "There was nothing inappropriate about it."

He studied her carefully. "Fine. The helicopter is preparing for takeoff." He shot a warning glare directed at Shane. "I will be right there." He paused. "Watching you not touch her again."

She let him go and he spun away, walked about ten feet and turned. Arms crossed across his massive chest as he glared at Shane. He was seriously going to watch them. She hesitated before turning. Shane had paled considerably over the confrontation and had retreated enough to put a lot of space between them.

"He's protective." She kept her voice low. "Thank you."

"No problem. Maybe I should take the next flight." He took another step back, darting a nervous look at Shadow. "I was going to ride back to Homeland on the helicopter with my unit but a drive sounds nice. I'm sure there's a rental car place in town."

"It's fine. You shouldn't have to go to that trouble." She glanced back to find Shadow still regarding them angrily. "Stop it. Tell him he can share the helicopter."

He hesitated but then shrugged. "Fine. You sit on the other side, not near her."

"You got it, Shadow." Shane rushed past. "Nice seeing you again, Beauty."

Beauty watched the task force member scurry away, giving a wide berth to the angry Species. She wasn't sure if she should be irritated or flattered that Shadow was so protective. It had distracted her from her embarrassment with Shane. Shadow uncrossed his arms, approaching her.

"Let's go. I put our bags in the helicopter. Officers retrieved them from the cabin. They are ready to leave."

"Are you okay?"

He blinked.

"Shadow? It was innocent."

"I don't like anyone touching you."

He was a man. *Male,* she corrected. Species weren't exactly typical of regular men. Breeze had warned her Species could be possessive. She was beginning to understand that now. Shadow really would have attacked Shane if she hadn't gotten in his way.

"I understand. I'll try to remember that if there's a next time. It's not as though too many men are around me."

Another task force member joined them. Beauty recognized him and smiled. Trey Roberts grinned as he clasped Shadow's shoulder. "I'm glad you're still alive, buddy. I heard you did some serious ass kicking. I bet you don't hate me now nearly as much for all that gun-range practice I put you through."

Shadow's attitude changed as he grinned. "No. I still resent the hours you yelled at me but I know I needed it." He reached out, hooked a hand around Beauty's waist and pulled her into a protective position against his side. "This is Beauty."

Trey glanced between them. "We've met. It's nice to see you again, Beauty." He put his hands on his hips. "I was there when she was rescued. Are you ready to come back yet, Shadow? The team misses you. I know you said you'd return by the end of next week but we sure could use you now."

Beauty heard the words and pain jabbed at her heart. *He's going back to the task force?* Her gaze jerked to Shadow's face but he was still smiling at his friend. *Tell him no*, she silently urged. She couldn't lose him. He'd lived off Homeland when he'd worked with the task force. It would mean she'd never get to see him, or very rarely.

"I promised Wrath I'd spend some time at Homeland." Shadow shrugged. "He thinks we need to connect with our people. It's been good getting to know them and living with my kind."

More pain shot through her heart. He hadn't mentioned her at all. Did that mean she wasn't important to him? Her focus dropped to the ground in case he glanced at her. She didn't want him to see how his words hurt.

"Well, we miss you." Trey released his hold, stepping back. "We got some new toys that I think you'll like. I bet you miss the action."

"It is a slower pace at Homeland."

Trey laughed. "I heard they put you on patrol in the interior. I bet that gets boring. Species don't cause too much trouble. They should have you assigned to the gates where the action happens."

"Fury decided I would appreciate not having to deal with humans after living amongst them."

"Yeah, we're annoying bastards, aren't we?" Trey chuckled and patted Shadow's shoulder again as Beauty glanced up. "Come back soon. We had some upgrades done to the living quarters. I think you'll really love the new digs. The bedrooms were enlarged and so were the bathrooms. I want to move in, they look so good. Tim even added in new big-screen TVs and put in fridges next to them so you don't have to walk to the kitchen to get your soda fix."

"That sounds nice."

Too nice, she concluded. Worry nagged at her that their relationship was over before it had really gotten started. They were having sex together. Didn't that mean something to Shadow? It was a commitment to her but he might not see it that way. It would break her heart if he just walked away.

"Tim felt bad about Lauren having to live in such rough quarters. You know his daughter is mated to a Species." Trey glanced away and waved to someone. "It's time to go. Load up and call me tomorrow to tell me when you're coming back. It can't be soon enough. Your replacement is kind of driving me nuts. Thank God it's only temporary. He growls too often, not understanding I'm riding his ass for his own good."

"Feline? They don't take orders well."

"Nope. He's canine." Trey walked away.

"Let's go." Shadow tugged on her waist.

She willingly went with him, her mind in a tailspin. What would it mean if he went back to work for the task force? The end of them seeing each other? Would he possibly invite her to live with him off Homeland? The concept left her feeling cold inside. There was no way she could live around a bunch of humans and feel safe after the life she'd led. She trusted Species men but could she ever relax around the men Shadow worked with? She highly doubted it. One of them had already betrayed the NSO.

Shadow would leave her alone inside his quarters while he worked. Fear gripped her just considering how anyone on the team would have access to her at the task force headquarters. They could be similar to the guards who'd once tormented her. Shadow would end up killing someone if that happened. He hadn't even liked Shane touching her arm. He'd really go insane if someone approached her for sex.

There would be no other women around to keep her company. There would be no protective Species to make certain no one bothered her. As much as it sometimes annoyed her, those women were also comforting. She'd lose access to her friends. It wouldn't just be a short trip to Reservation to stay in a cabin if she lived with Shadow. Her uneasiness increased. There was no way possible that she could leave NSO lands.

The helicopter was loud and a bit scary as Shadow swept her into his arms and settled her inside. Some of the team was already seated but they kept to one side of the interior. Shadow followed her in, had to duck his head, and guided her to a seat. She allowed him to belt her in while he settled down next to her until they were hip to hip, thigh to thigh. He put his arm around her, drawing her close.

She felt safe within the circle of his hold. Shadow always had a way of settling her fear. They'd need to talk about what he planned to do about the task force. It was impossible to discuss the subject in the helicopter. She'd have to wait until they were alone. Beauty decided it was probably going to be the longest ride of her life. Her eyes closed as she leaned against

Shadow, holding on to him, afraid their time together might come to an end soon.

I love Shadow and losing him is going to rip me apart, she admitted, fighting back tears.

Shadow knew something was wrong. Beauty's fingers dug into his arm through the shirt he'd tugged on after Trey had tossed him a spare. He held her tighter when she turned into him. Flying might terrify her, something he could relate to since he didn't enjoy it either. He'd had to adjust while working with the task force as flights were part of the job.

His friends on the team seemed threatening suddenly. They wouldn't harm Beauty. The reasonable part of his mind knew that but his protective instincts were kicking him in the ass. The men were too close and the scent of her fear drove him a little insane. He resisted glaring and snarling at them. A few smiled when he caught their gazes, while making sure they didn't pose any danger to Beauty. He forced his lips to curve but kept them closed, hiding his sharp canines. It wasn't their fault she was afraid of males.

He hadn't liked Shane touching Beauty but believed it had been innocent. Of course it had taken him time to control his anger. His teammate was easygoing and spoke well of females. He had a lot of sisters he talked about often. Shadow had viewed hundreds of photos of them— the male was proud of his family. Shane wasn't a threat to Beauty.

He inhaled, the sweetness of her fear a little diluted. Trey caught his attention, a reminder that he was expected to return to the task force. That would mean leaving the female he held. They hadn't known each other long but he couldn't imagine just walking away. They'd agreed to share sex and she only wanted him but he wasn't certain how long she wanted him around. He'd hate to lose his position with the task force if she planned to tell him to get lost soon. He was feeling deep emotions where she was concerned and they were only growing stronger. They needed to talk.

First though, he'd have to meet with Justice and the other Species males. Douglas Miller still posed a threat to Beauty. It wasn't acceptable, having him out there plotting more attempts to harm Species while the son of a bitch tried to recapture Beauty.

She'd be safest inside the women's dorm while he attended those meetings. It was situated almost at the center of Homeland and they'd corrected flaws in the building design after a previous attack. He'd demand a team of females be assigned to guard her around the clock too.

As much as he didn't want to leave Beauty, he needed to. He wanted a say in what was going to happen to keep her safe. He could be of more use working with the task force to eliminate the threat than holding Beauty's hand. He'd even have to sideline his plans to go after the member of the team who'd given the mercenaries his location to help them get to the Gift. The male would die for his betrayal and for putting Beauty at risk of being returned to her abuser.

They'd have to work out their relationship after the danger passed. He only hoped she'd want him to be part of her life. Giving her up would be nearly impossible. Everything inside him ached in a bad way at the prospect of saying goodbye. Their time together had been short so far but he hoped to change that into something permanent.

Mate. That one word did odd things to his heart. It beat erratically and he realized how much he wanted her to always be his. They'd sleep together every night and he'd wake to her in his arms. No uncertainty was present as he searched his feelings. He wanted that, with her. They would grow closer and he'd experience the happiness Wrath had discovered with Lauren.

Beauty snuggled tighter against his chest and he adjusted his body to make her more comfortable. She felt right in his arms and perfectly fit there. It was where she belonged. He smiled, his gaze studying the males again for any sign of a threat.

Trey winked, smiling but Shadow recognized the longing reflected in the male's eyes. He'd felt it himself when he'd watched Wrath with Lauren. It was the heartfelt desire to have a deep bond with a female. Wrath had been lucky to find that and now Shadow had Beauty. He wasn't going to push her away ever again because of fear caused by the damage he'd once suffered. He wouldn't allow his past to ruin his chance at having a future.

He would have to speak to Slade, Fury and Justice about living arrangements if Beauty agreed to be his mate. They couldn't very well live in the dorms. They'd need their own space. Perhaps they could be assigned to a house next to Wrath and Lauren. He really liked that idea. It would give Beauty a female friend nearby and it would be more secure if both he and his best friend were in close proximity to guard each other's mates.

The concept took hold as the miles passed. Lauren and Beauty were both soft natured and should get along well. He stroked his hand down Beauty's back absently, enjoying the freedom of touching her. He couldn't get enough of how wonderful it felt to have her so close. He just wished they were alone. A kiss would be better...or freeing her of her clothes. The need to inspect every inch of her body was deep rooted, just to make certain she wasn't harmed. He would love to kiss every bruise or scratch he discovered, then make love to her.

His dick filled with blood and he shifted his ass on the bench seat to close his legs, keeping his erection trapped down. The sweats were lousy for that and he wore no underwear. Regret came for not taking the time to shower and change into other clothing while they'd been at Medical.

He'd hunt down Douglas Miller quickly and efficiently to take out the threat to Beauty. There was no other option. As long as the male remained alive and free, he would use his vast resources to keep sending mercenaries after her and paying Mercile doctors to recreate drugs to hurt their people.

It would also feel good to destroy the male who'd harmed his Beauty. He growled low in his throat, unable to hold back the anger. Beauty must have felt the vibration it caused inside his chest because her head rose and her beautiful brown eyes peered up at him questioningly.

He smiled, assuring her he was fine. He stroked down her spine and arched his back a little to indicate she should rest while the flight was in progress. They couldn't talk. It was too loud without headsets. The entire team would hear each word if they spoke through those.

She got his silent message and relaxed against him. Shadow closed his eyes, content to just hold her while he made plans. Once he made sure Beauty was safe, he could ask her to be his mate. If she said no, he'd just have to convince her. He wasn't above using seduction. All those damn videos he'd been forced to watch while his semen was stolen had taught him a thing or two about what females enjoyed.

One way or another, he'd convince Beauty to stay with him forever.

Chapter Twenty

Beauty watched Shadow with a sense of fear and dread as he leaned down and brushed a kiss on her forehead. He was leaving her at the dorm to go to a meeting. While he didn't seem happy, he wasn't expressing a lot of regret either.

"You'll be safe here. You're home."

She wanted him to stay but kept silent.

"The females are going to guard you."

"I'm safe at Homeland." She wasn't sure why two women had dragged chairs out of their apartments to sit in the hallway to watch her door.

"You are." He straightened. "I'll just feel better knowing they are there."

"The security is tight. No one can get inside the dorms. There are locks, the windows are bulletproof and no one can smash their way inside. There are even cameras. Officers would be all over anyone unauthorized if they even approached the building."

He hesitated. "Some of the females have male visitors."

"They couldn't get inside unless someone walked them through the doors. Do you think any of the Species men are a danger to me?"

"I didn't say that."

"Is there something I don't know?"

"No."

They watched each other. Beauty suddenly touched him, her fingertips resting on his biceps. She stepped closer, having to raise her chin. He was really tall, something she tended to forget when they were seated, especially when she was on his lap and it made them about the same height.

"Shadow, you're being overprotective. I understand. You almost died protecting me earlier. I appreciate that but I'm in no danger. This is my home."

He lowered his head to bring them closer and his hands encased her hips. "Humor me."

The tension dissipated as she smiled, amused. "There are a lot of things I'd do for you." It was fun to tease him. "Or to you. Are you sure that's what you want?"

She grew a little brazen, her gaze slowly raking down his body to the front of his sweatpants. There was no missing how he physically reacted to her attention when the outline of his cock became noticeable, growing thicker and larger. He wanted her as much as she did him.

A soft growl made her glance up. Shadow's eyes had gone sexy, that passionate look in them something she identified immediately. His hold on her tightened and he lowered his face more.

"You're purposely being troublesome."

"I don't want you to go." It might seem needy to admit it but it was the truth.

"Keep looking at me there and I won't." He suddenly released her though and stepped back enough to break the physical contact. "I have to go. They are waiting for me."

"Justice and the others?"

"Yes. I've yet to give a report. I need to do this."

"May I go with you? They might have questions for me."

She'd do anything to avoid being left behind, worried he wouldn't return. Attending a meeting full of men didn't sound fun but at least he'd be at her side. She had a bad feeling the term "out of sight, out of mind" might apply to her when it came to Shadow.

He suddenly lowered to his knees. "Come here." His arms opened wide.

She quickly closed the distance. She liked it when he hugged her tightly and she wrapped her arms around him, burying her face against his neck. He was so big and so *Shadow*.

"What is really wrong? Tell me."

She hesitated. Men didn't like clingy women. Every book she'd read had taught her that and it was exactly how she felt. She didn't want him to leave, was afraid it would end what they'd begun, and she didn't want to return to her solitary life.

"Beauty?" He squeezed her tighter, not exactly a warning but the message was clear. He wouldn't release her until he had answers.

"I don't want to lose you," she blurted.

He adjusted a little so they had to stare into each other's eyes. He put one of his hands on her bottom and gently squeezed. "Is that why you are purposely delaying me?"

She loved his hand on her butt, so close to other places she wanted him touching her. "Yes. Everything is so new. What if you don't come back?"

He held her and buried his face against her neck, nuzzling her with his nose. He inhaled her scent, his chest vibrating against hers when he softly rumbled a sexy sound. "You couldn't keep me out of your bed if you tried, love. I'm on my knees for you. Do you think just anyone could drop me to them?"

"You're just trying to appear nonthreatening."

He chuckled and his lips teased the sensitive area just under her earlobe. His hot, wet tongue slid across the same spot. Beauty's fingers weaved into his hair, holding him there. He squeezed her ass again but slid that hand back to her waist. It was disappointing.

"True, but it wasn't the only reason. I want you to know you leave me vulnerable."

She pulled back and so did he until she could see his eyes. Honesty brimmed there as she studied them. "What does that mean?"

"You only want me, right?"

"Yes."

"No one else?"

"Never."

A smile curved his lips. "I feel the same. You're all I want. We have a lot to discuss but for now they are waiting for me in Justice's office. You don't want to get me yelled at, do you?" His tone became teasing. "That male is scary when angry."

"He is." She smiled back. "Okay. I'll be good and allow you to leave without delaying you more. Just hurry back."

He grew somber. "I don't know how long it will take. I have some things to do."

"Hours?"

He hesitated. "Perhaps days. I'm not sure. I will be back and we'll talk."

"Okay." She didn't have any choice and he was promising to return. That's all she could ask of him for now. "I'll miss you." Admitting that put her pride at stake but it was a chance she was willing to take.

"I'll miss you as well." He glanced at her breasts. "So much."

She laughed. "Hurry back to me then."

A knock sounded at the door. "Shadow? Security just called, asking where you are." It was Kit, her irritation clear. "Quit playing with the Gift and move your ass."

Shadow frowned. Beauty clenched her teeth. They regarded each other and she spoke first.

"That woman is a bitch," she whispered.

"I heard that. Get a move on, Shadow."

He rose to his feet, releasing her. One look down his body made him utter a soft curse. Beauty followed his gaze and grinned. He'd gone from semi-aroused to full-blown impressive in size. There was no way to hide the state of his body.

He turned, walked to her sink, and turned on water. Beauty watched in fascination as he wet his hands, reached up to the back of his neck, and rubbed.

"What are you doing?"

He shot her a grin. "Attempting to think of something besides you being so close to a bed." He closed his eyes, repeated the process of wetting the back of his neck and finally turned off the water. His cock wasn't as hard when he stepped around the counter into view. "Stay inside and I'll be back as soon as everything is taken care of."

"Okay."

She hated to see him go but she held still until he left her apartment. Kit stepped inside when he attempted to close the door. He paused, staring at her, but then walked on when the feline smiled after pointedly staring at his groin.

"Isn't he cute?" Kit closed the door behind her, leaning against it.

"You can't have him. He's mine." Beauty glared.

"I wanted to make sure you were okay. We heard what happened." Kit stayed where she was. "We almost lost you to the humans."

"I'm sorry if it disappoints you that it didn't happen."

The other woman's expression blanked, then she frowned. "I'm not as bad as you think. I don't dislike you. I'm glad you're safe."

"I annoy you. You think I'm weak." There was no use pretending otherwise. Beauty spoke her mind. "It would probably make your life easier if I had been stolen."

"That's not true. Tiny and Halfpint would have wailed and needed constant care if you had been lost." Kit sighed loudly, straightening away from the door. "I actually like you now. You showed backbone when you stood up to me. I was genuinely worried about you when we got the reports of the attack. I came to see if you wanted to talk to someone or if you just didn't want to be left alone."

Surprised at the confession, Beauty took a step closer. "Thank you."

"I guess I'll go." Kit spun, gripping the door handle.

"Kit?"

She glanced back, opening it. "What?"

"I'd like for you to stay."

The door closed with Kit still inside the apartment. "Okay. You hungry? I am. I just got off shift. They made pizza downstairs. Should I call the kitchen to ask for one to be sent up?"

"That sounds good. I love pizza."

"With meat, right?" Kit made a face. "They made some with just cheese. Why would they do that?"

"I don't know." Beauty smiled. "It is strange, isn't it?"

"We're not the vegetarian types. We're carnivores. Can you imagine handing a lion or a wolf an apple for their dinner? They'd take off your fingers for the insult."

341

"True." Beauty relaxed, liking this side of the usually prickly woman. She didn't point out that she was primate Species. "I love meat on pizza."

Kit lifted the phone. "Then we'll eat some. You can give me all the details of what happened."

Beauty nodded, glad that she wouldn't be alone to worry about what could possibly keep Shadow away from her for days.

* * * * *

Shadow grabbed a quick shower at the dorm and wore his NSO uniform to the meeting. He was almost an hour late when he arrived. Fury, Slade, Justice and Brass were eating pizza when he entered.

"There he is." Justice arched an eyebrow. "Finally."

"I showered and changed." Shadow shrugged. "I apologize."

"We decided to eat." Fury waved to the food. "Want some? Ellie made a few extra for me to share." He grinned at Justice. "She also wants two additional ovens added at the dorm's main kitchen. They are cooking more instead of eating at the cafeteria."

"Four aren't enough? Plus they have the ones inside their apartments." Slade frowned.

"Females enjoy cooking together in a group. It's a good way to bond." Fury glanced around. "She wants them. Let her have them." He narrowed his gaze at Justice. "Don't say no. It would disappoint my Ellie and make her unhappy. She will call Jessie and then your mate will be unhappy."

342

Justice chuckled. "My mate is sexy when she's angry but the females can have the ovens. It's not much to ask." He picked up a pen and scribbled on a tablet. "Note made. It will be taken care of."

Slade nodded. "Two ovens is far cheaper than what we just spent on updating the gym equipment inside the men's dorm."

"We do tend to break shit easily." Brass shoved a few slices of heavily loaded pizza onto a paper plate and passed it to Shadow. "Sit. I'll grab you a soda from Justice's fridge."

Shadow sat, using part of the large desk as a table. The relaxed attitude of the room was welcome. He'd expected anger after making them wait. He'd taken a bite when the meeting officially began.

"Breeze called in the details of what happened at the cabin," Justice informed him. "She is stuck at Medical so we held a conference call with her. What took place in the woods after you left her?"

"Is Breeze well?"

Fury nodded. "She doesn't like being kept for a few days but young Dr. Harris insisted she be given the healing drugs. It will lessen the chance of her scarring from the wound. They need to keep an eye on her while she's on them. Males aren't the only ones to grow aggressive. I am almost glad she's there instead of here. I'd hate to be her nurse."

Brass laughed, handing a drink to Shadow, before he took a seat on the couch. "Better them than us. She's a wonderful female but I feel bad for Destiny. Breeze will make him miserable just to stay amused."

Fury chuckled. "Obsidian didn't want him anywhere near his mate after what happened."

343

"What happened?" Shadow glanced around the room.

"Would you want another male around your female if he made it clear he wanted her too?"

Enough said. "Understood." Shadow opened and sipped the soda. "I tracked the humans down after I left the cabin. They'd treed Beauty after taking her from the bedroom upstairs. I removed their weapons and they were arrested."

Brass snorted. "A human you attacked is still in surgery. The doctors couldn't save one of his nuts. You smashed it."

Shadow remembered the mercenary he'd taken down. He felt no regret. He said nothing.

"I'm surprised they are still alive." Fury gave him an understanding look. "I would have killed them."

"Beauty wouldn't walk out of sight." He wouldn't lie. "She'd seen enough violence. I wanted them dead but wasn't willing to do it in front of her."

"We're glad they are alive." Justice leaned forward. "They know how to locate Douglas Miller. Tim is questioning the ones we captured. Miller's in Afghanistan. They gave him up easily."

Brass chuckled. "Bestial might have had something to do with that. He went into the cells with Tim to persuade them to be agreeable. Tim is good at intimidation but not as convincing as an enraged Species male. They tend to believe we'll eat them alive."

344

"True." Justice hesitated. "We also have a lead on who might be behind the drug given to Moon but they were unsure of exactly how Miller acquired it. We'll know more once the human is caught."

Anger filled Shadow. "We don't have the authority to go to Afghanistan."

"Lucky for us, we know someone already there." Justice held his gaze. "Jessie has a brother who works for a private security firm that protects American workers. I made a call. He was sympathetic and is assembling a team. It will take some time but Jake will capture Douglas Miller and have him returned to the States. They will hand the bastard over to us just as soon as they are able."

"I want to be there." Shadow wanted to personally kill Beauty's abuser.

"No." Justice shook his head. "We need him alive. He has to tell us exactly what was done to Moon and tell us where he got the drug."

"He abused a Gift Female." Shadow wasn't about to let it go. He wouldn't rest until the bastard was no longer a threat to Beauty. "He sent mercenaries into Reservation after her. He's too dangerous to be allowed to live."

"He'll suffer for his crimes but death is not the answer," Justice growled. "Calm now. The Gift isn't the only victim he's harmed. Species were hurt when that team attacked Reservation and Moon is still feral. The drug hasn't worn off. Every hour that passes harms him more. The doctors and specialists we've called in agree on that. They are frantically trying to identify the drug but so far haven't been able to. None of the treatments are working to calm and return him to his natural state."

It ate at Shadow's gut to leave Douglas Miller alive. He didn't deserve to breathe for what he'd done to Beauty. He'd kept her locked up in chains and forced his body into hers. The more he thought about it, the more enraged he became.

"Easy," Brass ordered, watching him with concern. "We understand but death is too swift. She suffered endlessly. Why shouldn't every day he takes breath be hellish? Do you understand? Justice's mate's brother will find Douglas Miller. It could take some time since it's pretty bad over there but he will get him. I met Jake when he visited here. He's a tough human with predatory traits. He would fit in with the task force if he wished. You'd like him."

"I don't care if I'd like him or not. It's my right to seek revenge for Beauty."

Brass' eyebrows rose. "I see."

"She's mine," Shadow snarled, still furious. "He forced her to submit to sex and hurt her. He named her Mud." His rage built. "Kept her from sunshine and exposed her to vile humans who threatened her with harm. I don't want him to suffer. I want him really to be in hell after I take his life."

Brass slowly stood. "You've deeply bonded to her."

"Yes." Shadow wouldn't deny it.

"So fast?" Brass looked skeptical.

"It doesn't take long," Justice mused. "Trust me on that, my friend. I spent a few hours with Jessie and she was deeply embedded under my skin."

Slade grunted. "Or a few minutes. I woke in a hospital after I was freed from Mercile with this angel leaning over my bed. I had her pinned under me in seconds, ready to claim her as mine. I wanted her immediately and I will never stop wanting Trisha. She's my mate. The attraction was so strong. I almost lost her later though because I didn't realize she was the same female when we met again."

Shadow gaped at him.

"She'd dyed her hair another color and I was pretty drugged at the time. My memories of her were affected." Slade grinned. "I knew my attraction was unusually strong when I met that mouthy little doctor. I just didn't put it together until she admitted who she was."

Shadow pushed the plate away, his appetite gone. "I need to do something."

"Be with your female," Justice gently urged. "Trust me on this. That's the only cure for the rage you feel. Help her heal from the damage done by showing her all the things she missed while in captivity."

Shadow considered it. He looked at Brass. "Tim wants me to return to the team. I'm needed there but Beauty couldn't live at headquarters. I can't go back to working with the task force."

Brass appeared shocked. "You are implying she'd want to live with you. Are you talking about mating with her? How does she feel about that?"

347

"We need to talk about it still." His chest tightened at the prospect of her refusing to accept him on a permanent level. "She admitted I'm the only male she wants. We agreed on not sharing sex with others."

"Ellie and I have discussed Gifts at length. They are different from our other females, who tend to reject settling down with one male," Fury stated quietly. "They learned to protect themselves against bonding with males to avoid being emotionally crippled when they were taken to different ones for the breeding experiments. But Gifts spent most of their time alone with no bonds at all. They didn't have an opportunity to form any since only their abusers had access to them. It's possible she might welcome being mated to a male." He silently regarded Shadow. "You're the first one a Gift has wanted to interact with. She must feel strongly for you."

"Did you share sex with her?" Slade arched an eyebrow.

"I don't feel comfortable discussing this."

"It's relevant and they did share sex," Justice announced. "Breeze confirmed that privately before I brought everyone into the conference call with her. Breeze stated Beauty handled the experience in a positive light."

Shadow hated the way everyone smiled at him. "Enough." It embarrassed him slightly.

"I guess your fears were unwarranted," Brass teased.

"I won't discuss it."

"Do you want to mate her?" Justice crossed his arms over his chest.

"I plan to discuss it with Beauty. I want to." He took a deep breath. "We'd need housing away from the dorms. I'd want to live next to Wrath and Lauren."

348

"Agreed." Justice picked up his pen.

"I'd like papers drawn up."

Justice looked up from his notes to stare at Shadow. "We only have them for humans. It's a legal issue with their rights and to protect them by officially making them Species."

"Mates have papers." Shadow refused to back down. "I want it official if Beauty agrees. She deserves to know I'm serious."

"We could come up with something," Fury intervened. He smiled at Justice. "Couldn't we? Ellie has our papers framed in our bedroom."

Justice grinned back. "We could do that. Jessie hung ours in the office at home."

"As soon as Beauty is out of danger, I plan to ask." Shadow reached for the pizza. He should eat.

"Why wait?" Slade paused. "There's nothing you can do right now. You aren't returning to the task force since a Gift shouldn't live at headquarters. There're too many human males and you'd never want to leave her unprotected around them. It's hard to work if you refuse to leave your quarters. Douglas Miller will be caught but you won't be a part of it. Your priority is Beauty."

"I know she is." He still wanted to argue the future of Beauty's abuser but it was clear the matter had already been settled. He wouldn't be allowed to kill the bastard. It didn't sit well with him but he'd learned to take orders. "There's the matter of the team member who activated my emergency transponder and gave those coordinates to the mercenaries to track Beauty's location. Tim promised to allow me access to him."

349

The males glanced at each other. Justice spoke first. "Tim shouldn't have done that but we know who did it. It was Chad, the one who runs communications for the team. He was having money problems after a divorce and that's how they got to him. You aren't allowed to kill him but let's just say I wouldn't punish you if your fists *accidentally* made some contact with his body a few times. I have a mate and I wouldn't begrudge you a little payback. Just don't cripple him for life. He'll spend the rest of his as a guest at Fuller. We don't kill our enemies when we don't have to. We're better than them."

Shadow considered those words. They might make sense but he'd still sleep better at night knowing Beauty's abuser was dead. He'd also have to settle for Justice's offer of only hurting the team member who'd risked Beauty's life. It didn't mean he had to like it though.

Chapter Twenty-One

Beauty had just stepped out of the shower when the doorbell rang. She frowned, wrapping a towel around her body, and entered the bedroom. It was just after eleven at night. Had Kit forgotten something? The woman had not only stuck around to share pizza but had been downright friendly. They'd talked for hours.

She hurried into the living room but paused by the door. "Who is it?"

"It's me."

Surprise and excitement struck at hearing that sexy, deep voice. She twisted the locks, opening the door to face Shadow. He had changed into his work uniform since she'd last seen him and he looked a little tired around the eyes as she stared into them.

"You're back. How did you get inside the dorm?"

"A group of the females were downstairs watching a movie. They opened the door." He cleared his throat. "It's no secret that we are seeing each other."

She backed up. "Come in."

He hesitated. "I want to spend the night," he clarified. "Is that okay?"

"Yes." She was glad he hadn't been gone for days and that she wouldn't have to sleep without him. The experience of being in his arms was addictive and something she no longer wanted to do without. "Always."

He moved to the side and lifted a bag, carrying it in. It was big and looked heavy. She wondered what was inside it. He dropped the thing a few feet inside the room and closed the door behind him, twisting the locks. His gaze held hers.

"I wanted to be here sooner but I had arrangements to make."

"What is in the bag?"

He shifted his stance, his expression unreadable. "My belongings."

"That's bigger than the bag you took to Homeland."

"It contains everything I own. I packed up my quarters tonight."

The stabbing sensation to her heart was pure agony. She spun away to hide the tears that refused to be denied. They burned behind her closed eyelids, a few of them escaping down her cheeks. Shadow would only do that if he'd decided to return to the task force. He'd leave Homeland in the morning and she wouldn't be able to see him except when he visited.

Maybe he believed she could be happy with occasional nights or weekends spent together when he could return to Homeland for work breaks. She could even understand his logic. Species women wanted their space but she wanted to scream that she wasn't like them. All the ways she'd been singled out as Gift suddenly mocked her. She'd resented the special concessions, had wanted the distinction removed, and Shadow had listened. He was willing to treat her as any other Species.

Careful for what you wish for, an inner voice mocked.

"Beauty?" He stood directly behind her. "What is wrong? Look at me."

She hesitated, trying to get her emotions under control.

"Beauty?"

She opened her eyes and rapidly blinked back tears, turning to face him. It was time to be totally honest. There was nothing to lose if he already planned to leave. She could just be blunt and hope he'd reconsider his current path.

"Why are you crying? Did something happen while I was gone? Did that female upset you? I saw her come inside as I left."

"Kit was unusually nice today. She didn't do anything wrong."

"What is it?"

"I don't want you to leave Homeland to return to the task force. I'll hardly see you. I know I should be grateful for having you in my life at all after spending so much time alone but I want more than that. I appreciate you seeing me the same way you do the other women but I'm different." Her shoulders straightened and she held his gaze. "I deserve more than a man who is barely around. I want it all, Shadow."

He seemed stunned.

"You know, a real relationship. I want someone who comes home to me every day and spends their nights with me. I want to cook you dinner and snuggle on the couch while we watch shows. I'm not even sure if we'd enjoy the same ones but we'd be together. I want to get to know everything about you, even the bad stuff I might find annoying. It won't matter because I'm willing to accept you for who you are, all of it, but I don't want to be alone anymore."

His lips parted but nothing came out.

She cleared her throat. "I want a true commitment." It made her feel a little dizzy to admit that but it was just nerves. The worst he could do was walk out. "Not just someone in my life when they can fit me into their busy schedule. I realize it's a lot to ask. You would have to remain here instead of enjoying the more exciting adventures you must have with the task force. It's also more dangerous working for them. You deal with the kind of men who came after me. They are bad and dangerous. That can't be good for you to see that every day. We're free now and should embrace the good things life has to offer. Maybe you enjoy the work but you enjoy sex too. Your team can't give you that but I can." She put her hands on her hips. "I can't compare work stories with you since I'm not permitted to hold a job as a Gift because it would put me in contact with too many men but I could give you a good home you would enjoy living in. I will worry about you while you're doing your job. It matters to me what happens to you and while they may be your friends on the task force, what I feel is stronger. I'm sure of that."

"Beauty... I—"

His features softened. He probably felt sorry for her. She refused to give up and cut him off. He couldn't just walk away.

"I know we didn't have much time together but I'm offering you all that I am. You can't just ignore that, Shadow. You owe it to both of us to see where we lead. I think we could be happy. I know I want us to be. We're both damaged but that makes us more suitable. There's something special between us, something strong, and it's not just sex."

"I—"

"Don't tell me you won't at least consider what I'm offering. You have to stay at Homeland to get to know me better." She took a shaky breath. "I won't beg but I won't be a doormat either. You can't have it both ways. You can't leave me here to go have a life but expect me to wait around for you as if I don't have one."

He lunged and jerked her against his body. "Do you ever allow a male to speak?"

She gripped his biceps through the material of his shirt, wishing for skin. "I don't want you to say something I can't stand to hear."

He softly growled as he released her waist and reached for something inside his back pocket. He held up a crisp, folded sheet of paper. "Do you know what this is?"

"No. Your orders to return to the task force?" It was her best guess.

He shook his head and then released her completely. He lowered to his knees in front of her. He licked his lips, his features tense. "Mate papers. I had it drawn up. We just need to sign it. It's just one paper actually but it's a less involved process to bind us together than the ones involving humans. The outside world holds no claim on us that they might ever try to sever."

Her legs turned rubbery and she ended up on her knees in front of him.

"I packed up my belongings because there wasn't a reason to keep a room at the men's dorm. I want to be with you and you're here." He cleared his throat, staring deeply into her eyes. "I came to ask you to be my mate and tell you that if you agree, housing is being made available to us soon. We can have a house next to my best friend and his mate. She's nice and I think she would be a good friend." He took a deep breath. "I'm offering you everything too, love. Me. I don't want adventure or to leave Homeland. You aren't there and I just want to be with you."

"Yes." She nodded frantically, blinking back tears again.

"We are both damaged." Shadow suddenly grinned. "I wouldn't have it any other way if it means I get you."

"You've got me." She held out her hand. "Let's sign them. Is that all we need to do?"

He grinned. "We should also have a lot of sex to celebrate afterward."

She managed to rise to her feet and dropped the towel. Shadow's gaze lowered, halting on her breasts. Sexual hunger sharpened his features and the soft growl of approval from him turned her on.

"Why wait? I want you now." She smiled. "But there is one thing I want to do."

He pulled his focus away from her body. "Name it. It's yours."

"Take off your uniform first."

He put the paper on her coffee table and bent to rip off his boots. She grinned at his haste. He nearly fell over sideways at one point but then righted, shoving his pants down. He really did want her. The clothes were gone, leaving one aroused man standing just feet away.

She lowered to her knees again and he bent a knee to follow. "Don't. Stay just like that."

He straightened and held immobile. She walked on her knees closer. "I read about this and I wanted to try it. You can stop me if you don't like it but at least allow me to do it once."

Beauty reached up and wrapped her fingers around his stiff shaft. He gasped at the sudden move or perhaps the implication. She licked her lips to wet them and dropped her gaze to his sex. He was beautiful all over but his cock fascinated her.

"Maybe I should sit." His voice came out gruff and husky.

She lifted her gaze, appreciating his muscular abs, wide chest, and settled on his handsome face. "Why?"

"You have no idea what the sight of you there does to me."

"Tell me."

"I've never wanted a female more. I hurt from the need. It's a physical pain."

"You do the same to me."

"You know female Species never do this, don't you? I can't come with your mouth around me though. I might choke you. I shoot semen hard. It would be too much."

"I just want to play a little. Will you allow it?"

"You can do anything you want. I'm yours."

Emotion swamped her. "I love you, Shadow. I hope you'll learn to love me back."

He suddenly pulled out of her grasp and reached down, gripping her under her arms. It was her turn to gasp when he lifted her, spun and stormed into her bedroom. She clung to him.

"What are you—"

When they landed on the bed it jolted her to silence. They were on their sides facing each other. His mouth was on hers, kissing the breath right out of her a split second later. One of them moaned—she wasn't sure who—and it didn't matter. His hot skin plastered against hers felt incredible.

He broke the kiss, panting. "You love me?" His blue gaze studied hers. "You are sure?"

"Yes."

"Good. You've made me very happy. I've never loved before but this has to be it. You are everything I want and need. You make me complete and having you in my arms is the most right thing in my world. Every thought involves you and how to keep you close."

"I was afraid it would scare you away if I admitted my feelings."

"The only frightening thing would be if you refused to sign the mate papers."

"Do you want me to do that right now? Let me go and I'll get them."

"Later." His mouth brushed hers. "There're so many things I want to do to you. I can't decide which should come first."

"Roll onto your back." She splayed her fingers across his chest, pushing lightly. "You said I could play. That is on the top of my list."

He turned, lying flat. "I'll be a good mate."

"I know you will and so will I. We'll figure it out together."

She brushed her fingertips along the length of his cock, enthralled when it moved, jerking slightly. There was a lot about men she didn't know but she'd learn. It would be fun to discover everything that turned Shadow on and have him do the same to her.

"I don't read much but I have watched a lot of videos." Shadow smiled. "Ever hear of sixty-nine?"

"The number?"

"The position."

"Is that a sports thing?"

"Um, no." He licked his lips. "You want to play with me with your mouth and I want to play with you with mine. You put your knees right here." He pointed to just above his shoulders on both sides. "Face toward the headboard. Do you understand?"

Her lips parted in shock. "You want me to spread my thighs open over your face while I'm stretched down your body to your lap?"

"Yes." He grinned widely. "Exactly. Just release me with your mouth if I warn you to. I have a feeling I won't last long. It's my first time. I probably shouldn't admit that but we're mates. I won't keep any secrets from you. We're two who have become one."

Curiosity and excitement overruled any shyness she experienced. He was right. They were mates. He was hers and she was his. There was no need to hide anything or waste time being embarrassed. She shifted up and spread her thighs, careful to place them where he wanted. She realized how close his mouth was to her pussy.

"I won't smother you?" It was an honest concern to her.

His hands took hold of her hips. "No." His attention shifted lower. "I like this view. Scoot a little closer and spread your thighs more."

She bent, bracing her palms over his hips. His hands slid to her lower stomach and his thumbs spread her sex open. His hot breath fanned her intimately as she settled over his face. The first swipe of his tongue across her clit sent pleasure spreading upward.

"I love that."

He growled, adding vibrations into the mix of the slow licks that made her ache. She wet her lips and lifted one hand, firmly gripping the shaft of his thick cock. He growled louder at her first touch, his tongue lapping faster. It felt so good it became difficult to concentrate on what she wanted to do to him. Shadow hit one spot over and over, pushing her to a fast climax.

Beauty loved ice cream and one of the books she'd read about sex suggested oral sex with a man was very similar. She stuck out her tongue and ran the flat surface from just above her thumb to the tip of his cock.

Shadow paused, snarling. She took that for a positive sign since she could relate. She wiggled her hips a little, the ache to come growing worse. He licked her again, firmly teasing the bundle of nerves with just a little more pressure.

She opened wide—he was thick—and carefully took him inside. Her tongue licked as she fit her mouth around the crown. His body tensed under hers, his stomach muscles growing taut. She moved then, taking him a little deeper and tightened around the shaft, creating a suction as she lifted up until he almost slipped away. She lowered, the taste of his pleasure sweet as pre-cum beaded the tip of his cock.

More moans tore from her and she realized her hips were moving. She couldn't stop wiggling them, wanting to come so much it hurt. She moaned louder, her hand began to stroke his shaft where she couldn't reach with the well of her mouth, and Shadow reacted by pressing his face tightly against her pussy. He lightly raked his teeth across her clit and she yanked her mouth away from his cock to cry out as the first spasm of release tore through her. Fear of biting him forced her to stop.

Shadow moved fast enough to make her gasp when one knee bent, he planted his foot on the mattress, and he used the leverage to roll her over. Her back hit the bed while she was still in the grips of the orgasm. His hot body no longer pressed against hers and she opened her eyes to watch him lift up and turn around.

He came down over her fast, pinning her under him so their faces were almost touching. One of his arms braced next to her ribs to hold his chest away from hers enough to allow her to breathe while his other hand reached down, gripped her just above the back of her knee, and forced it to bend next to his hip. He held it there, spreading her thighs apart enough to fit his hips between them.

He adjusted over her, staring into her eyes, and then she cried out when he entered her body with one slow thrust after aligning his cock against the entrance of her pussy. Her clenching vaginal muscles protested a little, making it a very tight fit while he penetrated her but she was wet and ready to take him. His eyes nearly closed as he snarled. He buried his cock in her and did small, fast jerks in and out of her pussy. It drew out her climax, putting her on sensory overload enough to buck under him.

"Beauty," he snarled and shook violently.

Heat shot inside her as he came. His face lowered to press against the curve of her shoulder and his teeth gripped her there, the sharp points of his fangs digging into her skin but it didn't hurt. He groaned, still coming, and slowly grinding his hips against her.

Her fingernails dug into his upper arms where she clutched at him just to anchor her to reality. They were both breathing hard, hearts racing as they lay there recovering. He eased the pressure of his teeth when he lifted his head.

"I'm sorry."

"For what?" Her fingertips surfed his broad shoulders. "That was amazing."

"I took you rough." He frowned, not happy.

"I'm not complaining. I enjoyed that."

"Are you sure?"

"Yes." She laughed, fingering his hair when her hands slid higher. "I like your taste. How did it feel with my mouth on you?"

He growled and his sex inside her flexed where they were still joined. "Really good."

"I like this sixty-nine."

"I saw a lot of things in videos."

"Really?" She was interested. "What else?"

He shifted to the side, glancing down her body with keen interest. "Do you ever touch yourself?" He met her gaze. "I would enjoy seeing that."

"I have but what you do to me feels much better. Would you touch yourself for me so I could watch?" The idea of seeing Shadow stroke his cock again was exciting in a naughty way that turned her on.

"Yes." His tone grew husky. "We could do it together."

That thought excited her. "Watching each other?"

"Yes. Do you know what I want to watch you do most of all?"

"What?"

"Sign the mate paper."

She laughed. "Let's do it!"

Shadow rolled away after slowly separating their bodies and quickly strode out of the room. She sat up, almost reached for the sheet to cover her nakedness, but then just stayed bare. They were mates. She didn't want to hide anything from him. She enjoyed seeing his body and he seemed to like seeing hers. Mating was about making the other happy.

"Where is a pen?"

"In the kitchen drawer by the sink."

He returned with the paper and a pen, sat on the edge of her bed, and dragged the night table closer. He turned his head, smiling. "Come here, love."

She practically crawled onto his lap, leaning more against him than not. He carefully unfolded the paper to lay it flat. She read the words, tearing up.

"It says we officially agree to belong to each other and that we have the approval of the New Species Organization. We are promising to cherish and care for each other." Her finger trembled a little as she used it to keep track of where she read. "It says no one has the right to make us live apart from each other and our loyalty is first to our mate and second to our people." She paused, looking at Shadow. "I like that."

"Me too. I promise all those things to you."

"I promise too." She looked down. "It says we are to swear to make the other happy and always be truthful and honest to one another."

"We can do that."

She held his gaze. "Yes, we can."

He focused on the paper and lifted the pen, signing the line above where his name was printed in ink. He winked, holding out the pen. "Your turn. You won't regret this, love."

"I know." She took the pen and signed her name on the line above where her name was printed. Her heart swelled when she was done, staring at both their signatures on the paper.

"I will take this to the office tomorrow and they will make a copy for the official files. We get to keep this one. Justice said it's customary to put it in a frame with glass to protect it from damage and hang it on a wall in a room that we spend a lot of time in."

Beauty pondered that for all of two seconds. "The bedroom."

"That's what I was thinking too." He took the pen, placed it next to their mate paper, and pulled her fully onto his lap. "I love you, Beauty."

"I love you too. Can you believe this? We're really happy."

"Yes. We are. We're going to stay that way. I will make sure of that."

"Do you have to leave me?" The thought left her cold.

"I just swore I wouldn't."

"You want to go after..." She hesitated, not wanting to bring the ugliness of her past into such an important moment.

"You're my priority." He understood what she hadn't said. "Others will take care of that. He can't hurt you anymore. All we need to do is move into our new home once they prepare it for us and enjoy sharing a life."

"I'm going to be a great mate. I'll cook you dinner and keep a good home but I want to also do something to help our society. I want to teach other Gift Females to embrace life so they know it's possible to have what we do, Shadow."

"I know you will." He brushed a kiss on her lips. "I will make you laugh and always be happy to come home to you after I finish my work shifts."

"It sounds wonderful. Thank you, Shadow."

"For what? I want you as my mate. I should be thanking you for agreeing."

"For giving me a real life and making it wonderful."

Shadow felt humbled. He couldn't believe he had a mate. Beauty was more than he deserved, more than he'd ever hoped to have, and she'd changed his life.

"I'm the one who is thankful," he admitted. "I'll never see lightning again without smiling. It showed you to me and made me give chase."

She laughed. "No more running during storms. I have no reason to do something like that again to feel alive. I just have to touch you."

They'd be doing a lot of that. He couldn't imagine keeping his hands off her and never planned to stop. He'd once been broken but she'd fixed him with her smiles, her courage, and her trust. He snuggled her closer, just holding her, and closed his eyes. For the first time, everything was perfect. He looked forward to whatever they would face because they'd do it together. She was his heart.